1

Also available by Gareth Howells:

Ten Tales of Transformation
Out Among the Ice Beacons

The story, all names, characters, and incidents portrayed in this novel are fictitious.

No identification with actual persons (living or deceased), places, buildings, and products is intended or should be inferred. Every plot device and all of the characterisations in the book is a work of fiction. If you can relate to any of it through your experience in the music industry, I hope you survived the ordeal and are still making music.

Music is unique - it's the only true magic in the world.

The

Brown Yelp Gang

By

Gareth Howells

Copyright 2019

Front illustration by Hunt Emerson

Preface and acknowledgements (and disclaimer)

I'm very pleased to be able to release this book. This is a fictional tale that is beyond far-fetched; it's truly revelling in its ridiculous premise and tone throughout the book. An interspecies rock band that has to deal with gangsters, bounty hunters, robot imposters, telepathic companions and lost guitar strings is not really strictly drawn from personal experience. It is worth saying, however, that my own personal experience of gigging for over 30 years has informed me of some of the characters in the book, some of the personalities of those characters and some of the pressures to get the sound right, or get to the gig, or get the audience on your side. When a show goes wrong, as it did in the first story I wrote about The Brown Yelp Gang, in my first book, it is disastrous and the potential for a long term struggle to claw back the audience's affections is palpable.

So, while this book is, of course, science fiction and totally ludicrous science fiction at its core, I have my own personal experiences littered through it. The first story called "No Sleep Till Corsylia" in the book "Ten Tales of Transformation", was a great learning curve for me. It was the longest story in the anthology, and a story that I really enjoyed writing. I knew that I wanted to return to The Brown Yelp Gang, as soon as I had exorcised the other idea I had, which led to the book, "Out Among the Ice Beacons". So this desire I had to return to the band that I have grown genuine affection for resulted in several different ideas to spring from, to give them a larger canvas to develop. For the longest time, the book on The Brown Yelp Gang was going to be a prison break story where I was going to somehow marry my love of The Magnificent Seven/The Seven Samurai and merge it with the demands of playing for the prison governor. After I toyed with that idea for a while, I decided that it would be fun to base the whole thing on more dealings with criminals, especially if the criminals were music promoters. Over the years I have worked with many music promoters that have been happy to exploit a situation or take advantage of a gullible, young band. There are some social media groups that call out the worst culprits, and the community can be quite good at spotting those characters. Bringing the story to that kind of level of real life referencing was a good move for me, because once I had done that, then I was constantly thinking of new ideas that I could bring in. Amongst the text there are a few nods to real life people, record companies or just stupid puns, but ultimately, I'm hoping that you find the story gripping and that maybe you might even begin to form the songs in your head, from just the lyrics.

I want to take this opportunity to thank some people, for being a part of this book. First and foremost, as always, I need to thank my wife who patiently puts up with me having late nights while I write and is always supportive with the different creative things I do. Being part of a busy, relatively successful band is a demanding thing for my wife as much as it is for me, and I am forever grateful for how much she supports us and is there for us if we forget our merch or something. My kids need to be thanked. They are a great support to me, and we all gig together frequently; especially my son, who has done pretty much every gig I have done with me over the last 4 years, and he is a phenomenal musician. This gratitude is also a reference to the family support of my band, but in general these three people give me the confidence and strength to make myself believe I can write, and that goes well beyond any thanks that I can give them.

I also want to thank my band, Bemis, for how happy they make me when I am on stage. For me, there is nowhere else that I feel that comfortable or that confident. The other members of the band have a lot to do with that, and I want to give them my heartfelt thanks. I want to give a special shout out to the man that I formed the band with originally, Richard Leo, who joined me on my adventures with Bemis when we were just a duo. He is a big part of my life, and a good friend. As this book is about a rock band, and about their relationship with their fans in many ways, I want to thank the people that continually support Bemis too. The supporters we have in the Surrey area in particular astound us with how much they support what we do and get to know our songs and develop a personal relationship with the songs; that is incredible, and we are all so grateful.

Whatever I do, I will be performing my own songs under the name of 'Bemis', and I am forever grateful that people value my songs and value the band. Thanks guys.

I also want to thank Hunt Emerson, who is an incredible artist, known for his work for Knockabout comics, for his BBC work, for Beano, for the Beat girl and his own fantastic books. He has provided the front covers for six separate Bemis albums now, and has graced this book with an amazing, evocative cover that I hope will make it easier to visualise the lunacy in the text. Thank you Hunt for being such a pleasure to work with, and for being such an incredible, and underrated artist.

I would also like to thank my main proof readers, Andy Brown, David Rozzell and Nikki Owen. They have all been invaluable in the process of writing the book. I have known all of them for many years, and I've always valued their friendship a great deal. Andy has been a long time follower and supporter of my band and has been enormously encouraging on many occasions. He also has the unique claim to have shared our Thailand gig with us; something that is etched very clearly in both our memories. Andy being a part of this book gives me a lot of pleasure in itself, and I am grateful to him for making this an easier read. David is a good friend who I have gigged with many times with our respective bands sharing the bill at different venues and different events. He would definitely relate to some of the issues in the book, through his experiences as a musician. Nikki is a close friend that has followed Bemis closely and knows some of the references I've made to my experiences, and has been a part of the live scene through her talented sons' many bands. I also had some great advice from my friend, Becky Jerams as I was writing the book, and I'd like to acknowledge that too. Close friends like Paul Hardy, Andy Logan and Gavin Thomas all made time to read early versions of the book, and I am very grateful to them for that. There are also good friends like Jeff Radford, Ashley Paddon, Viv Johnson, Raymond Dickey, Mark Duffield and many others that have given me crucial encouragement and advice along the way.

I feel I should say something about the nature of this book; where it stems from and how far it goes in relation to people I know or have known; people I have worked with on the music scene through the years. There is never a point in the book where an individual is mocked or used as a prop for a joke. There are probably quite a few moments where someone might recognise a trait, a habit or a tendency for a moment from someone they know personally. I would say that most of the parodies in this book are parodies that anybody that has had any experience as an audience member would relate to, let alone someone who has been on the scene from the performing side. So I don't think the parody aspect is particularly personal. Far from mocking the industry; I am hoping there is a spirit of the fun and adventure in gigging within the text and between the lines of this book. I have been performing gigs for over 30 years now, and those years have given me some bad experiences which have been exaggerated in this book, but also many of the things I love about gigging have been a big part of the book. Being on stage is my happy place, I couldn't love it more. I hope you get that impression from the adventures of The Brown Yelp Gang.

Without spoiling the overall plot of the book before you've begun reading it, I wanted to say something about the overriding motivation for the villain of the story. As I said, I don't want to be too specific here, in case it spoils the surprises of the plot, but there has been a shift in the last 15-20 years of more and more music becoming free, or part of a service that charges a nominal charge. Streaming is now the big drive from the industry executives, and you'll see labels being persuaded by those streaming companies like Spotify that their model is the future. Unfortunately, the music industry had a huge shockwave hit it with the digital revolution that followed the file sharing phase of the old Napster/Kazaa days. Now we are in the period between stable business models that jostles between the old and the new. Once the streaming services have figured out how to marry their new models with the more traditional method of payment for musical products, the public won't be in that mindset that seems to be growing where music isn't a commodity anymore, but simply something to take for granted in 'the ether'. This is crucially important. There are more and more demands on musicians to work for nothing, more and more demands for songs to be given to streaming services with a minimal payment back and less and less places for musical events to happen. It could be said that we are taking this all for granted, and that we are making it difficult for musicians to make a living from it. Giving up your day job would have been something you would strive for, by being picked up by a label or by building up a following on the live circuit; now you are encouraged to do it yourself, and become part of a trillion strong pool of noise that drifts through the internet dreaming to be heard.

So, I think we are in flux at the moment, with the music industry finding its way around marrying up the public convenience of streaming services, with getting regular payment to the people who made the music so they can be professionals, and spend all of their time on this beautiful and, actually magical, art form.

Music is the closest thing to magic we can experience. It transcends every barrier, and communicates emotion and experience in a powerful, sincere way that nothing else can. There is literally no art form that has that immediacy and accessibility more than music. Many art forms use music to enhance its own power; dance, film, computer games, television, acting, the list goes on. Music is a truly magnificent, wondrous fluke of nature. If you ever get the chance to make a living with music, you are very lucky, especially in the current climate.

I have waffled a little in this preface, and I'm still going to keep the waffle there, as this argument about the way music is being consumed is simmering away behind the motivations of the main villain of the story. Ultimately though, I wanted to make you smile or laugh reading this. If I have done this, that is fantastic. If some references have made you remember something you have experienced at a gig, or with a song you love, or a band you love, that is even better. It could well be that the situations, song titles and general behaviour of the characters in the book are so ridiculous that you just let the absurdity drift over you like a noisy funny looking blanket.

A few other things to mention here; there is a conceit running through the story that most of the aliens understand each other's language. This is obviously for convenience. There is one moment in the story where this doesn't happen, and I purely added that complication to add the translator. This was, again, simply because I liked the set up with the alien giving instructions and the translator translating, there was very little science involved. There is also a device running through the book that if

Trent is speaking, I don't bother saying which head is speaking if it's the middle head. I just found it made more sense to only get specific when it was one of the side heads. I hope that thread of convenience isn't too irritating. There will be other quirks in the book, but those two were glaring features in the book that I thought were worth mentioning. I really hope you enjoy this book, and the quirks of the characters within it. I have taken a sideways look at songwriting, support bands, venue management, band promotion, crowdfunding, band politics, audience feedback and general musicianship in this book...and all of that is drawn from my absolute love of performing gigs with my band.

....keep music live.

FIRST SET

Chapter One

"So, how *is* your hair?" Jimmy Lovejoy asked with a wry smile on his face. The spirited, expectant audience sniggered, as they recognised the reference Lovejoy was making to the Brown Yelp Band's biggest hit, "How is your hair". Every member of the audience had it, and knew every second of the track like they had made it themselves. It was a great way to start the first ever interview with the band's legendary band manager Jenken Janes.

"Nice. I see what you did there." Jenken tapped Lovejoy on the knee as he spoke, and looked around the television studio as he prepared for his first few moments of interplanetary scrutiny, gazing at the multi-species star struck audience as he thought ahead;

"My hair, as you know, Lovejoy, is always impeccable." Jenken slid his hands through his hair, to the back of his head, grinning as he underlined his point. "I've even dressed up especially for you, my old friend." Jenken's charm was glowing more than ever.

Jenken looked down at his shiny purple suit as he spoke, with the sound of the audience whooping and clapping in appreciation, all captivated by Jenken's rare presence on Lovejoy's show. They were old friends. Jimmy Lovejoy and Jenken Janes had known each other since Lovejoy had started his hugely successful celebrity chat show twenty three years ago. Back then, if you were getting somewhere in show business, and lived on one of the planets in the Corsyl System, you would eventually be invited to one of Jenken's notoriously wild parties. It was at one of these parties that they struck up a friendship that grew with every misdemeanour, slander case, drug bust and divorce. They were both on their ninth wife, so there was a lot to talk about when they met. On camera, in this brightly lit, garishly coloured studio, and in front of the line of cameras facing them, the conversation would avoid the ex-wives and concentrate on Jenken's controversial music career. The sea of expectant fans in front of them ran the gamut of species across the Corsyl system; reptilian, feathered, bark-like, sweaty, suited gaseous beings and a variety of more humanoid bodies filled the darkly lit room.

"Can I first thank you for doing this interview. I know you have avoided interviews for your whole career." Lovejoy's voice was sincere and welcoming. "I genuinely appreciate it, my friend."

Jenken had avoided interviews, but mostly because he couldn't be bothered. In the last six years, however, it was because he had been on the run from the Corsyllian authorities. The last tour in Corsylia by The Brown Yelp Band had resulted in the band, and Jenken, setting up gigs illegally, and abandoning them when the authorities arrived. The band had decided to move their attention to a different Solar System, and for all intents and purposes, started their career again, thousands of light years from Corsylia, in the highly populated and commercially active Mackanine System. They had remained hidden from the Corsyllian security for this long by staying so far away.

Jenken's ego, and his drive to do something dangerous and new, like this very visible interview, was now changing all of that. He was always a showman, and couldn't wait to get people talking.

"I'm clearly not right in the head, Jimmy." The audience laughed. "If someone rushes in to arrest me I may have to abandon the interview." Jenken smiled as he said this, knowing that the secret location of the interview and the personally invited guests made that scenario unlikely.

"So why now?" Lovejoy changed direction with a direct reference to Jenken's absence from public forums.

"Listen, I'd be quite happy to stay minding my own business forever, but I am managing a band and I thought it was about time I had tried some more personal PR." His tone was facetious, as if it was an obvious change in behaviour. The audience were silent, hanging on every word.

"Okay, so is there something in particular that has brought you out into the open?" Lovejoy was keen to catch up with his old friend's off world activity, and ultimately, knew the answer.

"Well, I guess we've been away for a while. The Brown Yelp Gang is still going strong. In fact, we've never been better. The songs are mind blowing, and seriously, the band is sounding like it's never sounded before. We have two new band members who are bringing a new energy to the band, and the band is keen to show you their new stuff." Jenken's love of the band was glowing from the expression on his face and it was effortlessly spreading around the room.

"Where have they been?" Lovejoy asked, audaciously.

Jenken sniggered; "You can't get that out of me, I'm afraid. We will be releasing some new music next quarter and you'll be able to hear that on any of the five Systems close to Corsylia. The new songs are going to spin your ears off your head, you'll love them Jimmy. As for where we are playing, I can't risk it. We're still running from the Dengen Plant incident, all those years ago. We have made a new home, and made new fans, and all is good. That's why I'm here I guess to tell you all that." He smiled at the audience. "In fact, I've brought along a recording the band has done."

There was an audible gasp in the audience.

"Wanna hear it?" He shouted, facing the excitable crowd behind the cameras.

They inevitably cheered. Some of the audience were so overwhelmed with his words that they couldn't contain themselves. One fainted, and one let out a noise that

19

sounded like a startled "Up!" In reality, in their native language that sound was actually the words "I can't believe I'm here!", but it sounded like "Up!" to the uninitiated. The audience were selected from the band's most passionate and supportive followers, so this was a big deal. Jimmy Lovejoy hadn't heard the recording Jenken had brought with him yet, and was almost as thrilled as the audience.

"Okay people, we have an exclusive!" Lovejoy shouted with excitable anticipation to the audience, whipping up their fever even more. "Jenken Janes, the man behind the wildly successful and unpredictable rock band The Brown Yelp Band has brought with him a new recording for us." The anticipation he was trying to build with the introduction was instantly creating an unbearable tension in the room, as the audience were now gripping their seats with excitement and a few of the feathered Thanthemites were emitting a quiet, high pitched squeal through the hole in the top of their heads as they waited. Lovejoy looked behind him;

"Are we ready?" Jimmy shouted, building the tension.

"Are you ready to hear Trent's three beautiful voices?" Jimmy referred to the three headed lead singer. The crowd screamed in response.

"Are you ready for Lazy Riff's guitar?!!" Jimmy screamed this line, knowing the Riff fans were more vocal than the others. True to form, the screams coming from the audience were ear piercingly high.

"Are you ready to hear Plak and DK's snouts play those pretty melodies?" Jimmy was getting louder, and almost destroying his voice with the snarl he was putting on with this tension building performance.

"ARGH!!" The audience were finding it hard to cope with their excitement.

"Are you ready for Deet's multi-layered, multi-fantastic rhythms?" Jimmy was almost finished, which was just as well as he was losing his voice.

"DEET! DEET! DEET! DEET! DEET! DEET! DEET! DEET!" The chant from the audience was deafening.

"Well, let's roll then!" Jimmy lifted his arms up and clenched his fists, lifting his head back as if he was about to reach some kind of state of absolute pleasure.

A low, booming, bodiless voice was heard from the wings; "Okay, here we go."

The voice was dramatically lengthening each word and raising its pitch to further push the thrilled audience over the edge;

"I give you lucky, lucky people..."

Another dramatic pause...

"The...Brown...Yelp...Gang..."

Members of the audience were making noises that were more like screams of pain than any recognisable exclamation of joy. The noise was deafening.

"...with their new song called 'What's the name of your name now?'"

Lovejoy raised his right arm as if he was controlling the recording himself, and, as his arm swooped down in a dramatic arc, the song played through the huge speakers along the walls. The crowd exploded with pleasure as the first bars began. As the guitar riff anthemically blasted through the speakers, with the rhythm section of the band layering the sound for epic effect, audience members hit their seats repeatedly, slapped each other in excitement and screamed at the roof of the building as they "listened" and danced in the aisles. The atmosphere in the room was electric.

The song carried on through the first section and veered wildly into a mix of Korillian Opera and Mappist Rock. The mix was bizarre and intoxicating in its full frontal assault on the chat show audience. Tears streamed down the audiences faces as this blend of styles buoyed the unmistakable three part harmony of the lead singer, with all three of his heads creating the purest vocal sound that had ever been laid onto a Brown Yelp Gang recording.

Trent, the three headed singer, mesmerised the audience with his poetic words;

"What's the name of your name now
What's the name of your name now
What's the reason you came now
What's the point of my song

What's the lift of my leg now
What's the stretch of my arm
What's the name of my name now
What's the point if you're wrong"

Such profound lyrics were seldom heard on any System.
The audience all looked at each other in awe of the lyrical
power they were witnessing, desperately trying to articulate
their pleasure. The sweet combination of vocal harmony,
deep, probing lyrics, Korillian Opera tones and pounding
rhythms of Mappist Rock was classic Brown Yelp Gang.
The song meandered through another three verses, and
then swung into a flute Jazz solo, which raised Jimmy's
eyebrows, as he knew none of the band could play the
flute. Then the song went back to the initial guitar melody,
and the Brown Yelp guitarist, Lazy Riff, played eight layers
of harmony and disharmony on top of that first melody to
create a climactic ending. Trent, the singer, ended the song
with notes that went the lowest he had ever sung, and the
highest he had ever sung, with his third head creating a
counterpoint in the middle. The band having a three
headed lead singer, typical of his Calpian physiology, was
often used for powerful effect by The Brown Yelp Gang.
The audience sat in silence for a moment as the song
crashed to its epic ending. Jimmy watched the crowd as
they processed what they had just heard. Jenken was

looking directly at them, grinning with satisfaction, knowing it was exactly what the audience wanted. Then, after that moment of stillness, the audience erupted with applause and screams of appreciation. Jimmy joined in with the applause and shook his old friend's hand. Almost laughing as he tried to mask his elation, Jimmy was visibly awestruck;

"That was quite something Jenken." He said, still with his eyebrows raised.

"Thank you, Jimmy." Jenken turned to the crowd. " - and thank you!" The crowd continued their applause. A woman in the back of the audience shouted, "We love you Jenken," unable to contain her emotional response to the song.

"Oh no, is that an old girlfriend?!" Jenken replied, in jest.

"I notice there was a flute solo in there."

"Yes, that's right Jimmy. That was played by Lazy Riff's wife."

An audible gasp emitted from the audience.

"Wife?" Jimmy leaned forward from the surprise.

"Yeah. They got married a little while back. She's a Denuvian Priestess. She's huge, like nine feet tall or something."

Denuvians in general were very tall and thin. Their culture was peaceful, meditative and reflective. Aria was a powerhouse of a personality; just what Riff needed. She towered above all of the members of the band, both in height and force of personality. Trent's assumed authority, often mockingly called 'lead singer syndrome' was often challenged by Aria's wisdom. This brought a new dynamic to the rehearsals and a new sulky expression to all of Trent's three heads in those moments. Her beautifully smooth skin, wispy jet black hair and blue, satin robes added to her allure, and made it that much more difficult for people to argue with her. A Denuvian priest's mission was to travel across different planets and offer guidance for achieving peace and love. Aria did this, and also brought baked Fallet Fish with her on her travels, as the Fallet Fish were great delicacies on the Denuvian home planet, Pwom. Fallet Fish were hallucinogenic and created controversy on some of the planets they travelled to, and consequently the Denuvians were driven out occasionally for the threat to the native planet's lifestyle choices. It is quite possible that Lazy Riff was seduced by the lifestyle, and possibly while being under the influence of Fallet Fish, when he met his wife.

"So she's in the band?" Jimmy asked, intrigued.

"Well, she is with them all the time, but I don't think they've said she's in the band yet."

Jenken's words were hesitant and staggered, as if he wasn't sure of the answer. Clearly there was more to this relationship between Riff's wife and the band that Jenken was keeping to himself.

"Well, she's a great flute player." Jimmy added.

"She is. It's a Denuvian flute, so it's played through a hole in her bottom. It's fascinating to watch."

"I can imagine." Jimmy replied, not really meaning it. He moved on quickly;

"So you're releasing this song soon?"

"Absolutely. It will be out within the next solar cycle. Watch out for the announcement on the information network." Jenken spoke with an excited, proud tone.

"Right, well thanks for bringing that track. Can I ask you about the band?"

"Of course. Fire away."

"Well, I guess they're all there right? Trent, Riff, Plak, Deet and DK?"

The five original members of the band had stayed together through thick and thin. Plak had left the band briefly when the Corsyllian security were chasing them around Corsylia about the Dengen Plant usage. Plak hadn't been enthusiastic about taking the drug in the first place, and certainly felt that running around Corsylia trying not to get shot was not why he joined a band. He rejoined the band shortly after the incident had resulted in their rebirth on the Mackanine system. Plak remained the sourer member of the band, always reluctant to slip into the lifestyle the others liked, and always threatening to leave the band. His close friendship with DK kept him on the road.

All five original members had been busy carving a new fan base in another System, with their new two members of the band.

"Yeah, they're all there. All five of them. All good. All happy." Jenken nodded as he spoke, pleased with his own success in keeping them happy as much as anything else.

"All still playing the classics, like "I can show you in next week"?" Jimmy asked, speaking as a long term fan of the band.

"Oh yeah, they won't stop playing the old classics."

Jimmy's face lit up, as he particularly loved that one.

Jenken continued;

"Now it seems, people love hearing "Do what you want but I won't shave it off". People really love that one at the moment!"

"That's off one of the early albums isn't it?" Jimmy tried to keep up.

"Indeedy. The third album, in fact. We called the album, "Shave it off", and I don't know if you remember, but the cover had Trent with his hair all shaved off on it." Jenken giggled as he said this.

Trent, the lead singer, was a three headed Calpian; they were wolf-like beasts that were naturally very hairy. It was big news at the time that he was seen without his celebrated coat of fur. Trent discovered how valuable and loved his body hair was; especially when he saw shrewd opportunists selling fake replicas of his hair on the electronic network.

"Oh, that's right!" Jimmy remembered the cover, "was it actually all shaved off?"

"No, it was a skin suit he put on. If you buy the 42 inch copy of the album, you can see the join. If anybody tried to shave Trent, he'd bite their hands off."

Jimmy nodded, fascinated to hear the secrets of the album that featured some of his favourite songs. Jimmy had the 42 inch version of the album, and every other version. He was a true Brown Yelp uberfan.

"So, what is this I hear about another new member?"

The audience gasped again. They had been light years away for a long time, so this was dramatic news to the fans in front of them.

"Ahh, that would be Teddy." Jenken smiled as he said her name.

"Teddy?" Any detail about the new member was news to Jimmy.

"Well, strictly speaking, her name is Translating Emirate Diplomat Envoy, but that's a horrible mouthful. So she's been called Teddy since we've known her."

Jimmy was intrigued. His face opened up in deep thought as he processed the new information.

"Nice." He nodded slowly. "So she's a diplomat droid?"

He pictured the familiar image in his head of the tall, humanoid metal machine that accompanied politicians around the sector.

"She is, but not your ordinary diplomat." He looked to Jimmy, anticipating a planned addition to the interview. Jimmy suddenly remembered, through the fog of his fanboy fascination.

"Oh yeah, you brought a hologram of her to introduce your new player!" He slipped back to his excited high pitched tone, to maintain the atmosphere for the audience. With a wave of his arm, the stage manager ushered for the hologram to appear in front of the audience. There was an instant wave of gasps as Teddy appeared in hologram form in front of them. Teddy was a stunning sight for them to take in, being one of the latest examples of advanced cybernetics, designed to be visually appealing as well as housing the most advanced artificial intelligence. She was the size of a typical ministerial droid, and clearly had some additional features that weren't familiar to the audience. They whispered to each other in wonder as Jimmy continued to ask about her role in the band.

"As you can see, she's not from around here." Jenken said, proud of the band's success in the Mackanine System. "Around here a droid like this would look like a human, but she's shapely in a different way!" The crowd laughed at his cheeky, audacious low level humour.

"I can imagine, joining your band, she's not that square!" Jimmy joked, in reference to her actual shape.

"She puts the others to shame. Give her a room full of Pannik Juice and she'll be drinking it hours after you've passed out."

The crowd laughed, united in their enchantment and passion for seeing her in action.

"As you can see, she has all these extra metal plates fitted to house all of her virtual music effects from her main operating system."

"Whoah!" Jimmy loved this, and reached out to touch it, forgetting for a moment that it wasn't actually there.

"She is amazing and a fantastic addition to the band, it's great."

"What does she play?" Jimmy asked.

"Not an instrument as such." Jenken thought for a moment for how to phrase it. "Through her digital music internal software, she brings atmosphere and augmentation to the songs."

"Augmentation?"

"Well I'm not sure if they're notes, but she adds noise....coming from her subroutines and circuits inside, all being processed and mixed through the front boards here." Jenken pointed to Teddy's plates on her torso.

The mesmerised audience were snapped out of their spell with one sweaty fish-like creature in the audience suddenly bursting out with an impromptu "Woo!!" from his chair. He wasn't embarrassed by their attention. He simply looked at those around him and shouted "Woo!" again, followed by an aquatic sounding gurgle as he cleared his throat. They all turned their attention back to the interview.

"That sounds amazing, Jenken." Jimmy said, sycophantically. Then he slapped his knees to give out a long sigh;

"Look, Jenken, I wish I could chat to you all night, but sadly we have other guests tonight, and not a lot of time left." Jimmy reached out his hand. Jenken offered his hand, and Jimmy lifted Jenken's hand and licked across his palm, as was the custom for Corsyllian chat show farewells. Jenken wasted no time, aware of the guests waiting in the wings, stood up, and turned to the audience. He spoke like the showman he was, and managed to make every member of the audience think he was speaking to them personally,

"The Brown Yelp Gang love you, don't forget that."

The crowd went wild in response to his declaration of love.

"Remember to look out for the new album. The special edition has a weapon with it. 5 to collect."

The crowd went wilder. Someone at the back shouted;

"Brown Yelp forever!!"

Jenken smiled at the slimy creature who shouted it,

"No! – YOU, forever!" Jenken's words made them scream with even more love and passion.

He turned to the front row, extending his arm out to them;

"Wanna touch it?"

The fans in front of him giggled with nervous tension. Three of them grabbed his arm and immediately let go, overwhelmed by the experience.

"I got another one here." Jenken lifted his other arm to them. Then, as if he was merely teasing them, he laughed and walked away. As the crowd stood up and screamed his name, he kept walking toward the exit at the back of the studio, not turning around, but waving at them in a casual, indifferent way, that set them off even further. As he continued walking through the studio corridor, he could hear Jimmy Lovejoy desperately attempting to calm them down. One of the people further back in the audience shouted, in a distressed voice,

"I want to touch his arm!"

The screams, cries, chants, shouts and bleeps in the audience halved in volume as he closed the first door behind him. One of the studio producers was there to greet him in the corridor as he left the interview. The producer looked directly at Jenken Janes and smiled at him after a triumphant interview;

"Hello Mr Janes. I trust you had a good interview?"

"It was glorious thank you. I need to find my dressing room. It has my other clothes in it, and my other personal belongings."

"Absolutely Mr Janes. As you requested, there is a freighter on its way here, to take you back to - "

He stopped, as he had no idea where Jenken came from.

" – Um...to take you back to wherever you are living."

"Thank you. I will wait in my room, if you could remind me where it is?"

The producer led Jenken to his room. It was a bare room, with a clarity and simplicity in its lack of furniture that Jenken requested before he arrived. The ship the band travels on is a tip, with the seven members of the band and the four tech crew as bad as each other for their tidiness. This was his chance for a room without clutter. A room without instruments, or without any self-amputated limbs from the lizard-like tech crew. A chance to relax and think clearly now that the band is ready to make its next move, in what they hope will be the third career for the band.

Jenken settled back on his four seater chair, and closed his eyes, to relax. He now felt an enormous sense of achievement and a relief that his secret interview seemed to go without a hitch. Moments later he was humming the quiet, soothing melody of "Who's got your nose", while he rested his eyes.

He didn't notice the female bounty hunter walk into his room, or the swift, professional way she raised her gun to his nose.

"You weren't quite discreet enough Jenken Janes," the bounty hunter said, poised and hovering above him.

He practically leapt out of the seat when he opened his eyes and saw where the voice was coming from.

"Elsa Grabbinot." He said, with an almost monotone voice.
"You finally found me." His voice was resigned and matter of fact.

"It took me long enough, you slippery git."

"Ah, you say the nicest things." Jenken facetiously commented, clearly speaking to an old acquaintance.

"Don't get up." She said, still pointing the gun at his nose.

"OK. Can I get you to make me a drink?" Jenken was courageously vying for the upper hand in the conversation, without the benefit of a gun pointing at her nose.

"I will not be making you a drink." She said, emphatically.

"In fact you will be making me one."

"Will I?" Jenken replied, still ignoring the gun near his nose.

"Yes you will. A drink of humble pie."

He looked at her with furrowed eyebrows. He didn't dwell on her choice of metaphor.

"What do you want, Elsa?"

"You owe my boss a lot of money." She said, blankly.

"I owe a lot of people a lot of money." Jenken boldly stated.

"Well, this one needs paying." She still held the gun at close proximity to his nose.

"Can we talk without that?" Jenken asked, with his eyes indicating the gun below his eyeline.

"No, I need to deliver this message, and I don't think you will listen to the message without my little security device here."

"Fine." Jenken sighed. "What's your message?"

"I have been sent by Carlo DeMarco."

Jenken immediately sat up, knocking his nose on the gun as he moved. He had previous run-ins with Elsa before, as he had frequently owed money to many people, and managed to avoid the consequences most of the time. Carlo DeMarco was cause for concern. As far as he knew, he hadn't upset or angered DeMarco. In fact, he couldn't remember dealing with him at all.

"Elsa, I have never done any kind of deal with Carlo DeMarco." Jenken's voice was uncharacteristically shaky.

"No you haven't." Elsa's words were not reassuring. "You have dealt with his son, though."

Jenken looked away, thinking back to his previous business shortcuts and deals within deals. He had no idea what she was talking about.

"Trans-gateway Solutions. Ring a bell?"

Jenken's face transformed as the realisation of his past coming back to haunt him was fully formed in his mind.

"That was DeMarco??!" Jenken asked, desperately hoping that he had misunderstood the entire conversation.

"Oh, come on. His goons were all over the bar. You can't tell me you didn't notice them?" Elsa was almost mocking him. Jenken retracted back to his seat, a little embarrassed.

"If I remember rightly, that was a fair bit of money I ended up with." He said, casually.

"40,000 credits."

"Oops."

"Are you seriously going with just "oops"?" Elsa was stunned at Jenken's attitude.

"Look, I have a knack of masking my panic with humour. If I crack some amazing jokes, you'll know I'm wetting myself."

"Eugh" Elsa screwed her face up at the thought.

"The point is," Jenken continued, "obviously I see how serious it is."

"Good. So where's the money?"

There was a slight pause.

"I spent it." Jenken was regretting every pointless purchase now, as he sat there in Elsa's charming company. As he recalled, he spent most of that money on a robot personal assistant for each of the band members. That was clearly not necessary, and not affordable. It didn't last either, as these robots decided to rebel and run off with the band's instruments and start a band themselves. He always vowed to find The Slaves of Time and at least get their instruments back!

Running off with DeMarco's money was a confrontation waiting to happen, and here it was, in front of him, now raising the gun back up to face his nose again.

"Elsa, you are highly trained in many combat disciplines and far stronger than me. You don't have to point that in my face." Jenken pleaded, truthfully.

"I know, but I enjoy it. It makes me feel like I am getting somewhere." Elsa replied, passively. Jenken scoffed, and carried on,

"Look, I am fully aware of what I've done and can promise you that I will give DeMarco his money back as soon as I can."

"I don't think that's going to be good enough."

Jenken kept his head still as his eyes darted around the room, with the empty, featureless nature of the room now coming back to bite him. There wasn't anything around him to use as a weapon, and nowhere to go. He was aware of the studio technicians along the corridor but they may as well not have been there for all of the help they could be. He thought he could string her along a little longer.

"DeMarco is a reasonable man."

"No he isn't." She replied bluntly.

"Alright, maybe not." Jenken backtracked. "I can be more use to him out here getting his money back than whatever you have planned."

"You don't know what I have planned." She said, not particularly mysteriously.

Jenken suddenly raised his voice, in a moment of great release.

"CAN YOU REMOVE THAT GUN FROM THE END OF MY NOSE PLEASE?"

"Where do you want it?" She lifted it slightly so it wasn't quite in his face in the same way, still aiming it at his head.

"In your holster." He nodded to the holster on her left side.

"Nah." She said, slowly. "You need to know how serious this is."

Jenken noticed Elsa releasing a long sigh as she produced a small pocket size video screen from her right side pocket. With one hand she activated the video poised to play on the screen.

As it played, and Jenken's face contorted in shock as he watched, Elsa explained what he was seeing.

"This is Plak. The taller one of your two Movine Brown Yelp Gang people. He's bloody annoying, I have to say, but there you are. I'm threatening you with his death if you don't come up with DeMarco's money."

The video showed Plak, alone, chained to a concrete wall, in an anonymous, dark room, calling out for help.

"What the hell?!!" Jenken screamed in shock. "Are you insane?"

"Yes, I have a certificate about that."

"Why have you kidnapped Plak? What's it got to do with him?!!" His pitch was now raised higher than he thought possible.

"Nothing. That's the sad part really. He is annoying though."

"Let him go. I know I'm in danger owing someone like DeMarco money."

"I don't think you do, Mr Janes."

Jenken let out a sigh of resignation as he gave up protesting.

"Okay, how long have I got?" His words were monotone and full of regret.

"One Corsyllian lunar cycle." Elsa demanded, slowly emphasising each word for effect.

"...and what happens to Plak in all this time?" Jenken was not happy, but understood he needed to know what he was dealing with.

"He will be safe. I will feed him and occasionally give him company."

"Your company?" Jenken asked.

"No, sod off. Like I said, his whining is really annoying. I've paid for someone to visit him and whine at him about their life. He'd like that."

"You've paid for someone to visit him to talk to him?" Jenken was finding this all too much to process.

"Bounty hunting ain't just shooting and...shooting buddy." Elsa's words were still aggressive, despite the inane way she argued her case.

"No, I guess not. I just manage a band, what do I know?"

"All you need to know is that you have to get out of here and get DeMarco's money."

Jenken sat there, still watching the video of his friend Plak, chained up in this unknown prison Elsa had given him. He looked at Elsa with an acquiescent look on his face. He put his hands in the air, in submission.

"Seriously, Elsa, I am in your hands. Don't harm Plak and I'll have DeMarco's money in the blink of an eye.

Elsa vacantly raised her eyebrows and threw him a look of anticipated disappointment,

"I don't want to kill your Movine guy. Don't let me down. I've got bills to pay too."

As she walked out, Jenken shouted after her;

"I need Plak back anyway. DK can't do the harmonies by himself."

Plak and DK were a close knit team. Their roles in the band were inseparable and legendary. Their harmonies were iconic.

...and not everyone was like Trent.

Chapter Two

When they first escaped the security force on Corsylia,
after the Dengen plant incident had become too intense to
deal with, they commandeered a small freighter ship to use
as a vehicle to get out of Corsylia as fast as they could.
They crossed the System boundary with the aid of a scary-
looking wormhole that they tried turning back from, once
they got too close to change course. Their initial fear of
dying from the journey was unfounded, and in fact, the
next two years of gigging and travelling through this newly
discovered star system were mostly positive. There was the
odd hiccup, sometimes with an occasional lost instrument,
or with the regular pressure on Jenken Janes to get them
more elaborate, ambitious gigs. The biggest recent issue
they had was a problem now resolved where Lazy Riff
disappeared for a few weeks; seduced by a Fenusian
woman with hypnotic telepathy in her arsenal of lust. They
were saved by the coincidence that the gigs for those weeks
were in smaller venues, so they pretended they were
stripping down the sound for artistic reasons. Then every
morning they would frantically resume the search for their
missing guitarist. This was a few months ago and they were
now feeling back on an even keel. Plak having been
missing from the group was not an immediate concern, as

Elsa had kidnapped him from a visit he had made to the local supply store.

The Brown Yelp Gang was a tight group of musicians from different star systems who were now like a small, unique family. The lead singer, Trent, with his Calpian forthrightness and the ego that gave him the confidence to lead a band, was often the most vocal about the band's situation. His Calpian physiology sometimes created issues of clarity with his three heads arguing with themselves over the slightest thing; the biggest bugbear for the left and right heads being that nobody seemed to care what they thought. For them, it was always about the middle head. Being in the business for a number of years didn't lessen that annoyance. Despite this, when they sang harmony together it was glorious. It was, ultimately, the kind of perfect harmony you would get from someone sharing the same body.

This was, of course, only one of the many characteristics that made The Brown Yelp Gang so legendary across many different star systems. The guitarist, Lazy Riff, was one of those musicians that men wanted to be and women wanted to nurse. His wayward, free spirited days in the early years of the band were being shaved into submission by the presence of his new love, Aria, the flute playing Denuvian priestess. They were inseparable. For the rest of the band, they enjoyed the Fallet Fish that Aria seemed to have an endless supply of, but weren't always sold on her musical decisions. When she played in a different key to the rest of them, Riff would insist that the dissonance was part of the writing of the song. Clearly plying the band with hallucinogenic fish was an easy way to pacify them.

The one member of the band who wouldn't have been manipulated with mind altering food was Plak, who had missed the last Fallet Fish gathering as he was helplessly detained somewhere by Elsa Grabbinot. Plak would have refused the Fallet Fish and would have been very vocal about her mistakes. In fact, it became a source of frustration for him that he could hear the mistakes and the rest of the band couldn't, even hours after Aria served them their dinner. Plak's absence was sorely felt by the whole band and backstage there was a situation brewing that Jenken couldn't ignore.

DK had been looking for Plak all day, to go through some of the songs again. He was particularly concerned about the song, 'Kiss your Proboscis' as they hadn't performed that, or rehearsed it, in several years. That featured a significant harmony from the both of them that would sound ineffectual with just DK's phrase. Movines were a species of pear-shaped bipeds whose smooth, hairless skin covered a body that led to a long protruding snout that acted as their instruments. At the end of the snouts were small flaps of skin that vibrated when the Movines made a sound. This acted like a double reed and, through these great snouts, fluid wind music was produced. The synchronicity of both Movine lines together was a potent thing to hear and DK felt vulnerable and "ordinary" without Plak. As DK started to panic, it was clear that Jenken would have to admit to what had happened to Plak, and his resolve to get him back.

It was the first day on the "Return to Corsylia" tour, a tour designed entirely to see if they could get away with coming back to the system they escaped from those few years ago. So far, they hadn't had any heat from the Corsyllian security, which was a very good sign. In fact, the signs were so positive with the way they were being treated by everyone from the mechanics at the space dock to the staff at the venue that the band began to forget about the Dengen plant incident and the subsequent hunt for them entirely. This created a very relaxed atmosphere backstage. The band was starting their tour of Corsylia with a medium sized venue that only held 50,000 beings on any one night. This was medium sized on Corsylia, as some venues were huge floating cities, above the capitol. The venue was called "The Atomic Wombat", and had an enviable reputation. The band had been there since the early morning, milling about waiting for the sound check. DK had been frantically contacting anyone he could to get some answers about Plak; and Jenken was avoiding them, trying to think of the best way to get the money as quick as possible so that Plak would be freed.

Deet was the band's drummer, a particularly talented and ambitious native of the beautiful planet, Hurl. He was a symbiotic twin; both these twins became the drummer, Deet. The insides of the larger host had freakishly grown to be even more resonant than most of the Hurl people. They were known for the power of their percussive chests, but Deet's host possessed a reverberating chest that rang out well beyond what was expected on his planet. This is partly why he was such a star on Hurl. On a planet where the native population could naturally create rhythm from their chests, Deet was capable of surpassing any other Hurl musician with the power of his drumming. Deet was the first one to notice how close they were to the sound check time.

"Where's DK? We need to sound check before the hour is up." Deet said to Lazy Riff, Aria and Teddy, who were the only people in the large Green Room with him.

"Where's Trent anyway?" Aria added, compounding the issue.

Riff looked up from his noodling on the guitar as his wife spoke.

"Hey guys, I've spent today delving into the blues. I've found a lovely little thing here. Have a listen."

Riff, oblivious to the questions about the band members' whereabouts, played the blues progression he was working on that day. The others ignored him, looking at their watches to try and send messages out to locate Trent, DK and Plak.

"It's a blues song I'm calling 'You blinded me with love and now I can't find you'. I think it's a goer."

They were still ignoring him, and still checking for replies and sending more messages out.

Riff looked around the room, aware that he was being ignored.

"Hey!" He exclaimed, with a start. "Where are Plak, DK and Trent?!"

Deet looked up with a sigh,

"That's what I asked you a minute ago, Riff."

"Yeah, sure." Riff scoffed, and returned to his blues song on the guitar.

"We can't sound check without them." Aria said, concerned about the lack of response from the messages.

"Nope. This is annoying, though. Our first gig in this system and we've already got this bullshit." Deet was happy to vent, feeling helpless to find them.

"Why don't we just call them?" Teddy said, with the typical mechanical logic you would expect from her.

"Tried that. Plak and DK aren't answering and Trent has his watch here in this room." Deet pointed to one of the tables in the Green Room, where Trent's communication watch was lying. He turned to Riff again;

"Riff, what do you think?"

Riff looked up again from his guitar,

"I think it could break up the set a bit, a bit of blues. We haven't done anything like that a while. It might be very 20th century, but people like that kind of thing."

"What?!" Deet raised his voice, exasperated by Riff's answer.

"Alright mate, steady." Riff said, taken aback by Deet's angry tone. He turned to his right, where Aria was standing. "What's got into him then?"

"Riff, we are missing some people here, and we need to sound check." Aria was beginning to get annoyed herself. Before the conversation could develop any further, Jenken ran in with his usual energetic, enthusiastic manner.

"Hi guys. How are we doing?" He was smiling at them all and clapping his hands and rubbing them like it would somehow make them spring into action.

"Where is Trent?" Deet said, killing the mood with his blunt delivery.

"Trent is on his way up mate, it's all good. He had to do an errand for me."

"DK?" Deet asked.

"He's on his way up, he'll be here in a second." Jenken replied.

"- and Plak?" Aria asked, with a similar tone of not being impressed.

"Ah." Jenken's tone changed. "That's a different story. I'll tell you about that when Trent gets up here." He looked sheepish, but fully intended to tell them everything once

47

Trent and DK have returned to the room. "Just make sure you're ready to get on stage in a minute for the sound check."

His words were greeted with a collective huff, which he heard, but stayed focused.

"I'm making a Jakadian Tea. Anyone want one?" Jenken asked the room as he mixed his own tea. Aria and Deet mumbled a decline, while Riff was more willing.

"I'll have some of that, Jenks." Riff said, exuberantly. "That will wake me up after burying myself in the blues for hours." Riff laughed as he said this, amused by his own retro morning.

"Ah, talking of the blues, Riff." Jenken replied. "Do you guys ever think of doing that song from the first album, 'Hole in the hole'? That was a great song that, and I don't think you've ever done it live have you?"

"Jenks mate, we've never done it because it's ridiculous." Riff replied.

"It's impossible for us to do it live." Deet chimed in. "Trent barely managed it in the studio. The delay setting is set for each note to be repeated for fifteen minutes. He got totally confused."

"Yeah, it was quite funny actually." Riff started laughing, remembering the long recording sessions with Trent trying to remember where he was in the song. "Hole, hole, hole, hole, hole, hole, hole, hole..." Riff couldn't contain his laughter. Deet was also smiling at the ludicrous nature of the song.

"Do you remember the a capella section in it?" Deet turned to Riff, still smiling.

"Yeah. It was that poem wasn't it?"

"A poem that Plak wrote I think." Deet frowned as he tried to remember.

"That's right. It was a poem about holes." Riff said, smiling.

"He wrote a poem about holes?" Aria said, with an unconvinced tone to her voice.

"Only Plak would write a poem about holes." Deet replied, shaking his head, smiling. "Where did you say he was again, Jenken?" Deet asked again.

"I - I - I was just - " Jenken was interrupted by Trent and DK returning to the Green Room.

Trent whispered something to Jenken then grabbed a towel and headed for the bathroom.

"Er, hold on, Trent. I need to speak to all of you about Plak." Jenken sounded nervous.

DK found a seat beside Riff and sat forward, eager to hear about his friend and partner in the band. Trent turned around and waited, halting his stride into the bathroom. They all looked at Jenken with baited breath.

"Perhaps you should all sit down." He motioned to the chairs that were dotted around the tables in front of them.

"What's going on, Jenken?" Deet asked, more sternly.

"Is Plak OK?" Aria asked, concerned.

"Not really." Jenken said.

"What the hell has happened to him?" Trent became animated very quickly.

"It's the past coming back to bite me. Plak is suffering because of something I did."

"That doesn't make sense. You've done something to Plak?" Riff had put his guitar down on the floor next to him, something he rarely did.

"No it's not something I've done to Plak. It's something related to what I did once."

"It would be clearer if you just said it, Mr Janes." Teddy had a point. There is no substitute for just saying it.

"Yeah, okay." Jenken took a deep intake of breath and then exhaled. "Plak is held somewhere, chained up somewhere, I don't know where. It's some kind of threat that I need to clear a debt or he'll suffer."

The band was shocked. You could hear a pin drop in the room. Trent was the first to break the silence.

"What was the debt?"

"It was 40,000 credits."

They all gasped, audibly. DK was silently boiling over, just about containing his anger.

"40,000 credits? Bloody hell!" Riff exclaimed.

"Who do you owe 40,000 credits to?" Deet asked, with a tone of incredulity to his words.

"That's the thing." Jenken didn't want to say it out loud.

"What's the thing?" Trent asked, impatiently.

"I can't think of anyone worse." Jenken said, with a resigned tone. He was feeling terrible revealing this to the band, especially knowing that Plak was in the middle of all of this, vulnerable and probably terrified.

"Just tell us, man." Riff pleaded.

"Okay. I owe that money to -" He hesitated for a moment, nervous to finish off the sentence - "Carlo DeMarco."

"You're kidding?!!" Deet gasped.

Lazy Riff whistled, showing his astonishment. Trent was more concerned about the consequences.

"Hold on, you're saying that Plak is tied up somewhere in mortal danger because you owe a stupid amount of money to Carlo DeMarco?" Trent's voice could be heard from the stage below them.

"Yes, that's true." Jenken said, humbly.

"Wow." Trent said, sitting down and throwing his towel across the room.

"That's quite something." Deet said.

"You've endangered the life of one of the band for one of your pointless, dodgy deals!" DK was keeping his anger under control but speaking out now.

"Look guys, this is bad. I know it's bad, but we can sort this out. We need to get the money together and then Plak will be fine." Jenken had a pleading tone to his voice.

"How am I going to do my bits in the songs without Plak?" DK shouted, directly at Jenken.

"I can reproduce his part amongst the sounds I'm creating, DK." Teddy replied, reassuring him with her technical wizardry.

"Great! We're going even more electronic now." Riff scoffed, completely dismissing the help Teddy was offering.

"It's fine, that will be a great help, Teddy. Thank you." DK declared, aiming the words mostly at Riff.

"Get this gig done, and we'll get a plan together for getting the money and getting Plak back." Jenken said, with his instructive manager voice.

He then left the room, going outside to make some calls.

Riff, Deet, DK, Teddy and Aria went downstairs to the stage area, with Riff taking his equipment with him in an unfeasibly awkward trolley. In this trolley were several guitars, an effects board that featured 24 effects pedals and his own makeshift Theremin. The tech crew had taken all of the amps and monitors out of the ship and onto the stage earlier that morning. Trent followed on, after his quick trip into the bathroom to freshen up.

As he reached the stage area, he asked Deet from the back of the stage,

"Who have we got opening for us tonight?"

"Aww god, you wouldn't believe it." Deet said, with a frustrated tone.

"What? Who is it?" Trent was intrigued.

"You heard of Malitaine Malicouse the Third?"

"You're joking?"

"Nope. That's who is on before us."

"That miserable bastard will make everyone walk out."

"I don't get it. Why do people want to listen to him?"

"I know." Trent was as annoyed as Deet was. "I feel for the guy. The last remaining person of his whole species, all wiped out by occupation and war."

"Yeah, I feel for the guy too..." Deet agreed. "...but EVERY SONG?!!"

"Yeah, every song is about his species being killed off."

"It's like he's asking for the same thing to happen to him."

They both laughed at Deet's poor taste.

"He's a good lutist, though." Trent offered.

"Is that a word?"

"Yeah, it's a word."

"That's good...and I agree, he can play that little stringed thing well."

"Just as well really...considering the songs." Trent concluded. They both laughed.

Then they all took up their positions on stage to begin the sound check. Trent was at the front with his microphone; his three heads sharing the one mic for the visual effect. Deet was lying down on the back board riser he had propped up so he would be able to see the audience as he beat his chest. Riff was plugging into his effects board, stage right. DK was stage left, getting his microphone positioned to capture the melodic lines coming from his snout. Aria was behind him, positioning her microphone correctly for her flute, and Teddy was plugging herself into the PA system, standing beside Deet at the back.

After the sound engineer had checked that everything was coming through the PA correctly, he motioned for them to test a song out. Teddy began the ambient sounds of the introduction to "We're back and we're livid". As the music from Teddy's circuitry swelled into a sustained crescendo, DK and Riff burst forth with the song's main melody. Deet came in 4 bars later, and the band sounded bombastic and perfectly in time. Trent's three heads all smiled at each other and began the vocal refrain that never fails to get the crowd chanting.

"We're back, we're livid, whatever, we'll live it."

As the song reverberated around the hall of the concert venue, The Brown Yelp Gang settled into their new songs again, looking forward to showing them to the old crowd in Corsylia.

The sound check went without a hitch. DK struggled to concentrate due to worrying about Plak, but he played his parts correctly and Teddy made up for Plak's absence with electronic versions of Plak's melodies. Trent and Aria were adding extra ad-libs into the vocal and flute parts. Trent's left head was being particularly fruity with his ad-libs and often made the other heads turn around in pleasant surprise. As the sound man and lighting 'man' gave them the thumbs up to decamp, the band walked offstage from the back, and Trent's heads complemented each other on their performance at the sound check. Deet bounded off the stage with the buzz he always got from the sound check; for him it was the start of the gig. There was a big gap in the middle, but from when he started beating the rhythm out on his powerful chest and they began adjusting the mics, and controlling the sound on the desk, the gig was on, for him. Riff had a more laid back approach. He barely played in the sound check and sometimes performed in the sound check off his head on Freak capsules. This grated on the band a little, as it would take much longer, while people tried to communicate to him, in vain attempts to penetrate his drug-fogged mind. On this day, there were no Freak capsules, no Dengen plant and no Fallet Fish to alter his perception. When his guitar was out of tune, he heard it.

Backstage, the band's attention turned back to what they should do about Plak. They all sat around the Green Room with Jenken to formulate a plan that could get him back as soon as possible. Riff played guitar while they talked.

"So we need to get 40,000 credits?" Aria was the first to get the ball rolling.

"Indeed. 40,000." Jenken was business like, and not quite as sheepish as he was before the sound check.

"So if we pooled together our band's resources now, to see how that changes things, does that help?" Deet was quick to be as productive as he could.

"The band has enough for the travel and food and living costs around the tour, knowing we may not get paid straight away."

"How much is that?" Trent asked, blissfully unaware of the cost of touring through the Corsyl system.

"Fuel for the journey around this system is 8,000 credits alone. The rest of the costs come to about 5,000, depending on how much you want to eat or drink, or how much you want to spend on some of the 'friends' you might meet along the way." Jenken looked at Riff when he said this. Aria lifted her eyebrows at this suggestion.

"Hey, man. I'm a new man now. Trapped in a beautiful relationship with this incredible goddess here." He pointed to the chair where Aria was sitting, and halted his guitar playing for a moment.

"Priestess, not goddess." She corrected.

"You're my goddess, Aria." He swooned.

"Oh, please." Deet rolled his eyes.

"I'd say it was a good save, but I just think you were trying too hard." Aria cut his fawning down with a look as much as her words.

Riff gave out a slight "humph" sound and went back to playing guitar, mumbling something that sounded like 'I got those priestess stare blues'. Aria didn't take the bait.

"Okay, so if we strip down our eating and drinking..." Trent began.

" – and don't travel." Deet interjected, sarcastically.

"Well, we could look at alternative ways to travel?" DK spoke for the first time.

"I may have a solution to that." Teddy said, from the back of the room. They all turned around, surprised to hear a contribution from the often silent, often recharging, robot.

"Go on." Jenken said, intrigued.

"The transports that take robots to and from planets for repairs and trade are big, bulky freighter ships with outdated facilities and engines that barely run efficiently."

"If you're going where I think you're going with this, you're really selling it."

"No, the whole point is it will be very cheap."

"How cheap?" Jenken was listening.

Teddy looked like she shut off for a moment, appearing like she does when she recharges, then came back alive after a 6 second gap.

"A freighter that could fit all of our crew, the band and some equipment would just cost 2,000 to hire for one lunar cycle."

The atmosphere in the room changed, instantly.

"Wow, that's a hell of a reduction." Trent said, holding up his arm to high five her. He slowly lowered it when there was no response from her.

"That must be for a reason." Deet replied, cynically.

"Well yeah, it's because it will be dirty, hard work and risky." Jenken added.

"It could make it possible for us to get Plak back though?" DK answered, nodding optimistically to the band, hoping for an agreement.

There was a moment of silence while the band looked at each other in thought. Riff stopped playing the guitar and looked around. He had missed the last bit of conversation, so was hoping someone would repeat something. As it didn't look like that would happen, he tried to force it; "How's that going to solve it, though?" His eyes widened after he said it, in embarrassed hope that his sentence made sense.

"How is what going to solve it?" Deet said, finding it hard to connect his question to the conversation.

"You know, the thing we just said."

"What, the freighter?" Deet replied.

"Yeah." Riff guessed.

"It'll save us money won't it, fretbrain."

While Riff tried to think how their freighter would save them money, he listened in for more clues.

"So I guess we're talking about selling ours then?" Trent added.

Riff let out a loud "Ahhhh!" of recognition, which the others ignored, being used to his confusion.

"If we sell our freighter, we could get at least 30,000 for it."

Riff whistled again, saying "Nice" to punctuate his astonishment. Then it dawned on him.

"Er, guys, then we wouldn't have a vehicle." Riff felt like he was stating the obvious but clearly someone had to say it. They all looked at him with frowns that made it crystal clear that he had missed something.

"Have you been listening to anything we've been saying?" Aria barked, with a tone that got his attention like nothing else.

"Yeah, course." He sat up, and nodded. "Freighters and all that."

They weren't convinced but carried on, with or without him.

"So, we sell the freighter, get a cheap one built for robots and...what else?" Trent recapped.

"An auction?" DK suggested, with a rising pitch so extreme, that it was obvious that DK wasn't even convinced of the idea.

"An auction of what?" Deet said, bluntly.

"I have some old paraphernalia I could muster up, to be fair..." Jenken thought, out loud.

The band seemed interested by this and murmured their approval.

"You could get a lot for these hands!" Riff stated, wide-eyed and theatrically, raising his arms in the air and letting his guitar drop in his lap.

"Well, you need them to play don't you, ya tree." Deet was quick with the insults.

Riff quickly retreated from his display, suddenly aware of the lack of logic in his contribution.

"Can we get the fans to help?" Deet suggested, meekly.

"They helped us last time...?"

The thought was like a huge truth bomb that had been let off in the room. Every member of the band was hesitant and unsure about how to react. Finally, after the longest silence the band had witnessed that day, Trent spoke up, "What was the name of that superfan that spent all of his savings on a trip to the Fillaphion System to see us? That was clearly the wrong side of mental."

"Yeah I remember the guy. He had a huge beard. Like, crazy long." DK recalled.

"Didn't he name his beard after us?" Deet added.

"His beard?" Aria scowled, unimpressed.

"Yeah, he named it Riff." Riff added.

"Sorry, why would anyone name their beard after you?" Aria asked, still reeling.

"After us?" Riff corrected her.

"Yeah, us."

"Why would you name your beard after anything? He did, though." DK said, dryly.

"Well, him anyway. He might be a way in." Trent interjected.

"Is he the one that created that huge posse on the information stream?" Jenken was now getting involved, animated by the thought of the fans helping out.

The information stream was the method many different star systems used to communicate. Branching out to different planets across the system, but limited to within each system, this network of communication beacons was crucial to the news getting out to the neighbouring planets, crucial for contingency plans when governments failed or predatory aliens tried to conquer a sector of the galaxy. It was also a great way to spread the game of "Furp". This game was essentially an intergalactic Mexican wave of people plastering the word "Furp" in different places. Kids love it.

The last time the band were in Corsylia, their fans took part in their defiance against the authorities as the Corsyllian security attempted to arrest the band for high level drug use. It wasn't unreasonable, given the way they mobilised before, to put their trust in their fans once again.

"I have to say, I do like this idea." Trent declared, quietly, almost to himself.

"We can't tell them why though, surely?" DK said, with a hint of panic in his voice.

"No, we don't have to give them every detail. We can spin it. Make it about a new album." Jenken suggested.

"We're already plugging an album, that's already made!" DK objected, with a sigh.

"Who cares?!" Jenken smiled, trying to capture a spirit of adventure that had left the band when he told them he owed Carlo DeMarco 40,000 credits.

"You think we can get away with plugging something that doesn't exist yet?" DK was sceptical.

"I've seen this before, on the Traaline System. It was on the largest moon orbiting Yanikk. There was a band there getting money for a record they hadn't made yet." Trent was more animated as he remembered.

"How does that work?" DK was pulling a face of disgust.

"They just asked their fans for money!" Trent said, widening his arms to accentuate the point. It was that simple.

"- and the fans gave them money, just like that?"

"Honestly, DK. It was crazy. They told me they were going to make an album out of the money...eventually." Trent was chuckling as he said this last point.

"Whoah, we have to try a bit of this!" Jenken was getting more excited the more he thought of this.

"I don't like it." DK said, looking around the room for support.

"Hey, fella. Do you want to get Plak out of...wherever he is?" Deet looked straight at DK, almost as if he was giving him the final choice.

DK looked around at his bandmates. Riff was occupied with his guitar playing again, and hadn't actually heard the last suggestion concerning the fans, but everybody else in the room was looking back at DK, expectantly.

"What do you think, DK? Wanna get your boy back?" Jenken was beaming with excitement as he tried to lift DK out of his doubts. There was a moment of tension that you could cut like a knife. Riff noticed it, and stopped playing for a moment.

"Is it time to go on?" He asked, unaware of the time.

"No, we have another hour, Riff." DK snapped, unimpressed. "Okay, fine, let's do it. We'll fleece the fans of their money for a non-existent new album."

"- and just to clarify." Trent directed his question at Jenken. "What do we do when the fans find out we've tricked them into giving us a ton of money?"

Jenken thought for a moment. Again, the members of the band all listened. Riff was listening now, trying to join the dots of the snippets he heard. After a few seconds, Jenken threw his hands in the air, and like the showman he was, shouted with a beaming smile,

"Let's cross that bridge when we come to it!"

Chapter Three

Malitaine Malicouse the Third was the last of his species, and he let everyone know this, at every gig, in every song. From the laid-back gentle lilt of his song, "Where is everybody?" to the melancholic drone of "Me, myself and I", and the even more laid-back, ambient, soundscape, "The Empty Plains of Fellaceese IV", his message was clear and unavoidably sombre. Fellaceese IV was where he grew up and where his species lived. They seldom left their world and had endured a bitter history of occupation from the neighbouring planet's warrior race of Tarken aggressors. Malitaine had only known hardship and an ever present fear of the Tarken people. It was a miraculous stroke of luck, and an uncharacteristic change in focus, that took Malitaine off-world for his first ever music festival gig. He had overcome his own fear of travel at this most fortuitous moment in his life. The timing couldn't have been better as, during the afternoon of the second day of the festival, his planet was decimated by cannon fire and bombs raining down from the Tarken forces orbiting the planet. In less than a day, his species were almost completely wiped out, leaving him the surviving member of his race with a new sound, and the relentlessly repeated subject matter in his lyrics. The music commentators on other planets in the system had remarked on how much

they missed his first big hit, "I'm so happy I could fly".
Maybe one day he would bring it back to his set.

On Corsylia, he was supporting The Brown Yelp Gang,
and his particular brand of morose navel gazing was not
going down well. As he started the chorus to his first song,
"All of them, gone", the crowd started chanting "Cack!"
which is the Corsyllian word for "No!" Their voices were
ruthlessly cutting as the unforgiving mood of the Brown
Yelp fans swept through the venue. If Malitaine was in any
doubt about what the word might have meant, they also
started throwing bits of the floor at him. It was often a
rough crowd at "The Atomic Wombat" and the venue had,
over time, removed most of the items that could be thrown
at the performers, in response to previous gigs. Taking the
floor away was not an option, and the enraged audience
managed to peel large chunks of it off to throw at the poor
singer-songwriter on stage. Malataine's style was not the
kind of sound that would pacify them, and they were eager
to hear The Brown Yelp Gang. It was painful to watch;
almost as painful as it was to hear.

After a brief twenty minute set, that felt to Malitaine like
twenty years, the stage was clear for the setting up of the
Brown Yelp Gang staging and equipment. It took them a
while to remove the debris that had been hurled at the
poor support act, but soon enough; the stage was
transformed into the Brown Yelp Gang spectacle that their
fans would be expecting. For this tour, the crew were

setting up a kitchen design on stage, responding to Jenken's idea of a food theme to the staging, as a lot of the songs from the new album had food-related lyrics. They decided they would create more of a theatrical concept for the shows with a backdrop that referenced new songs like 'Put your berries where your mouth is', 'Cheese dream' and the epic album closer, 'Sweet, Brown and Sweaty'.

So, within forty minutes of the crew working on the stage behind the huge, silver curtain, all of the gear they needed was on stage and the line check had been successfully done without any issues. The stage looked like a classic Corsyllian kitchen from the often imitated, classic Yanten period, with cupboards coming out from all angles and the oven suspended on wires. It was a gloriously creative example of staging, worthy of a band with Brown Yelp's reputation. The band was backstage with aprons on, looking out for the signal to go on, with butterflies in their stomachs on their first night in Corsylia.

The stage manager's voice boomed across the huge venue hall;

"All right you lovely people." The crowd roared with a noise that was utterly deafening to anyone in its vicinity.

"Returning from Corsylia, this time without the aid of the Dengen plant...!" The crowd chuckled and nodded to each other in silent praise for the reference, "...and with new songs and new members..." His voice was now almost shouting in a high pitched scream, "I give you, The Brown...Yelp...Gang!!!"

The crowd went completely wild. The silver curtain rose and revealed the band standing in their regular spots, playing the first few chords of "Bake it the way I like it, baby". The crowd hadn't heard this one before, but within less than a minute they were singing along to the line, "Bake it the way I like it, bake it like you do".

The first song of the set was going down extremely well. The audience had spotted the new members immediately and were instantly fascinated by Teddy, at the back creating indescribable sounds to mask Plak's absence and, ultimately, as a way of expressing herself. They were also mesmerised by Aria's presence on stage. When she wasn't playing flute, she was gyrating and swaying with a mixture of personalised meditation techniques that Aria thought would suit the music. Trent and Riff had competition for the limelight here, but they had got used to it and enjoyed having a different vibe on stage after so many years. Riff was utterly in love with Aria, so would happily watch her slapping a tree repeatedly if she had the urge; he found everything she did glamorous and spellbinding. Trent was a red-blooded wolf-like three headed male, so he could certainly relate to Riff's frequent hypnosis. As the first song finished, Trent's left head shouted out to the shrill, energised crowd;

"How are you all doing?!"

The crowd cheered again, whooping and screaming in response. Trent's right head joined in.

"It's great to be back in Corsylia!"

Riff walked up to his mic, and slyly joked,

"Has anyone got any Dengen plant?" Most of the band looked at him with a knowing smile. Teddy didn't catch on to the sarcasm and gave him a worried look. The crowd responded with the kind of laugh that demonstrated that if he had simply read out the names of the people in the front row, they would have been on their knees laughing.

"We love you, Riff!" A voice from the back shouted.

"Is that me out there?" Riff said, to another wave of hysterical laughter.

Trent's middle head introduced the next song.

"Okay guys, this is an old one for ya. The last one was from our new album, 'Warm and Tasty'. This one is from our old album, 'Come out with your hands up!'"

The crowd erupted with joy at this revelation. The band didn't draw from this album much for their sets, so they knew this moment in the set would have a dramatic effect on the crowd. The band was grinning as they watched their fans lap up the live spectacle. One overexcited Corsyllian member of the audience at the front eloquently shouted, "THIS IS A THING!"

- and it was. The gig was going down like Platinum Soup. Jenken was backstage trying to get a buyer for the freighter they had, but he could see that the gig was going well.

Occasionally he walked over to a place backstage where the band could see him, to show his approval, and they reciprocated in their mutual respect. Years of working together had brought them non-verbal signals that said so much more than words could. For Jenken and the band, a simple slap on each eye was all that needed to be said.

After the fifth song, Trent was eager to introduce the new members of the band to the crowd.

"Thanks guys." He said, as the noise of the screaming and applause died down from the previous song's ending. "As you know, we've been away a while, and been creating new music for you."

A few "whoops" were heard throughout the auditorium.

One member of the audience remembered an old phrase from the 4th Brown Yelp album, and shouted it out to the band in the relative quiet;

"Who's your mother, Trent?"

"Ahh, nice reference, my friend." Trent acknowledged.

"We might do that one....if you're good!"

The crowd showed their appreciation again with cheers and screams.

"First, I want to tell you about two new cats that are bringing their music to us in our little family here." He looked over to Teddy first, and moved his arm to point in her direction. As he spoke, Teddy moved slightly forward on the stage to acknowledge her moment in the spotlight.

69

"Over here, at the back, we have the marvellous creative machine that we call Teddy!"

The crowd gave her a suitably joyous welcome. Then Trent turned to Aria, and smiled at her.

"...and over here, people of Corsylia, is the beautiful, radiant and utterly charming Aria, on flute."

Aria walked to the middle of the stage, smiled to the audience and played a short phrase on her flute, ending in a quick bow before she walked back to her usual position on stage. The crowd were equally noisy and welcoming to Aria. Arguably, more so.

Then, Riff immediately burst into the guitar introduction for one of their biggest hits, "Fallet Fever". Riff loved this song even more, now that he was with Aria; it had more meaning to it, in the light of his daily routine of drifting off into another plain courtesy of her Fallet Fish. Riff and Aria looked at each other as the song flowed into the first verse. Aria had added a flute part that had become one of the band's favourite elements of the song. Teddy played some extra ad-libbed notes in Plak's part, turning Trent's three heads from the front. The crowd were clearly and demonstrably loving it.

The gig continued in this vein for the whole evening. Any fears they had of being away too long, or of the new songs not having the same impact as the old classics, were decimated by this triumphant first gig back in Corsylia. They predictably finished the set with their biggest interplanetary hit, "How is your hair", a song that almost haunted them with its popularity. They liked to finish that song, and indeed their sets, with the crowd chanting "How is your hair" as they sauntered off, waving goodbye to the crowd. On this night, they did this, but this time with Teddy staying on stage to add some extra layers of synthetic atmosphere to the chanting. The crowd chanted in exactly the same way as previous audiences had at Brown Yelp gigs, but this time a whole new smile was overcoming them from the orchestration they could hear under their voices.

It was a great finish.

Backstage, the band was buzzing. By the time Teddy had got to the Green Room the band was guzzling the rare, purple Jump Wine; named for the energy and fearlessness it creates as you drink it. The atmosphere in the Green Room was almost feral. They were shouting incoherently, laughing, singing, whooping, slapping the furniture and generally releasing any physical manifestation of joy they could.

They were so entrenched in their high spirits that they hadn't noticed the short bald girl, dressed in silky rags, who was watching them in their revelry, from the far left corner of the room. Teddy noticed.

"Hello." She said, bluntly.

The band turned around, noticing her for the first time.

"Whoah! Who is this?!" Trent squealed.

"Security!" Deet shouted.

"Want us to sign you?" Riff asked, suggestively.

"Er...hello." She said, quietly, ignoring the inappropriate question from Riff.

She was sitting in the corner of the room, with her arms wrapped around her legs. She was humanoid, small, with a slim build and clothes that looked worn and dirty. Her baldness was striking: it was rare to see a young girl alone in Corsylia; a bald girl even rarer.

The atmosphere in the room had calmed down dramatically to a whimper of smiling faces and quiet giggles.

"What is your name, child?" Aria asked, gently, sitting beside her on the floor.

"Hello. My name is Lilly."

"Hello Lilly. My name is Aria."

"I know. I love your band."

Lilly looked around the room at the motley crew in front of her. She was familiar with all of them, having followed the band for a long time. Like a lot of people, she had followed them so intensely that she felt that she knew them. She didn't, but that wasn't the point. Perception is a funny thing. The galaxy is filled with entertainers living opposite lives to their public image, putting on a mask for the audience so all parties involved can forget about their real lives for a moment.

"I feel like I'm home being around you guys." Lilly said, confidently, starting to smile.

"Where is your home, Lilly?" Jenken asked, kneeling down to her level as he spoke.

"Originally, Earth." She answered. "I haven't been there for many years though. Me and my sister have been travelling from ship to ship, living day to day." The band all looked at each other, concerned.

"A sister you say?" Trent clarified.

"Yeah. My sister, Penny. We are always together. We always have each other's backs." There was no hint of irony in her tone, despite no sister being in the room with her.

"Where is Penny now?" Aria asked, again, with a soothing, friendly voice that came from years in the priesthood.

Lilly closed her eyes for a moment. The band looked at each other again, wondering what she was doing. Then Lilly opened them again, and turned to Aria.

"She is fine. She is in a cafe down the road, drinking Manok Fruit."

"Urm...are you sure?" Aria asked, a little confused about what she was seeing; it appeared that Lilly closing her eyes was linked to her knowing where her sister was.

"Yes I'm sure. We speak to each other all of the time, and feel each other's feelings."

Jenken suddenly became more animated and stood up, slapping his knees as if experiencing a "eureka moment".

73

"You're a telepath twin aren't you?" He asked, still smiling to keep the friendly tone of the encounter. Lilly looked up toward Jenken's direction,

"Yes, that's right. We are twins."

Deet hadn't heard of a telepath twin before. He had to ask.

"Sorry, Jenken, I'm a bit behind here. What's a telepath twin?"

"It's fascinating. At some point, on Earth in the last century, there were a few cases, and only a few, of children born as twins where they literally could read each other's thoughts and feelings."

Lilly listened, aware of the details, but intrigued to hear somebody else talk about her and her sister, Penny.

"I've never met one before." Jenken said, unable to hide his pleasure as he smiled at her, enchanted.

"I don't think any of us have." Trent added.

"I have." Riff said, picking up his guitar again.

"Have you?" Trent turned around to him, surprised.

"Well, not exactly, but yeah."

"What do you mean not exactly?" Trent was almost rolling his eyes before Riff spoke.

"I met a twin once, but she wasn't a telegraph."

"Telepath." Trent corrected.

"Yeah. One of them. She was a twin though. Gorgeous woman."

Everyone in the room turned away from Riff.

"She had five arms. Amazing woman." He was talking to himself now. "She could get anywhere on your body without you doing a thing about it."

"Can I get you some water?" Aria asked Lilly.

"Yes please." Lilly politely replied. She had been on the move all night, and was thirsty, tired and hungry.

Aria stood up and went to the other room to find some water for her. Riff managed to get more unwanted scowls from the others, as he began to sing an impromptu song on his ever present guitar;

"Lilly, Lilly, Lilly,

Don't Be Silly,

You look brilly...

Ant, Lilly..."

The other members of the band were biting their tongues, almost tempted to ask him to leave the room.

"Why are you here in our Green Room, Lilly?" Deet asked, somehow managing to sound less benevolent than the others.

"I am sorry for intruding. I wanted to talk to you all."

"Really? What do you want to know?" Trent puffed out his chest and immediately switched his tone to how he spoke to his fans, his tone full of showbiz and ego.

Aria had returned with the drink, as well as one for herself.

"I really want to join your band." Lilly quietly said, before sipping her water.

The band let out a unanimous, audible gasp.

"Sorry, did you just say you want to join the band?" Deet
asked, for clarity, not quite believing what she had said.
"I would absolutely love to." She smiled at them all; with a
smile they hadn't seen yet. The kind of blissful, contented
smile you would imagine she would have after emerging
from a sensuous bath carrying set of replacement clothes.
"What do you play?" DK asked, pragmatically.
"I do this." She closed her eyes again, and enigmatically sat
still, with her skin turning paler as she concentrated.
Slowly, as the band remained fixed in their spot, waiting to
discover her musical gift, a sound started to emanate from
the room. It was a sound collated from several sounds
being drawn from a number of sources around the room.
All of the glasses around the room were creating a pitched
note, a rattling sound was coming from the air vent along
the wall, and the walls themselves seemed to be releasing a
hum. The effect was incredibly subtle, and all the more
powerful for it. The band looked around the room, open-
mouthed and transfixed. Jenken was grinning as he
watched and listened. The shape of the music being drawn
from the room shifted into something more harmonious,
and more rhythmic. It swirled through the room like a
psychotropic trick. The difference here, of course, was that
this effect was being created by a girl from Earth, with
extraordinary gifts. After several minutes, when no band
member or band manager said a word to spoil the
moment, the music faded away slowly, and Lilly opened

her eyes and smiled calmly at the astounded faces around her.

"That was quite special, Lilly." Aria was the first to break the silence.

"Thank you."

"So, you can manipulate your surroundings to create sound?" Deet asked.

"To create music!" She emphasised the word music, like it was a magical word with supernatural properties.

"I'm hugely impressed, I have to say." Trent said, standing up to reach for more Jump Wine.

"Absolutely," Trent's left and right heads agreed, in unison.

"I echo our hairy singer's words." DK said, with a smile.

Jenken halted for a moment and addressed the band squarely,

"Hold on, are you saying you want another member in the band?"

"No," all three of Trent's heads replied, "but she's pretty good!" the middle head added.

There were quiet mumbles of agreement from the rest of the band. A tone of relief hovered around the hushed voices of the band as their unanimous response bounced around their tight circle. Jenken was sympathetic to the girl, especially as it was clear that something else was happening in her life, besides her wish to join The Brown Yelp Gang. For now, they could promise to make sure she would be

OK for that night, but then they'd be moving on to the next venue in the morning.

"Lilly, we are flattered that you would like to join us. It is obvious from what you said before that you know the band well. There are quite a lot of us now, and another mouth to feed isn't ideal with everything that's happening at the moment." Aria gave Jenken a look, as if to remind him to hold back on the life story for now. Jenken nodded to her in acknowledgement. "We can let you stay in our rooms here for just the evening as we're leaving the venue tonight to go to another City, a few hours from here. We cannot stay, unfortunately. We have loved meeting you, Lilly, and please go and see the crew in the morning to pick up something from our merchandise."

Lilly listened silently, gave a slight smile and stood up. With the band's eyes fixed on her, she looked at them all, and then choosing a position that met the middle of their positions in the room, she gave a swift bow. Then, without a word, she left the room, and left the venue. There was a short pause, followed by DK, Trent, Jenken and Riff letting out a loud sigh, releasing the tension. Aria maintained a casual, nonchalant manner that came from her regular meditations and years in the priesthood. She had, with the mechanical logic of Teddy's input, become a rational voice within the volatile personalities in the male members of the band. They were all fully aware of this, and enjoyed the new dynamic.

"So, that was interesting!" Riff began.

"I have never seen anything like it." DK added.

"Me neither. I love the idea. I think there was something else going on though," Deet said.

"Yeah, it was all a bit weird wasn't it?" DK replied.

"Layers building on layers, building on layers." Riff pondered, enigmatically.

"Maybe." Trent said sharply, turning back to the Jump Wine again. "Who wants more wine?"

All of the male members of the band raised their hand for more Jump Wine. Aria was happy with her water.

"Where are we going tomorrow again, Jenken?" DK asked, as he poured his wine.

"Ahh, tomorrow we will be beside the sea! At the port of Bragal."

"Bragal?" Trent had an alarmed tone to his voice. "That's full of pirates, gangsters and gun runners isn't it?" Trent was referring to its reputation as much as anything else. He'd never been there, but had heard of it.

"Erm..." Jenken chose his words carefully, "...it's one of the best paid gigs in this Sector guys. It might be a bit rough, and we need to keep our heads down, but it will be worth it."

The rest of the band was facing Jenken now, more than a little interested in the activity on Bragal.

"So, we're going to be safe in Bragal, right?" Deet was hoping it was a hypothetical question.

"Tomorrow's gig will give us 8,000 more credits for the funds. None of the other gigs on our tour will give us the same amount for one night's work." He was pacifying the band, but they were still aware of Bragal's reputation. "You know how important it is that we get this income flowing through..."

"What kind of venue are we playing at Jenken?" Trent asked, warming a little to the idea, with the money factor brought in.

"It's called the Sinking Wharf."

"We're playing on a sinking wharf??!" Deet exclaimed.

"NO! That's just its name." Jenken was waving his arms around as he spoke, to calm the band down. "It will be fine. More than fine!"

"That's a stupid name." Deet said, under his breath.

"Yes it is, Deet." Jenken heard him. "That doesn't matter. We put on a good show, get the fans into the new songs and collect our winnings!"

"Indeedy, Jenkaroo." Riff said, raising his Jump Wine as a salute.

"Oh, one other thing," Jenken said, to the room, "I've sent one of our lizard guys out to my ranch to get more merchandise. We nearly ran out today."

"That sounds promising." Deet said. "How much did we make on merch?"

"We sold several hundred Brown Yelp batteries, about 130 shirts, 67 wigs, 458, or thereabouts, copies of the new album, and just over a hundred rubber tyres."

"Wow, I didn't think the rubber tyres would sell." DK shook his head in surprise.

"I told you they were a great idea. I love buying tyres." Riff was glowing with pride on his idea paying off.

"Are you bringing over the other gear from the ranch?" Trent asked.

"Absolutely. I brought the essentials, not knowing what to expect...as well as the tyres." Jenken nodded to Riff. "Now we can be pretty confident that we'll keep selling after a night like tonight."

"Nice." Trent said, drinking more Jump Wine.

"For now, I suggest we all get some rest, as we've got to travel to Bragal tomorrow and another gig, before heading off Corsylia for the rest of the tour."

The band all looked at each other with a mutual feeling of pride, and unspoken sense of achievement after an eventful evening. The thought of Bragal's notorious reputation hung in the air as Jenken brought their thoughts back to the tour. Their determination to get this debt solved, and to recover Plak from his captivity, gave them all the determination they needed to venture out to a dubious and scary place like Bragal.

"Let's hope Bragal is friendlier than its reputation!" Deet stated, articulating what everyone was thinking.

"We must be mad." DK added, almost smiling.

"Of course you're mad. You're in a rock band!" Jenken said bluntly, and then left the room.

Chapter Four

Riff met the next morning with determination; he was determined to get out of bed as late as possible, without affecting the gig. He knew they were travelling out before midday, so he stayed wrapped up in bed until a few minutes before that. He knew the tech crew would pack away his belongings for him; they were used to him. He had a history of late nights and long lie-ins; sometimes he would be in bed for a fortnight, and the band had to scrape him out of his bed after his sweat had fixed him to the bed like wallpaper glue. Trent had risen from his sleep early, on a mission to get something organised for the band's economic predicament. He didn't want to let anyone know about it yet, before he could properly formulate how much material he could generate. Deet was out and walking off the previous night's gig in the early hours of the morning. For people from the Hurl planet, their symbiont nestled inside the chest of the larger host needed sunlight to replenish energy and vitality every day. Going out into the open streets of Corsylia would give Deet's symbiont a chance to get this sunlight, while the host would stretch and refresh his chest after the battering it got during the gig. Out of all of the Brown Yelp Gang, Deet's physiology needed the most care and attention. If he ever took it for granted that he was beating his chest repeatedly all night, it may get irrevocably damaged. Jenken had organised a bigger insurance policy for his chest, and more of the crew attend to him on a regular basis. The rest of the band didn't mind, although Riff sometimes got hold of the oil the crew use on Deet, for his own recreational use. For similar reasons, DK was massaging his snout and cleaning the reed-like flap of skin that cuts across the wall at the end of his snout. It was a delicate process that would last hours. He was rubbing and maintaining it through most of the morning, before they set off for Bragal. Aria spent the morning meditating, which was not unusual. If she didn't do this, her temper could get the better of her, and someone could get maimed or left with permanent psychological damage. Teddy was busy with her particular brand of meditation; recharging.

Jenken left the venue to hire the shuttle that they would be travelling in to get to Bragal. As he left the building, a shifty, bipedal, 6 foot bird-like creature was propped up against the wall outside, dressed in a smart, perfectly ironed yellow suit. He was a Pascinada; creatures known for dodgy deals and sleight of hand. He seemed to be just minding his own business, enjoying the blazing sunlight and light breeze on the busy walkways of Corsylia, but he was patiently waiting for anyone from the band to come out of the venue. Jenken knew the consistent motivation for the

Pascinadas and kept this in mind as the Pascinada caught his attention.

"Here..." His voice was sly and hovered just above a whisper, as if revealing a secret... "Mr Janes. Good show last night." The Pascinada's posture carried with it a confidence that exuded the authority of someone involved in a conspiracy.

"Thank you." Jenken stopped to give the Pascinada a nod in acknowledgement. Before he could carry on walking away, the Pascinada spoke again.

"I can give you something to help with your situation, Mr Janes." His voice remained quiet and conspiratorial.

Jenken was startled by the offer. Did this mean that this black market dealer knows about the 40,000 credits?

"What did you say?" Jenken remained calm, while he quietly panicked internally.

"I said, I can offer you some help for your situation."

"What situation?" He thought it best to see what this creature knew.

"Playing gigs, man. Going out there, in front of thousands every night." The Pascinada's tone lightened and his voice got louder as he painted the image of the tough touring schedule to his latest victim.

Jenken breathed a sigh of relief.

"You must be knackered my friend." The Pascinada moved away from the wall and toward Jenken now, still with a friendly disposition.

85

"What have you got?" Jenken asked, knowing he had little money but was curious.

"OK." The Pascinada became animated as he gave Jenken his patter. "You're gigging every night, right? You're full of tension, scared, frightened, can't concentrate. You need to concentrate. What do you need?"

Jenken hesitated, not really sure where this was going.

"Concentration?" He tried, weakly.

"What?? I'm not going to sell you concentration!" The Pascinada giggled to himself. "I can give you this though."

- and with that, he quickly, and decisively shoved a needle into Jenken's left ear. Jenken flew back as a reflex in shock at the physical intrusion.

"My God, man, what the hell did you just do?" Jenken's sight was blurry and, for a moment, the world was spinning off its axis. The shock of the attack on his ear was instantly overwhelmed by the effects of the drug that was now flowing through his blood.

"Just hold it one moment..." The Pascinada calmly responded.

Then Jenken was upright, wide eyed and silent, purveying the area around him.

"Amazing isn't it." The Pascinada was smiling back at Jenken with a knowing glow that only the most confident salesmen could wear.

"It's like every thought I have is waiting in a queue. It's weird." Jenken was staring out in front of him, as he tried to make sense of what he was sensing.

"Good weird though, huh? It literally clarifies everything in your head, so any nerves would just disappear like that!" The Pascinada clicked his fingers for effect.

"Well I guess so. I wasn't expecting anything like this. What is it?" He was still dazed and mesmerised as he spoke.

"It's called a Straightener, it's a compound that is applied to the tip of this needle. Just one tiny speck of it has this transforming effect. If any of your band wants some, I can sell it to you cheaper as I love your music."

Jenken took the compliment, even though it was almost certainly a sales pitch.

"If you are interested in waiting a moment, I could show you one other thing I can give you..."

Jenken was stunned by the Straightener and needed to sit down anyway. The Pascinada wasted no time and offered him a drink; a drink that would counter the effects of the drug. Jenken took it, placing trust in this stranger for expediency's sake. They both sat on a low wall running along the side of the adjacent building.

"This one is more for your three headed singer guy."

"Trent."

"That's him. Good voice."

"Thanks."

"Voices."

"Yeah, I know what you mean." Jenken gets that all the time. People who are used to being around Calpians tend to stress the head that is speaking when it is one of the side ones. That's not great for the side heads' egos, but it's sadly a fact of life for Calpians. It's also a constant source of annoyance for Trent.

"What is it you've got for Trent?" Jenken asked, intrigued after the effects of the Straightener needle.

"This one is beautiful." He shuffled closer to Jenken so that he was stepping inside his personal space. "Sing me something" Jenken gave him an incredulous look. "Go on, I won't bite." The Pascinada reassured him.

As many people would in this situation, Jenken chose a power ballad he knew, from one of the early Brown Yelp albums,

"You tore my heart in two, ripped it up, and made a paper aeroplane of it

You broke my heart and stamped on it again and again and again and again and – "

"That's great." The Pascinada interrupted him. "I say it was great. It's great that you did it, even though your pitching was terrible. Most of it was out of tune, and the last bit I couldn't really take hold of the tune at all."

"All right mate, steady on, mate, who crowned you the expert?" Jenken said, frowning at the criticism.

"No, don't misunderstand me. I wasn't trying to be nasty." The bird-like dealer pleaded.

"Do it again." He asked. "Hold on."

- and he produced a spray can from out of his side pocket. He then, without hesitation, sprayed Jenken in the face with it. After a coughing fit that annoyed the hell out of the mildly curious band manager, Jenken sang the same song of heartbreak and loss that he sang a moment ago.

His pitching was perfect.

Jenken turned to the dealer and shook his hand.

"This is impressive, my friend."

"I will be here all day if you want some. My van over there is full of all that." He pointed to his goods vehicle across the street.

"Thanks. To be honest, I don't know if I have the balls to tell Trent he needs a pitch correction, but I appreciate the offer." Jenken said, as he walked away in the direction of the bus hiring company.

Clearly, the Pascinadas must be big in this part of town, as the private shuttle company was run by a family of Pascinadas, all looking as shifty as the street dealer. Jenken managed to get a good price, despite several attempts on their part to fleece him for everything he had. When he returned to The Atomic Wombat, to pick up the band, Riff was up and the rest of the band was all present and fully rested. Teddy was fully recharged too, and giving her advice on how to make the trip to Bragal more efficiently.

Jenken, as he often did with Teddy, pretended to listen and take on board her suggestions, while thinking of other things as she talked. They all bubbled with nervous tension as the clean, comfortable hyper shuttle smoothly took off and headed for Bragal. Riff insisted on sitting at the front of the shuttle; He wanted to sit in that position so he could play the new song ideas he had; which caused obstruction to Jenken's flying and made Jenken desperate for one of those Straightener injections. Finally, after at least half an hour of distractions from the guitar and the elaborate explanations for the chords that came with it, Jenken snapped.

"Will you shut up Riff, and just do something quietly while I fly this bird to Bragal?"

"Ooh..." thought Riff, "...This bird to Bragal, nice alliteration Jenken. I can feel a song coming on!"

Riff carried on playing, this time looking for some music to hang the phrase 'bird to Bragal' on. Aria was listening in, and as she noticed a gap in Riff's attention seeking, she sidled up to the front pilot seat and spoke to Jenken;

"Hi."

"Hi Aria." Jenken replied, looking sideways to get a glance at her out of politeness.

"I wanted to talk about Plak."

"OK. Shoot."

"Well, it seems to me that we haven't explored an obvious point for discussion."

"What's that, Aria?" Jenken asked, aware of her wisdom and clear thinking.

"First can I ask you, how are you going to get this money to this bounty hunter? Do you know where she is?"

"I wondered that myself." Jenken admitted. "I guess I just thought that I would see how the next few days panned out, and see if she reappears."

"Fair enough." Aria conceded. "That does, kind of, make sense."

"Thank you."

"Thing is..."

"Yes?" Jenken was trying to concentrate on the traffic as well as the usual wildlife and weather obstructions you would get from a short, low level shuttle flight.

"We haven't talked about simply trying to rescue him."

"From Elsa?" Jenken was clearly too intimidated to contemplate this possible scenario.

"Well, yeah. I would be willing to attempt it."

"Are you used to combat?" Jenken frowned as he doubted her ability to hold her own against a trained assassin like Elsa."

"Part of the Denuvian religion was built around defending the faith. Pwom is full of rival factions and rival prophets, often threatening each other with a massacre or the killing of a prominent leader."

"Bloody hell." Jenken impulsively replied. "Sorry, but that sounds rough."

"Oh, religion is a brutal thing Mr Janes." Aria stated bluntly.

"Okay, so you're saying you are equipped to handle a fight with Elsa Grabbinot?" Jenken found the conversation compelling, but was determined to keep his eye on the view of the sky in front of him and tilted his head slightly back to be polite to Aria behind him.

"I'm saying I should give it a try. We are coming up with several ways to get this money together, and no doubt we should get the money together...but our timetable would be different if we weren't worried about what she was going to do with Plak at the end of the lunar cycle."

The other members of the band were oblivious to this conversation. The nearest member to Aria was Riff, who was busy obsessing about guitar chords and melodic shapes. The others were too far behind to hear her above the noise of the shuttle's engines. They were also fully engaged in an intense game of 'Squirrel, Duck, Squirrel', which DK had brought along for the journey.

"So, what do you propose?" Jenken was now receptive to the idea, and intrigued by this new warrior class priestess he had behind him.

"Once this Elsa bounty hunter reappears, I follow her when she leaves, to find out where she has taken him. Then, once I know where he is, I figure out a way of getting him out and then Bob's your Grandad."

"Bob's your Uncle."

"Whatever the weird Earth phrase is."

"It's an odd one isn't it? Maybe Bob was a popular name when that phrase was invented."

"When was that?" Aria asked, almost interested.

"I don't know."

Silence followed as the conversation had been led to a dead end.

Jenken picked it back up again;

"So, yeah, that seems like a plan. I'll ask Teddy to look at your flute parts. See if she can get that going as well as Plak's bits."

"She'll be fine. She's a talented robot that one." Aria said, slapping Jenken on the shoulder before returning to her seat further back in the shuttle.

Plak had been treated remarkably well considering he was chained to a wall in an unknown location and, worse still, totally against his wishes. Elsa was a good captor to have, as she kept him watered and fed, and frequently locked the warehouse up so he could get out of his chains to help the blood circulation and prevent too much scarring. For a few hours a day, he was allowed to run around the warehouse and do whatever he wanted. As a Movine, he often used the time to massage his delicate snout, especially as, for him, this was what earned him his income. He missed the band and missed gigging, but was terrified of Elsa, so didn't do anything to upset her when she was around. She hadn't

93

told him much about his situation and just kept repeating the phrase 'when Jenken pays his debt, you will be released'. How much that debt was, and if indeed it was money, was a mystery to him, but Plak had faith in Jenken and the rest of the band. He remained staunchly optimistic.

As she had indicated to Jenken, Elsa found Plak deeply irritating, so she hired a resident of Corsylia to entertain Plak and keep him company. She was a young female Bask Lizard, like the tech crew on tour with the band. She was desperate for the money Elsa was offering, and thought of it is glorified babysitting, so wasn't fussed about any moral dilemma that may be attached to the job. She had been hired muscle for many years and had managed to conceal a powerful weapon of a body in a small, slender frame. Their first encounter was tentative but a good indication of how different it was from a typical captor and captive encounter. Nesta entered the warehouse nervously, as she didn't know what to expect from the vague description of the captive Movine she had from Elsa. She had been told that he was chained up, and that he was a tall Movine, but that was it. As she walked in she could hear him playing a tune to himself, and she rightly assumed it would have been played naturally through his snout.

"Hello?" She whispered.

Plak stopped his tune immediately and sat up straight, startled, with dozens of scenarios running through his head.

"Is that you, Elsa?" He clearly hoped it wasn't.

"Hello? Plak?" Nesta repeated, walking closer into the back of the warehouse, where Plak was chained up.

As she came into view, Plak beamed an enormous smile as he realised he had the company of someone new, and possibly someone that could rescue him.

"Hello. Do you know me?" He asked. "How do you know my name?"

"I have been asked to come here and talk to you."

"Can you unchain me?"

"I can't, I'm afraid." Nesta was very polite and sounded genuinely disappointed that she couldn't rescue him.

"Ah, I see." Plak deflated back into his captive stupor.

"Take a seat."

Nesta looked around for a seat. She could only see random mattresses, broken wooden doors and wire railings strewn about the high ceilinged room. She realised after a few moments that he was being facetious. That was many levels before rude, so she was OK with it.

"I have been employed to talk to you." She said cheerily.

"Oh, that's nice." Plak replied, not meaning it.

"So how are you then?" She said, clearly not starting the conversation well.

"Not great, I'm chained up in here for some reason." He rolled his eyes as he spoke.

"Yes, I guess that's true." She looked at the floor, slightly embarrassed, then came up with a more positive question. "Are you hungry?"

"I am actually, yes." Plak remained monotone in his reply, not impressed yet with his company.

"I'll go and get you something."

"That's very kind of you." He said, almost changing to a more engaged tone.

"I'll be right back."

- and she trotted off, almost skipping, out to a nearby food store to buy Plak some food, her tail swished with unbridled joy behind her. Plak watched her go, slightly baffled and frustrated, and totally unaware of what Jenken had done and how he had anything to do with it.

Jenken's concentration, flying the shuttle to Bragal, was interrupted by Trent's left head, shouting from the back of the shuttle;

"So, who is opening for us tonight, Jenken?"

"A bit different tonight." Jenken replied, still looking ahead, but shouting to the back of the shuttle.

"Different, how?" Trent asked.

"It's a family band. Could be interesting."

"What family?"

"It's the Bickle Family Band. They're famous for all their songs being built around them arguing."

"Sounds crazy." Trent was still shouting, above the game of Squirrel, Duck, Squirrel; above the sound of the engine, and to project his voice to Jenken's seat at the front.

"Yeah, they're more like an anti-family band really. I've seen them before. It's a bit of a mess." Jenken laughed as he said this.

"Why the hell did you book them as support?" Trent asked, confused at Jenken's damning of the band.

"They're fans. They said they would do it for nothing, just to say they'd played with us. I couldn't turn that down. Besides, they're big around here."

"Takes all sorts." Trent shouted.

"Take some sauce?" Jenken was confused by what he heard.

"TAKES ALL SORTS." Trent shouted even louder.

"Oh right. Absolutely. I was going to say, not sure what you'd do with sauce."

"Clean your ears out with it." Trent mumbled to himself, facetiously.

Trent returned to the game of Squirrel, Duck, Squirrel. He had been out of the game so long that he was now back at square one as a Duck, while the others had surpassed the Squirrel stage and were now Horses. Jenken smiled to himself as he thought about the chaos of the Bickle Family Band, and what might happen at the gig tonight. Riff continued to play guitar.

Less than an hour after the short conversation about the Bickle family, they arrived at the space port of Bragal. It was a busy port, as this was one of the most popular trading areas on Corsylia. This was also the city with the highest crime rate and the most complex network of organised crime on the planet. The drug and gun barons in Bragal could get you anything, and would double cross the deal in a heartbeat if they could profit from it. The nefarious residents of Bragal had their own codes and their own moral compass. A few months of living in Bragal would bring a normality to that amorality that could scar you for life.

As the band left the shuttle, and wandered out of the main docking bay and into the city streets of Bragal, they could all sense the fear and heightened tension in the streets. People shouting across at each other from different sides of the street; vehicles clashing into one another, on the road and in the air just above them; gunfire in the distance; security forces chasing criminals down the street around them; long scowls coming from the people serving street food as they pass them. It was the middle of the day, before the cover of darkness descended on Bragal, and it already felt like a dangerous, unpredictable place to do business. The idea of putting on a gig in front of an audience populated by these people they were passing was giving them more trepidation the more they thought about it. Jenken was walking at the front, as he knew where the venue was. Deet was just behind him.

"So, you say this place we're playing is really friendly?" Deet was fishing for reassurance.

"I wouldn't say friendly, but it will pay us well."

"So, not friendly at all?" Deet was really trying hard for reassurance.

"Not really." Jenken wasn't as blunt as this when he was selling the gig to them the previous night.

"We're nearly there. We'll just say hello, find our Green Room and see if the crew are there yet with the gear." They carried on walking for a few minutes longer. The occasional sudden sound, like a bomb, a scream, or a block of plaster from a building falling in front of them, put them on edge, but soon enough they were at the venue, The Sinking Wharf. To the right, behind the venue, they could see the sea stretching out into the unknown. Despite the dangerous location, the sea maintained its usual appeal and romantic spirit. The band gazed at it, with the eyes of land locked musicians.

"That looks really spectacular doesn't it?" DK said, to the rest of the band.

"It sure does, Deeks." Trent agreed, patting him on the shoulder as he caught up with him.

"Well, we'll probably have time for a proper look later. Let's just say hello first." Jenken mobilised the band and motioned to open the door to the venue. He was suddenly halted by Trent, tapping him on the shoulder.

"What's the matter, Trent?" Jenken asked.

"Look over there." Trent pointed to a Bask Lizard selling Brown Yelp Gang shirts on the pavement a few yards from the venue. Jenken was determined to get to the venue and meet the promoter and settle in, but this had to be investigated. He motioned to the rest of the band, who had now latched on to where Trent was pointing.

"Well, let's go have a look!" Jenken said, with a smile.

As they walked over to the shirt vendor, his tail stopped swishing and his faced turned very serious, thinking they were going to turf him off the pitch and away from the venue completely. In fact, they were more interested to see what he was selling. They were bitterly disappointed.

"Erm....mate." Riff said, pointing to one of the shirts. "That one says 'Brown Yell Gang'!"

The rest of the band groaned. The Bask vendor was embarrassed.

"- and what's that?" Trent was appalled by another shirt, "that says, 'where is your hair'. It's 'How is your hair', dummy."

The vendor was getting more upset, the more they pointed out his terrible mistakes.

"You've got six designs here and three of them are mistakes!" Deet scoffed. "Here, you've got an image from the first album with the title of the last one!"

"Ya cock." Riff added, needlessly.

The already insecure, and hugely intimidated, street vendor ran off down the street, crying. Jenken saw the opportunity immediately.

"Right." He turned to the band. "Teddy, you guard this bunch of shit shirts. I'm going to get one of the crew to sell them so we can add the credits to the debt fund."

"Good thinking, Mr Janes." Trent said, smiling.

"Really?" Deet wasn't impressed.

"Do you want Plak to die?" Jenken barked, dramatically.

"Well, no." Deet considered himself chastised.

Teddy stayed with the shit shirts, and the band went into the venue; Jenken leading them, as he knew the promoter from way back, and ultimately was the right person to speak to the staff.

"Hi, we're the band for tonight."

"The Brown Yep Gang?" The hapless security guard asked.

"No, The Brown YELP Gang." Jenken was now starting to get impatient.

"Ah, yes, sorry. I don't really listen to your kind of music."

"Charming." Aria said, under her breath.

"What kind of music do you listen to?" Jenken asked, making conversation to ease the tension, as they were all led up the stairs.

"Korillian Opera, mainly."

101

"That's interesting. That is genuinely one of our influences. The songs they write mix the tones of Korillian Opera with Mappist Rock, fused with Calpian rage and Movine traditional melodies."

"Hmmph." The security guard released a sound that was the auditory translation of him trying to work out what that would sound like.

"It's a toxic mix that you can't get enough of, once you've heard it." Riff shouted from the back.

"Once you Brown Yelp, you never need help....picking another track to play." Jenken couldn't get that to sound fluid, however he said it, but he kept trying, thinking it was a good catchphrase.

"Well, good luck to you all. I guess I'll be hearing this heady mix you're talking about tonight when you're playing in there." His tone of voice hinted at a total lack of excitement about this prospect. They had reached the top of the stairs and were being directed through the main auditorium. "Go through the main room here, and there's a door at the back, to the left. Go through that door and up the stairs and then knock on that door. Ray is in there." They were looking around at the venue as he spoke. The mirrored walls gave a powerful, dazzling effect, making the room look fresh and shiny, despite its constant use and age. The band walked through open-mouthed, turning their heads around the whole room as they walked. Trent had the advantage of not needing to turn his heads so much, but was equally enamoured.

"Whoah, this is a beautiful venue." Trent's left head said, softly.

"It's less beautiful in a few hours from now, when the ugly crowd start piling in." The security guard stated, cutting down the glamour of the venue instantly.

"Fair enough." Trent's right head sniggered, pulling a face that said "awkward" to the rest of the band.

"Yeah...can't wait to meet them." Deet added, sarcastically.

"Anyway, I'll see you later, have a good sound check." The security guard mumbled almost to himself, clearly not star struck by the gang's presence. As he walked off, the band watched him go, a little surprised at his demeanour."

"Well, he was happy." Trent said, to the others.

"Good to get a dose of humility sometimes, I'd say." Aria replied. "Not everyone thinks you're a God among men."

"Yeah, but he does." Deet sniggered, nodding his head in Trent's direction. They all smiled. Trent took it on board and smiled with them.

"Let's meet this promoter guy and get this sound check started." Trent made a play for changing the subject.

"Ray is a good man. Today should be a success." Jenken said, as he led the band through the main auditorium and through the door that led to the next floor. Jenken quietly knocked on Ray's office door.

"Who's that?" A snarly, slobbering voice boomed out of the room.

"It's me, Jenken Janes. I've got the band here."

"Ahh, come on in. It's open."

Jenken turned the knob of the door and walked into the room. The rest of the band followed him in, nervously. They had walked into a long, thin room with a low ceiling. Hunched over a table that was dwarfed by Ray's colossal size, Ray sat munching on live Raggets, amphibians local to Bragal. The noise of the Raggets screaming as he ate them was making the band wince. They were small creatures with little defensive capabilities, and a common delicacy in Bragal. Ray was clearly far too tall to fit in the room, as he was bent over from half way up his back. Regardless of the awkward position Ray looked to be in, the band found him extremely intimidating.

"Hi, Ray. Good to see you again." Jenken said, humbly.

"Mr Janes. Good to see you old friend." His voice always sounded angry, whatever he was saying. "So this is the famous Brown Yelp Band."

"Gang." Trent corrected him.

"What?" Ray swivelled his head to look directly at Trent's middle head, glaring at him.

"Er...it doesn't matter." Trent retreated swiftly.

"Yeah, that's the Brown Yelp Band." Jenken replied, brushing over the interruption.

"Want one?" Ray lifted a Ragget from the bowl he was eating them from, the juice from their crushed bodies dripping off the Ragget as he offered it to them."

There was a general, subdued murmur of a 'no', all of them too scared to be too forthright with their refusal.

"Suit yourself." Ray said, and threw the Ragget into his mouth, whole. Despite the large mouth it was thrown into, the Ragget made a dash for an escape, its legs writhing about in the corner of Ray's mouth. The noise coming from this Ragget was more determination than pain. "You want to sound check?" The question was shouted at them, as a foregone conclusion.

"Yes, please."

"No need to answer." He pressed a code on a keypad that was beside the bowl of Raggets. "When you go downstairs the crew will be there."

"Sorry to ask, Ray." He really was, being terrified of this huge beast in front of him. "...but just wanted to check when and how we were getting paid."

"8000 credits, in your hand, as soon as you've walked off stage." Ray said, without looking at them, engrossed in the dismemberment of a particularly large Ragget.

"That's great, thank you." Jenken looked to the rest of the band for approval, but they were transfixed on watching the wet mess being made by Ray violently shoving Raggets into his mouth while they screamed in agony at every bite.

"It's no trouble. You boys will put on a good show. I always pay my debts, it's fine." Ray's words struggled to cut through the gnawing and drooling of his crude eating habit.

"Have the Bickle family arrived?" Aria asked, slightly off topic, but of interest for clarifying their schedule.

"They arrived, argued, threw their instruments at each other, and left." Ray snorted.

"They left?" Jenken hesitated from walking out of the room with this news.

"Yes."

"Are they coming back?"

"Probably not. The mother of the family screamed 'I'm not working with you again', the father screamed something similar back, and the daughter snapped her harp-type thing in half with her foot."

The band balked at this unusual physical achievement, imagining how strong her feet must have been.

"What happened to the son?" Jenken asked, "What's his name again?"

"Barrett."

"Yeah, Barrett."

"He's still here. Talking about ending it all." Ray was matter of fact about all of this, seemingly indifferent to one of his acts falling apart.

"What should we do?" Jenken asked, sincerely.

"Play a longer set."

Plain and simple. They had their instructions. They were all too intimidated to argue.

"Yes, Ray, will do." Jenken agreed, looking at the band for confirmation.

"Yes, Ray." They all said, slightly after each other, each revealing their anxious unease just being in the same room as him.

"Now go and sound check." Ray blurted. "I'm eating." He glared at them with his bulging eyes, giving them an even bigger sense of foreboding about the whole gig.

They all walked out, briskly and with all of them unnaturally holding their breath. When they reached the bottom of the stairs and opened the door into the main auditorium, they could see the crew setting up the PA and lights. Teddy had abandoned the bootleg shirts and was waiting for them with the tech crew.

"Well, THAT was intense." Deet said, as they all caught their breath.

"Was it me or did you all feel like we were next on the menu?" Riff asked, with a high pitched whine to his tone.

"Let's just get this gig done, get the money and get out of here." Jenken said. "I will get the merchandise ready while you sound check. I noticed the noise of our guys hauling in the gear as we came in just then."

The band nodded and turned their attention to the stage, and the stage hands around them. They were, like a lot of the population of Bragal, bulky Frergen beasts like Ray, although not unfathomably large like he was. Their manner was polite and professional, which was refreshing after their encounter with Ray. As they sound checked, Jenken helped the tech crew to assemble the merchandise table and replaced the price stickers on all of the merchandise with a 20 credit increase. When the tech crew gave him a quizzical look, he responded like he did before; with a stern reminder of what they were up against;

"Do you want Plak's blood on your hands?"

Nobody wanted blood on their hands. The prices went up without question.

Chapter Five

As the band were getting their equipment ready, and Deet was positioning himself in the right place for his rhythm to be picked up by the microphones, Trent slipped out to the front to have a quick word with Jenken.

"Jenken, buddy, I need a word." Trent had slipped out earlier in the day to find a database retrieval service somewhere near The Atomic Wombat. The database retrieval services were buildings where you could locate files you had submitted to the information stream from any location, and download them. All members of the band were looking for ways to raise money; Trent had come up with one that hadn't been discussed yet.

"Yeah, sure Trent. Is everything OK over there?" Jenken pointed to the stage area in the other room.

"Absolutely, it's not that." Trent replied.

"Although we haven't got any water." The left head interjected.

"- and we could do with some snacks backstage," the right head added.

"Yeah, fine that's true, but that's not what I wanted to talk about." The middle head insisted.

"O....kay..." Jenken looked at all three heads, hoping to accommodate Trent's wishes. "What do you REALLY want to talk about?"

"I had an idea." Trent's middle head began.

"Could be a crazy idea or it could be an earner." The left head winked as he said this.

"What is it?" Jenken was getting impatient now.

"I went back to the old files, to see what I could dredge up. It could be a goldmine, as it happens."

"What did you find?" Jenken asked, genuinely interested.

"Stuff like, do you remember when we visited that hospital for flying Kinzu warriors? We sang a happy birthday song to that Commander-in-Chief, do you remember?"

"That's like, 30 seconds long." Jenken scoffed.

"Yeah, true, but there's other stuff. There's all the demos!"

"You kept the demos?" Jenken asked, raising his voice in hope.

"Well, a few of them, yeah." Trent replied.

"How many?"

"Four."

"Okay, well that's something." Jenken replied, a little underwhelmed.

"That includes 'How is your hair', though." Trent said, smiling.

"That's more like it. What else did you find?"

"More random moments like the alternative version of 'Woman, I need your hands': do you remember we did a

110

version where every chorus we sang 'where's your sister'. We thought it was hilarious."

"Okay, so you have that." Jenken wasn't feeling it, but was keen on the idea.

"There's that..." All three heads looked at each other trying to recall what else they found. "There was also the nightclub mix of 'Fallet Frenzy', that will go down well."

"Nice."

"Ah!" Trent had a eureka moment. "We found, get this -"

"- go on..."

" - the entire musical rock opera concept we started. That album we didn't finish called, 'With limbs like these", do you remember that?"

Jenken scratched his head trying to recall the specifics.

"That wasn't a lot of songs, was it?"

"Well, it was three." Trent admitted. " - but they'll go down well too."

"A rarities compilation."

"Just to download through the information stream, no fuss." Trent was on the hard sell.

"I like the idea." Jenken was nodding and smiling.

"If you're a fan of the band, it doesn't have to be good does it?" Trent stated.

"Yeah, I think you're right." Jenken agreed.

"Oh, and we found the song we did for the Bask Lizards, in the Bask language."

Jenken thought for a moment, looking at Trent sceptically.

111

"What was that called?"

"I can't remember but it had that weird intro that Plak played before we all came in."

"That wasn't in the Bask language, Trent. You had a cough that you couldn't get rid of."

"Ahh, that's right. Well, we have that too." Trent wasn't deterred.

"Sounds good. Send it all to me tonight and I'll get an electronic package together, and create a bit of buzz about it overnight."

"Will do." Trent nodded.

"Good call, Trent, that could be an earner."

Trent returned to the sound check and Jenken turned back to the merchandise table. When Trent returned, he discovered they had been wondering where he had been and were impatiently wishing to get the sound check over with so they could get to know the port a little more. Riff had heard about an instrument shop that he was itching to explore.

"Where have you been?" Deet shouted out, as Trent approached the stage.

"Just talking to Jenken about an idea I had earlier." Trent answered, dismissively. "Are we all set?"

"Yeah." Deet shouted from the back.

"Well, let's see what we sound like!" Trent said and grabbed the microphone set up for him. Riff played the intro to 'I Bet You'd Even Look Good In A Cocoon', and the band came in, sounding tight as ever, with the sound engineers adjusting the settings as they played.

Plak had been stuck to those chains, in that undefined location, for days now. He was getting tired, disheartened and thoroughly miserable. After the initial capture, when he was chained against the wall and eventually left on his own overnight, he hadn't seen Elsa much at all. Elsa kept paying for Nesta to visit daily, and she did. Nesta had a habit of appearing for a moment, and then promising some food, and then promptly skipping to the store nearby to buy food for Plak. It was almost a routine. Her visits became longer and longer too. The first one was just under an hour, but by the third day Nesta and Plak were exchanging life stories and joking around for hours. Plak was having a much better time than he thought he could, chained to a wall in an unknown location.

"I don't like this, you know." Nesta said, on the third day. "You seem like such a nice guy."

"I am." Plak agreed.

"I have never met a Movine before. Are you all as nice as you?"

"Most are nicer really. The other Movine in the band is really nice, you'd like him."

"Do you miss them?" Nesta said, almost asking the obvious.

"I believe I do, Nesta." Plak said. "I even miss Lazy Riff, and he often tires me out with the way he doesn't listen and does his own thing all of the time."

"Lazy Riff?"

"Yeah, he's the guitarist. He's a good guitarist, but annoying with it."

"I don't know how long you are going to be here for, Plak." Nesta apologetically stated.

"It's OK; I know it's not your fault."

"Whose fault is it?"

"It's got something to do with my manager, but I don't know what yet." Plak said, without any hint of curiosity. He was simply stating the facts as he could see them.

"Well, I guess the worst thing for you is that you should be out playing to an audience." Nesta said, being far more empathetic than Elsa would have wanted.

"Ah yeah, that's killing me. I was so looking forward to these gigs." Plak looked at the floor as he said this, genuinely heaving with frustration.

Nesta watched him for a moment, in silence, crouching next to him. Then, suddenly she bounced back up to a standing position, and cheerily told Plak of the idea she just had, that she couldn't wait to put into action.

"I'm going now, Plak, but when I come back tomorrow, I will have my Bluesophone with me, and we can make some music together! What do you think about that?" She was grinning from ear to ear.

"That's a lovely idea, Nesta." Plak raised a smile, which came as a surprise to him. "You are making this whole experience far easier than it could have been. Thank you." Nesta was already near the wide metal doors to the warehouse at this point.

"Don't think anything of it, Plak. I'll see you tomorrow." She shouted behind her as she left.

As he retreated back into his solitary thoughts, Plak thought to himself, '*what a lovely lady*'.

The second gig of the tour was another success. With the Bickle Family Band out of the gig and, in fact, still arguing around Bragal, the band decided to simply loosen the set and have longer solos, and more fun with the audience. The crowd loved the aprons and kitchen style staging the band was using to push the "Wet and Tasty" album. One of the things they spontaneously developed in the set was asking if any fans wanted to come up and join them on stage for a song. This worked out extremely well and, for almost 20 minutes, the only members of the band on stage were Teddy, Deet and DK, while the others went to the bar and watched from afar. The new songs went down well again, and the old classics were met with a cacophony of singing along from the audience and some wild moments of unbridled joy from some members of the audience. For a large part of the gig the audience began chanting 'La-rry, La-rry, La-rry': requesting one of the members of the audience who played earlier to go back on stage as he was such a good guitarist. Riff wasn't happy, but just sternly and silently indicated to Larry to stay put for the rest of the gig. During "Fallet Fever" on this night, Aria had the urge to let go of all of her inhibitions, and threw herself to the front for her flute solo, and promptly played a solo that led the song for another 13 minutes. The rest of the band were looking at her, looking for a signal that it was the end of the solo; each fourth bar was expected to be the last one in the solo, but each time, for 13 minutes, she just carried on, playing extremely fast and beautifully melodic. She was playing trills, working her heavy breathing into the rhythm of the melody and taking the flute into musical areas the band had never heard before. They were absolutely stunned. At the end of her solo, Aria leapt to the front of the stage and held her flute in the air, screaming, "Krallit Sinseet Plantiq Notriq!!" at the top of her voice. This was Denuvian for "I love this band!!" It was lost on the audience, but the spectacle of how she played that solo certainly was not lost on them at all. It was the main topic of conversation as the crowd were walking out during the dying sounds of "How is your hair." Each member had their spotlight, and they all made the most of them; Aria had gone even further and surpassed anything she had done on any stage before. Riff's lust for her was exponentially increased with every phrase she played during that song. He nearly passed out.

The extended set they were given had worked out well too. They had made an enormous impression on Corsylia, which was particularly important to them, after having to run from Corsyllian authorities when they bought the Dengen plant. Now, it seemed the nightmare that was the aftermath of that incident was over. The securities on Corsylia hadn't been a bother to them and the fans lapped up every second the band was on stage. If one of the members hadn't been chained to a wall somewhere in Corsylia potentially waiting to be murdered, it would have been their best tour so far. As it was, Plak was never far from their minds.

As they went back into the Green Room, to pour some customary Jump Wine, and celebrate another successful gig, they were greeted by one of Ray's Bask Lizard security team. He paid Jenken their money, with a chip that contained the 8,000 credits they earned for the gig. Once that was done, he didn't give them any time to settle into the room; immediately barking at them;

"The boss wants to see you. Now!"

They all stopped what they were doing and stared at him, stunned.

"Have we done something wrong?" Aria asked, confused.

"No. He wants to give you a proposal. You need to go now."

"You don't mess about do you?" Deet said, irritated by the security guard's manner.

117

The guard didn't reply and moved his arms in the direction of the stairs that led to Ray's office. The band obeyed, with their spirits pulled down as the usual post-gig buzz was replaced by intimidation and fear of what Ray was going to say to them. Jenken knocked on the door as the band approached it.

"I sent for you, didn't I?" Ray's low boom barked.

"Sorry..." Jenken meekly said, and opened the door.

They all walked in and were all stunned to see Lilly standing beside Ray, being held by her robe by one of the Bask security guards.

"We found this little thing backstage. She said she's with you." Ray shouted, dispassionately.

"Lilly!" Aria screamed.

"What are you doing here?" Trent added.

"You know her then?" Ray was astute at noticing the details.

"I had to come. My sister is with me this time."

"What?" Ray turned to his security guard and nodded to him. Without any more information, the guard knew what to do. He let go of Lilly's robe and walked out of the room, on the hunt for this other missing girl. Lilly closed her eyes, to concentrate, and warn Penny that a Bask Lizard would be looking for her. Ray didn't notice, but the band did.

"This is not why I sent for you, really." Ray began again.

"Oh?" Jenken replied, intrigued, but still very intimidated.

Ray entered a code into his keypad and almost instantly an out of breath guard appeared at the door; a different one to any of the guards they had seen so far.

"Get me 8 chairs. This is going to take a while."

"Yes, Mr Ray." The guard disappeared back into the corridor that led to the stage area.

"Now while Kevin is getting the chairs, I need you to sing." Ray glared at them with expectation.

"Pardon?" Jenken replied.

"Sing. All of you. Come on. I need to speak to you, but I want you to sing first."

"Er...what do you want us to sing?" Trent asked, a little confused.

"Anything. One of your songs."

There was a slight pause, and then DK, who was the most nervous among them, began to sing 'What's the name of your name now'. Slowly, as his voice shakily warbled through each line of the song, all of the band joined him, staring at Ray while they did it. It felt threatening, despite them being musicians, being forced to sing out of context. Deet couldn't even sing. When he joined in, Ray's face changed from a mix of blissful pleasure and needless aggression to suppressed nausea. Kevin returned with the chairs. Lilly had moved from Ray's table to where the band was standing on the other side of the room.

"Okay, stop." Ray waved his huge, furry hand at them. "Sit down."

They all sat down.

"Right. Now, were you wondering why you were paid so much for this gig?"

The band, and Lilly, looked around, realising that there was more to this gig than they first thought.

"We just thought you had decided we were worth 8,000 credits..." Jenken said, with an extra slight wobble to his voice.

"We were a few years back." Deet said, giving more context.

"We still are!" Riff added, his ego rising above his fear of the situation they were in. His bravado subsided immediately, once he noticed Ray's glare at him.

"Well, look at it this way." Ray interrupted, loudly. "How much did you get for last night's performance at The Atomic Wombat?"

They all looked to Jenken.

"That was 2,000 credits." His voice was deflated and vulnerable.

"Exactly." Ray punched something in his keypad on the table in front of him. "Want some Raggets?"

The band mumbled a gentle refusal as he finished his instruction to his men on the keypad.

"So this means, by my calculation, you owe me 6,000 credits." Ray looked at them all directly, having spelled out their position, and his stealth business deal that nobody agreed to.

"That's outrageous." Deet argued, getting a swift kick in the leg from Jenken, who was more worried about what would happen if they didn't comply with what was coming.

"So, as you owe me all of this money, I need you all to do something for me."

Kevin returned with a large bowl of Raggets, all fighting against their beaten and drugged state to climb out of the bowl. Ray nodded to him and began to savagely shove them into his mouth, producing a cocktail of drool from his unpleasant eating style and blood from the screaming Raggets.

"I can just give you the money back." Jenken suggested, offering the chip he'd just been given for the gig.

"Ha ha ha, it doesn't quite work like that." Ray's guttural laugh boomed around the room like a smack around the face to each of the members of the band.

"I want you to help me destroy someone that is causing me problems."

The band, and Lilly, gave out a collective sigh, now seeing how much more complicated their lives were going to get.

"Do you know the name Carlo DeMarco?" Ray asked, knowingly asking the obvious.

"He's the reason Penny and I are on the run." Lilly replied, to the shock of the band.

"Are you serious?" Trent's left head blurted.

"Yes." Lilly looked at him, expressionless. "He has been trying to use us for some big event he's putting on."

"The Great Big Beat." Ray added.

"That's it. Some kind of music thing."

"It's a big festival he's putting on, here on Corsylia." Ray's voice was full of contempt as he spoke.

"What's the big deal?" Jenken asked. "Why didn't you just say yes?"

"You don't understand. He wanted to strap me and my sister to one of his big machines and manipulate us while we performed. It would really hurt."

The band winced.

"It would probably cause us permanent damage to our brains." Lilly continued, with the band listening to her full of sympathy. "We kept saying no to him, and he kept pushing it, then he kept us in his bar basement for a while. He wasn't going to pay us or give us any kind of reward for it."

"Bloody typical, if you ask me." Riff added, feeling incensed by that last part more than the harassment and kidnapping.

"So, DeMarco is forcing you to strap yourself to some kind of machine for a festival?" Aria was visibly upset as she said this to Lilly.

"Yes, that's right. We've been looking for people to help us. I don't know why we thought of you, but I suppose over the years we have felt like you were friends."

They all smiled, feeling complimented.

"Plus, I don't know any soldiers, bounty hunters, security guards, gangsters or wrestlers."

They all mumbled their understanding as she shared this crucial bit of information.

"Well, this is interesting. This girl will be part of your mission." Ray spat out the words, showing little empathy or emotion.

Lilly reacted with shock, almost making a double take as she finished speaking to the band.

"What do you think I can do?" Lilly asked, innocently.

"Whatever it is that Carlo DeMarco wants you to do. Clearly you have talents."

He wasn't wrong, but was evidently unaware of the specifics.

"Okay, you have us. We're not going anywhere. We don't want to get you riled up, especially as we already owe DeMarco lots of money." Jenken stated, attempting to be forthright and dominant.

"Ha ha ha!!" Ray laughed more than ever now. "This is fantastic." His voice had risen in volume such that Riff's hair was moving from each sound coming from him. "You owe him money. This couldn't be better."

"It looks like we all have a common enemy." Lilly observed quietly.

"To be fair, most people on Corsylia would say the same thing." Deet said, frankly.

They all muttered in agreement. Their mutterings were interrupted by Ray's thick, low tones, "Anyway, I've got you, you've agreed and we're all good. I'm bored now. You can get the rest from my second." Within a split second, the floor opened up and the band and Lilly all fell through to a chute that led to the lowest level of the building. They hadn't noticed Ray's hand on the lever, and hadn't seen it coming, screaming in shock as they slid down the chute. The drop was quick and the landing was abrupt. They landed with a painful bump on a concrete floor. Disorientated and unsure of how they had fallen through the floor, they all looked around. The room was full of chairs, with a lectern at the front and a screen attached to the wall directly opposite them. On the screen, was simply the word 'Orientation'. It was clearly a functional room, with just the chairs, lectern and screen for the band to ascertain what other surprises were in store for them. What looked like a 7 foot hill of hair stood behind the lectern, waiting.

"What is that?" Riff quietly leaned over and whispered to the rest of the group, pointing to the hill of hair.

"Urgh!" Lilly involuntarily blurted out, not being much help at all.

"It looks like a Hargendarce." Aria observed, correctly.

"What are they?" Jenken asked, as unfamiliar with this species as Riff was.

"They live in cold wastelands and caves surrounded by snow. This is hardly the right kind of climate for a Hargendarce." Aria was correct but confused. Then she noticed the large pool of sweat around the lectern, building up around the creature's feet. "Ah, look. He's baking in here."

They all looked. Mystery solved.

"What is going on?" Deet asked the world, utterly fed up of their unending adventure on Corsylia. "I just want to play my chest."

"Deet," Trent turned to his rhythmic companion, "you can't expect to travel across the galaxy with your band and just play music all of the time. Shit happens."

"Well, a lot of shit is happening to us on this tour." Deet groaned.

"What doesn't kill you makes you larger..." Trent argued, awkwardly. There was a silence while they frowned at him. "Something like that; point is Deet, its fine, and all part of life on the road!"

With Deet firmly put in his place, Trent looked back at the front of the room, where the Hargendarce stood.

"- also mate," Riff added, "you wouldn't want to just play your music in your hometown on Hurl."

The cold reality of their ambition hit home.

"No. You're right." Deet conceded.

"You gotta travel to get your music out there!" Jenken winked as he finished the pep talk.

Chapter Six

Not only was the Hargendarce race extremely hairy, to the point of their faces being hidden behind their hill of hair, and typically large and foreboding creatures, they also were obsessively defiant about only speaking their native language. They refused to pick up what was generally regarded as 'the common tongue' and in the frequent occurrences when they were off their home planet of 'Brrrr', they needed a translator wherever they went. Ray had brought this Hargendarce, his second in command, away from Brrrr against his will, thinking that his colossal size and infamous strength would be a great asset to Ray's habit of threatening people. He knew the deal with the language, and always had a translator handy. As the band dusted themselves off and, getting the vibe from the room, found a seat to sit in, an extremely thin man with an unfeasibly long face and spiky, grey hair appeared from a door on the right hand side, at the front. He stood beside the Hargendarce and quietly waited for his translation skills to be required. The band waited in their seats for a few minutes, nervously twitching and wondering when someone at the front was going to say something, or do something. Then they heard a scuffle behind them, and the tech crew had appeared at the bottom of the chute. As the

126

band did before them, they dusted themselves off and found a seat near the band, mumbling about being taken by force and thrown into a room with a trapdoor in it. The band whispered words of comradeship to them, unknowingly feeling that they should keep their voices to a whisper, instinctively feeling an oppressive demand for silence in the room.

Music began to sound above and around them, coming from invisible speakers set in the walls of the room. It was like a fanfare, but more aggressive and dissonant. It was like a fanfare for a demon, if a demon wanted one.

Immediately following that fanfare, Ray's voice was heard booming around the room;

"Children." The band and crew looked at each other confused. "You are here today to be given the full picture of your mission, and the full extent of my intentions against the man you know as Carlo DeMarco."

Jenken mumbled to the band that they knew him as Carlo DeMarco because that was his name.

"It is important to understand that you are my property until this mission is successful." Ray's disembodied voice continued. "You have been chosen because of your skill set, and DeMarco's fondness for your music."

The band realised that this odd monologue from Ray was written especially for them, even though it somehow seemed that it wasn't.

127

"I will leave you in my Second's good hands." The lights dimmed, and the Hargendarce made some grunts, as if in acknowledgement of his role to take over from there.

He made some more grunts, pointing at the screen as a picture of Carlo DeMarco appeared to his right. The tall, thin grey haired man translated as the hairy host spoke; "Here is the man in question, Carlo DeMarco." More grunts from the Hargendarce. The tall man continued, "Study this picture. This is the man you will be working alongside for the next few weeks."

There were mumbles and quiet objections from the captive audience. He continued, as did the translator;

"Carlo DeMarco has been successfully manipulating a multitude of businesses, almost every security council in the sector, and many musicians, sound technicians, marketing think tanks, composers and ice cream vendors for many years now. It has to stop. He has forced musicians to play for him under duress; forced music venues to give him protection money, closed down concert halls, then opened them up again with a new lick of paint and a new name, under his rules. He has insisted on conducting his business through favours, as a tool for sponging off the talent around him."

The band was intrigued, glued to the screen and the tall translator in front of them, and empathising greatly with the tone of the tall man's speech, aware of the rumours and the outrage built around DeMarco's business deals on the music scene. They whispered their suspicions to each other as the Hargendarce at the front, and the translator, continued on;

"You are the chosen operatives for an extremely important mission that Ray has been working on for a number of years. As such, he has already found out some important information that you can use in your investigation."

The translator's words came to a dramatic full stop, followed by a pause that brought an air of expectation in the room. Subtly, and without any of the band's crew in front of him noticing, the Hargendarce pulled a small lever to his right and the whole room opened up with each of the thirty seats in the room falling into a trapdoor suddenly activated by the lever. In an instant, the band and the crew had landed on the lower floor, 35 feet below the room they were in. The floor they landed on was made of a soft material, but the impact of the landing and the unexpected shock of the fall left them unprepared, landing uncomfortably on the lower floor. Deet practically bounced from the impact of the landing, having the advantage of an almost elastic physiology, ideal for his internal drumming. Everyone else cursed with their own variety of expressions of shock, while holding their backsides and backs in pain. The sound of the empty chairs falling with the band and clattering around the room below was deafening, and added to the overall shock of the

129

moment. They all stood up, slowly and painfully, to get a full view of where they had landed.

In front of them was what seemed to be exactly the same vision at the front; a Hargendarce beside a lectern, in front of a screen, with a humanoid man standing to the side. It was almost identical to the room above, but it was clear that the two creatures in front of them were different people.

"What the hell was that about?" Riff strained, through his teeth, as he held his back.

"Delegation I guess." Jenken replied, with a shrug. The truth was he was as confused as the rest of the band.

The Hargendarce at the front and, consequently, the translator, began to speak;

"You are now in the second phase of Orientation." The band awkwardly and angrily found their seats on the floor and picked them up, placing them correctly on the floor and sitting on them to listen to their instructions. "It is imperative that you hear all of the following details so you can proceed with the mission efficiently." The band at this point was squinting at the front, tolerating the pain, but distracted by worries over the extent of their injuries.

"There is a lot of information to get through, and not a lot of time." The band and crew looked each other, in irritated anticipation. "So you all need to look carefully at the following images and information, and concentrate very, very hard."

Almost immediately, a slideshow appeared on the screen passing through at an incomprehensible speed with text, that the audience in the room had no chance of reading in time, laced across the presentation. Occasionally, they could make out the odd word like "DeMarco", "guns", "HQ" and "Praxim 7". Praxim 7 was a significant inclusion, as it was a planet on the far side of the system, 60 million miles away from Corsylia. As the slideshow rattled through its information, the Hargendarce and the translator sounded like they were speaking in tongues, giving a commentary to the presentation at a rate that made it impossible to hear each word.

"Bloody hell, this is ridiculous!" Jenken exclaimed, straining to hear the words, leaning forward, open mouthed.

"What is this lunatic setting us up for?" Aria protested.

"This is hardly fair. Did anyone catch any of that?" Deet asked, reasonably.

"Nope!" Riff said, almost light heartedly as if he found it amusing.

"Er..." Trent's left head spoke up, above the complaints and confusion around him. "Can we see that again?"

"No time." The translator said, without a prompt from the Hargendarce.

Then the floor opened up again, this time with less of a drop, and they all fell into another lower floor, and found themselves in a dark corridor, with the slow, metal conveyor mechanism they had landed on moving forward to the darkness ahead of them.

"I AM NOT HAPPY!" DK shouted, exasperated and frightened by the whole ordeal.

"I'm with you, brother!" Riff shouted, as the moving platform under them picked up speed.

"I am going to have words with Ray when this is over!" Jenken shouted, with unusual bravado.

"Really?" Trent shouted back from behind him, "what kind of words? Words like 'sorry', and 'excuse me' and 'if there's anything more I can do' kind of words?" Trent's sarcasm had an angry, rather than a comedic tone.

"What is going on?" Lilly shouted, being the most scared and vulnerable among them.

"Stick with me, kid." Aria reassured her, "we're in this together, and there's no need for anyone to feel like they're on their own here."

The conveyor platform they had been dropped onto continued to wind its way around corners at a speed that threw its captive passengers against the walls around them. The journey continued for several long and painful minutes, with the tension of the journey getting more intolerable at every corner. They were shouting at each other, blaming each other for their situation, as the constant darkness and unnerving speed began to transform into a more leisurely pace and a light at the end of this seemingly endless tunnel.

As suddenly as the journey through the tunnels began, they reached the light at the end and the conveyor mechanism reached daylight, and the outside world. As the rail they were on disappeared below them, they were gently bumped outside, and into the sunlight of the streets of Bragal. Rolling around in front of this strange tunnel, they eventually picked themselves up, nervously looked around and dusted themselves down.

"I just want to play my gigs!" Riff shouted, to the sky.

"I hear you, brother." Deet added.

"Look." Jenken turned to all of the unfortunate members of his crew. "It seems that this tour is not going as planned."

"You think?" Trent's three heads said, at once.

"Let him speak." Aria replied, sympathetically.

"Thank you, Aria." Jenken almost bowed. "This is a royal cock up, I get that. The last thing we want to be doing is getting involved with Carlo DeMarco," Jenken thought about it a little more, "especially me!"

They all nodded in empathy, mumbling their support.

"The fact is, we will be hunted down by Ray if we don't do what he says, and no amount of signed picture discs will get us out of that one." He paused for approval, and could see on their faces that they were on the same page as he was with this. "We have to go along with this and see where it leads. Let's face it; we're getting help from Ray's people to get rid of DeMarco!"

"Potentially." Deek said, realistically.

"Well yeah, nothing is guaranteed."

"Thing is, Jenken." DK said. "What about Plak?"

There was a silence spread swiftly among them. With all that had happened in Ray's club, they had lost their focus on Plak, and his plight.

"I will make it my mission to find Plak, DK." Aria said. "I have discussed it with Mr Janes here, and I will be splitting off from you guys to try and locate that bounty hunter and Plak, of course."

"Sounds reasonable, Aria." Riff knew her skill with Denuvian fighting techniques was legendary on her home planet, Pwom, so was confident that she was the best equipped to search for Plak.

"Should we be splitting up anyway, wouldn't that make things worse?" DK asked, anxiously.

"Don't worry, DK." Aria comforted. "I will have Plak back before you can toot your snout a victory fanfare!"

As this conversation continued they were looking around to try and adjust to where they were, and figure out how far they had travelled on the moving tunnel they had been trapped in.

"Where are we?" Deet asked himself, and those around him.

"You are here." A nasal, thin voice said from behind them. They all looked behind immediately and saw a man looking remarkably like one of the translators that Ray had with the Hargendarce creatures.

"Who are you?" Jenken exclaimed.

"I am your shuttle pilot."

"What?" Deet was having a hard time with the idea that there'd be more travelling against their will immediately following this conversation.

"I will be taking you to Praxim 7." The tall man said, without any sense that there may be some debate within the group.

"We can't go to Praxim 7 now, Mr Weirdo." Riff said, politely.

"You can, and my employer insists."

"We've got gigs man." Riff persisted.

"You needn't worry about that. That is all in hand."

They all looked at each other, confused.

"What do you mean, all in hand?" Jenken asked.

"We have made arrangements for you to travel to Praxim 7 without any worries about your music commitments."

"What are you talking about, posh bloke?" Riff was getting angry now.

"Follow me." The man insisted, and turned to the right of the tunnel and walked toward a small, run down, seemingly empty building in front of them. Once outside, the man turned to the Brown Yelp Gang posse;

"Okay. This is very exciting, and I have to warn you that you may not be able to cope with how wonderful this is."

They all sniggered, thinking the tall man was completely mad.

"Is it a room full of groupies?" Riff asked.

"Is it a room of endless batteries?" Teddy asked, succumbing to an urge to join in on the frivolous banter.

"He's probably just going to lock us up in here." Deet declared, cynically.

"There are no groupies, batteries or cages in here." The tall man announced. "There is...THIS!"

His words were followed by a dramatic sliding of the main metal door at the front that revealed the warehouse inside.

A few feet away, standing proudly awaiting their initiation commands, were exact replicas of each member of The Brown Yelp Gang.

"Behold!" The tall man announced, like a Ringmaster, "Here before you is the latest in robotic technology. Trent, Lazy Riff, DK, Deet, Aria, Teddy and Plak all in robot form, waiting to take your place in your next scheduled gigs."

The band stood with open mouths, gawping at the robots in front of them. They clearly looked like robots, and looked incapable of putting on the immense, extra-sensory, extravaganza of a rock show that they were used to putting on for their fans.

"You think robots could put on a Brown Yelp gig?" Trent's right head shouted, outraged.

"You must be joking." The left head added.

136

"You're out of your tree!" Riff shouted, in disgust.

"Yeah, I'm sorry, but this won't work." Jenken addressed the tall man with his 'reasonable' business voice. This was the voice he usually reserved for the phone deals, but here he felt it could be useful amongst the outrage coming from the band.

"I wouldn't mind keeping the one of Aria with us on the shuttle though..." Riff added, which prompted Aria to shake her head in resignation.

"How is this collection of tin supposed to make us look like we're on stage? They are clearly robots." Aria asked, reasonably.

"The beauty is in the gullibility of the fans." The tall man said. "Your shows will be advertised with a new theme. The theme of robotics. This is your costume." He pointed at the robots with pride.

"What?!!" Riff was stunned. "You're going to pretend that they're costumes?"

"Not sure that's going to work." Deet said, disapprovingly.

"They're good costumes though, I have to admit." Riff's confusion was inevitable.

"Riff, they're not costumes, they are robots!" Trent shouted at his guitarist.

"Oh yeah."

"You can leave for Praxim 7, knowing that your gigs are in good hands." The tall man repeated.

"Good hands?" Jenken bellowed, maddened by their treatment.

"They're not even hands!" DK observed.

"It is fine." The tall man insisted. "Watch this."

With that, he proceeded to take out a controller from his right hand pocket, and began to press the keypad with a sequence that activated the robots. The robots immediately started to perform the beginning of the song, 'What's the name of your name now?'

It was painful, and had every robotic cliché that formed the basis of every screaming rant that Riff let off about robotic music. The words didn't flow together, the rhythm was staccato and formal, the melodies sat on the beginning and end of bars like static tiles being laid down on a construction site, and the replacement for Deet was producing an awful, tinny drum sound that betrayed the depth of Deet's chest.

"This is a joke, right?" Deet said, sickened by the 'music' he had just witnessed.

"Yeah, that is NOT The Brown Yelp Gang." Trent's heads said, in unison.

"Seriously, mate. There's no chance this will pass even the most casual fan's inspection." Riff added.

The tall man flicked a switch on his controller, and the robots interrupted that first big Brown Yelp hit with another song, this time 'Show me where you put it'. The band stood watching, nauseated by the lack of spectacle in front of them.

"Look, I'm not being funny mate, but this is shit." Riff said, plainly.

"This is an experimental phase. You are trying something new for the synthetic market."

The tall man's words were spoken as a fact, rather than as some kind of practical joke, which the band were hoping it was.

"This is an image thing?" Jenken tried to get his head around what was being proposed.

"You go to Praxim 7, these talented robots masquerade as The Brown Yelp Gang's new costume and image change. Electronica era- Brown Yelp Gang!" His tone was as insistent as when they first met outside the tunnel.

"We would never do that synthetic, electronic bollocks!" Riff declared.

"I would certainly never make my chest sound like that!" Deet added, still appalled by the fake sounding drums coming from his metal doppelganger.

"These brilliant creations will be performing your next 6 gigs. We have made all of the arrangements and their schedule has been mapped out."

"Six gigs?" Jenken thought about the implications. "That is about three weeks of gigging."

"Indeed." The tall man replied. "This should give you enough time to do what needs to be done for Ray."

139

"- and what was that again?" DK asked, now just keen to get moving and get this all over with.

"Find out what DeMarco is doing and report back. He is spending a lot of money on something, and Ray wants to know what it is."

"Right." Jenken said.

"Right." DK echoed.

"So..." Riff was still puzzled. "They know all our songs?" Riff pointed to the robots.

"Every one of them."

"Even the crap ones."

"Even the crap ones." The tall man replied.

"What about the extended version of 'See you in the fridge'?"

"All versions, even the ninja version."

Riff turned around to his musical colleagues.

"Wow, that's impressive." He said, genuinely impressed.

"Are you OK with this?" Deet checked, still outraged and sickened.

"No, but we don't have a choice do we?" Riff said, turning to Jenken.

"No, we don't really." Jenken sighed.

"See." Riff said, to them all. "We're bollocksed."

The tall, reserved escort took them to the shuttle without any more objections. There were angry feelings of being forced to travel against their will, leaving the worst kind of cover band in their place that they could possibly imagine. These feelings were dwarfed by their fear of Ray and what he might do if they didn't comply. One thing Jenken and Aria didn't abandon however, and that was their plan to rescue Plak. Aria waited for her moment and slipped over to the left during the walk to the shuttle. The tall man did notice, but decided to keep going, and sent a message via his communicator to Ray, saying that Aria had escaped the party travelling to Praxim 7. Consequently, Ray sent out several of his security guards to hunt for Aria around Bragal. Once they had found her, they could then send her on to join the rest of the band.

Aria knew she had a difficult job on her hands hunting down Plak's whereabouts. She had to get back to Corsylia, where Jenken first encountered Elsa and the debt with DeMarco was first explained to him. Once she was back in Corsylia, she knew that she would find it impossible to find Plak without discovering the whereabouts of the bounty hunter keeping him captive. So she resolved to find Elsa: then, as a result, hopefully find Plak. Aware that she was defying the wishes of the notoriously methodical and violent gang lord Ray, Aria moved stealthily through Bragal, and as soon as she was back in the main market area, decided a disguise was the correct move to make. Getting out of Bragal without alerting Ray's men would be a significant victory, as they were unlikely to follow her to

Corsylia. So this disguise was essential, but mostly for this initial step in her escape to find Plak.

Thinking that Ray would be sending out a party of security guards looking for a female Denuvian priestess, Aria had the inspired notion of disguising herself as a different species entirely. She approached a cosmetic surgery just off the beaten track of the main market street in Bragal, and walked in, confidently. She was greeted by a small, three foot high stout humanoid with light green skin and long, razor sharp teeth. His hands were claws and his feet were huge. He had the distinctive features of a Hobligon. Hobligons were excellent surgeons who often operated outside the law. Their expertise with a cosmetic knife was made even more valuable by the pleasure they took in conducting operations, projects, experiments and custom requests that were highly illegal and dangerously risky. Aria recognised the Hobligon and couldn't believe her luck.

"You are exactly the person, or Hobligon, I am looking for." She said, pleasantly.

"Oh, really?" The Hobligon by the front door answered.

"Oh, absolutely." She replied.

"Well it will cost ya." He wasted no time in warning her of the price.

"Oh, I know." Aria said, slipping into her seductive tone, on a mission to get a reduction in price.

The Hobligon giggled, aware that her tone of voice was exactly what he needed that day, having had a run of customers that had brought him to the brink of nervous anxiety.

"Ooh, we're going to have fun aren't we?" The Hobligon said, optimistically.

"I expect so, little man." Aria almost whispered, moving closer towards him and touching his nose, suggestively.

"Oh my," The Hobligon giggled. "You know what drives a Hobligon wild don't you!"

Aria wasted no time and bit his nose, with a hard, brutal bite that would make the average humanoid creature scream in agony. The Hobligon howled with pleasure.

"You, my lady, are spoiling me."

"I think we should spoil each other, little man." Aria was smiling, aware that her plan to get a perfect, and cheap, disguise was very possible with this little horny Hobligon.

"What would you like me to be?" She asked, fluttering her eyebrows at him as she spoke.

"Oh my, I get to choose?" The Hobligon was having the best day that he could remember.

"Absolutely. Let's go crazy!" Aria said, tempting fate.

"OK then." The Hobligon answered. "Let's make you into a Movine!"

"A Movine?" Aria wasn't expecting that.

"Yes." He said, getting very excited. "They have a lovely snout, and you could play a little tune for me."

"Play a tune?" She replied, confused. "I won't actually be a Movine."

"Ah yes, that's true." He conceded. "You will have a lovely snout though."

Aria thought for a moment and then concluded that any disguise would be fine, as long as she no longer looked like a Denuvian priestess.

"OK, so let's do it!" She shouted, feigning excitement.

"Oh, goody!" The Hobligon shouted, jumping up in the air with unbridled anticipation. "You will look amazing!"

"Just make sure I look different!" Aria insisted. "How long will I be affected once you correct it?"

There was a slight pause.

"You want it corrected?"

"Er...yeah." Aria's voice was insistent, but a little anxious.

"I can try." The Hobligon wasn't exuding confidence.

"There is certainly going to be some scarring."

"I can handle that." Aria said, thinking about the threat on Plak's life.

"OK that's lovely." The Hobligon leapt onto a circular, mobile platform. "Step up onto this table, here." He indicated the table in front of his platform, and produced some tools out of his front pockets. "I will have to take some flesh from your body to make the snout."

"I understand." Aria had a general understanding of the Hobligon's artistry. "Do I stay awake?"

"Oh no, that would be awful." The Hobligon chuckled.

Aria settled into her position, lying on the table, awaiting the inevitable anaesthetic injection. She was eager to get to the space port to find a pilot to take her back to Corsylia as soon as possible, but knew that she couldn't rush this cosmetics expert. She let out a long sigh, and prepared for the anaesthetic.

Hobligons don't use subtle methods such as injections and Aria, in her trusting resting state, didn't see the huge mallet coming. She was out instantly.

The journey to Praxim 7 was short and brimming with speculation from The Brown Yelp Gang about what DeMarco was doing with Ray's money. The tall man piloting the shuttle was obliviously leaving the discussion running without any insights or objections from him. That discussion was interrupted when the pilot began to play some music from the intergalactic radio service, often used by shuttle runners, called 'The Frequency Modulation Stream'. As soon as the Hurl-beat hybrid dance music started, Lazy Riff's intolerance for rival bands burst out of his opinionated mouth.

"This is bullshit!" He shouted, from the back of the shuttle.

"It's easy to ignore, Mr Riff." The pilot insisted.

"Deet, how do you cope with being infinitely better than everyone else on your planet?" Riff said, to the quiet, unassuming band drummer.

"I don't think everyone would agree, Riff." He replied humbly.

"To be fair, Deet, you've been voted the most rhythmically interesting Hurl every year in WOW magazine for eight years now!" Jenken interjected.

"Yeah well..." Deet was naturally still keeping a humble stance on this response to the Hurl band on the F.M.S. "...who reads the WOW magazine material now anyway?"

"You're the best drummer we've had Deet." DK said, adding to the compliments.

"I'm the only drummer we've had." Deet replied, truthfully.

"Yeah, exactly." Riff said, not quite linking the points together well.

The next song from the F.M.S. was another song that inflamed his ego.

"What is this pseudo-rock heavy spoken word instruction manual bullshit?" Riff shouted, more animated than with the previous song.

"Haven't you heard this?" Trent's left head replied, quietly humming along. His right head supported the left head with more, harmonised, humming.

"He's just talking about doing something up!" Riff's outrage was obvious, and very hard to ignore.

"I know this." Jenken exclaimed. "It's the New Blue Shoe Dudes." Jenken jumped out of his seat and leapt onto the space near Trent's seat, grabbing onto the back of his head rest, singing along to the chorus;

"You gotta bend it at the hinges, bah ba-bah, bend it like you want to, bah ba-bah," Trent sang along, in three part harmony, "hold it at the edges, bah ba-bah, and keep it off the ground."

Riff was not impressed.

"This is a stupid song."

"It's a classic." Jenken and Trent both argued, almost simultaneously.

"Who writes a song about construction like that?" Riff groaned, incensed and disturbed by the song on the F.M.S.

"Clearly they did." DK replied, calmly.

"What happened to them, anyway?" Trent asked. "Are they still going?"

"Last I heard they all became Civil Engineers."

Everyone on board the shuttle all nodded variations of 'ah, that makes sense'.

Riff calmed down and settled back into his seat, picked up his guitar and played scales to the annoyance of everyone else on the shuttle. The pilot continued to silently take them across deep space to Praxim 7. As far as the ongoing discussion on DeMarco's plans, the pilot knew more than the band did, but found their guesswork amusing.

For part of the journey, they travelled through the beautiful Luctus Nebula, where many people travelled for a break from normality, just stopping by to stare at the Nebula's shifting colours and amorphous patterns. It was often nicknamed 'the safest high'. Riff's mind was immediately

147

taken away from the discussion and taken somewhere peaceful and vivid, detached from the shuttle and the dire situation they were in. They were all succumbing to the Nebula's effects. Teddy was immune, being a cold, rational robot with only occasional feelings. She slapped Riff hard on the face, to get his attention.

"Riff, that's not going to do us any good, being taken in by the Luctus Nebula."

Riff rubbed his cheek to numb the sting.

"What the hell?!!" He resented the interruption. "Teddy, the Nebula is utterly harmless."

"True, but..." She had no rebuttal.

"Ah well, it can't be bad to get back our focus." DK said, thinking about Plak and Aria, and worrying about where they were headed. "DeMarco must be planning something big." He added.

"Absolutely. No one in their right mind would steal from Ray." Jenken agreed. "It must be a huge operation he has going."

"What do you reckon, Jenken?" Riff said. "Drugs?"

"Must be drugs." Deet added, emphatically.

"It's not necessarily drugs." Jenken replied.

"I think you'll find he has done very well with his drug network without Ray's money." Teddy's computerised rationale interrupted their discussion again. A few moments of silence followed her cutting moment of authority.

148

"Well, it must be dodgy." DK added.

"That's true. Maybe it's a political thing?" Trent suggested.

"Like the man behind the curtain." Riff added. "Throwing money at a bigwig somewhere to rule from the sidelines?"

"That's the safest way to rule!" Jenken concluded.

"If I ruled the Corsyllian System, I would get rid of doughnuts." Riff said, philosophically.

"Doughnuts?!" Trent barked.

"They're well dodgy." Riff elaborated, comprehensively. "I wouldn't trust one with my worst enemy."

The rest of the band struggled to understand his statement.

"I've got some out back." The tall man remarked, listening in, a smile on his face as he spoke.

"Urgh, no thanks." Riff reinforced his disgust with the kind of face he pulled when he played a solo.

"I would destroy all water." Teddy said, despotically.

"Wow, that's harsh!" DK replied.

"I have been shut down for weeks because of a spillage, or a misplaced bucket, or a waterlogged ceiling."

The band contemplated her unique properties.

"We'll be careful, don't worry Teddy." Trent said, putting his hand on her shoulder as he stood up to pour a drink. "Who wants a drink?"

They all muttered affirmative reactions, except Teddy who smiled at him as she said,

"Have you got anything dry?"

"We are under an hour away from Praxim 7, so I suggest you come up with a plan for how you will approach Mr DeMarco. I will be dropping you off above his main offices of operation."

"Above it?" Deet asked.

"Yes. I will not draw attention to this shuttle by landing it near the building. You will be ejected exactly where you need to work with him."

The band looked at each other.

"Have you got jetpacks or something for us to use?" Jenken asked, looking around the shuttle for something to help them land.

"In the back, on the left, is a small room. When we get close, open the door and unlock the cage in it. There's a saddled Mikkle Bird waiting for you to ride it."

"A Mikkle Bird?" Trent's voice couldn't hide his excitement. "I thought they were wiped out."

"Ray has a few."

"Ooh, get him." Riff said, widening his eyes and tilting his head, cheekily mocking his pilot.

"Can this bird fly us all?" Lilly asked, unaware of what one of these creatures looked like.

"Lilly, they are massive creatures." Jenken explained. "I am shocked they have one on board."

"Surely I'll be too heavy?" Teddy asked, more factually than out of concern.

150

"Yes, you will have to join them later. I will drop you off a little way out of the city." The tall man explained.

"I will stay with her." Deet offered. "She'll have more chance with someone to bounce off and help if needed."

"Fine." The tall pilot agreed. "I will give you all maps with the centres of operation that DeMarco oversees marked on them. You will all have to meet up with Deet and Teddy later"

"Don't do anything stupid, Deet." Jenken said, concerned that they'll be on their own.

" – and don't run off." Trent was more direct.

"Hey, it appears to me that we have to see this through." Deet said, with a resigned tone. "I will find you. Me and Teddy will find a different way in and we'll be there in no time."

"Indeed. I can be very resourceful, with my data banks of information and my negotiation programming. I can speak several hundred languages from many different star systems." Teddy said, unnaturally optimistic.

"There ya go. She's a tin pot genius. We'll have no trouble." Deet added, almost to convince himself."

"We will get through the DeMarco compound from the front entrance, disguised as maintenance droids." Teddy suggested.

The band all looked at each other.

"No?" Teddy said, sensing the lack of enthusiasm on the shuttle. "I'll think of something."

"We'll think of something." Deet agreed. "Tell you what though..." Deet added "...I just want to get on stage and play."

"Me too, brother." Riff said, lifting his arm for a high five with Deet.

Deet didn't comply. He never understood that high five thing that Riff and Jenken did.

Chapter Seven

Aria had left the Hobligon's clinic and was now walking the streets of Bragal, intent on finding an amoral pilot that won't ask any questions and take her back to Corsylia. She was now looking like a Movine, which was an advantage in this situation, as the Movines had such an innocent, gentle reputation. The operation was painless, and had only taken just over an hour. She was still getting over the shock of the Hobligon using her left leg as the matter that he would reconfigure for the extra features typical of a Movine. He gave her a prosthetic limb, but she couldn't help but wonder why he couldn't give her a prosthetic snout instead. Regardless of her misgivings about whether the Hobligon did a good job on her features, she was now fully disguised as a Movine, and very capable of walking the streets of Bragal without suspicion from the security forces that Ray had sent to look for her.

Aria hobbled through the market place at Bragal, with her radar up for a nefarious creature that might be persuaded to take her to Corsylia. She was a good character, and had a good filter for spotting the rough and ready, unscrupulous chancers so prevalent in Bragal. It was a short walk to the space port, which suited Aria as she was finding it difficult adjusting to her new false leg. She slipped into the bar that ran along the left side of the space port and ordered a drink of Rannick Juice. She quietly surveyed the bar, while sipping on her toxic brew. There were pockets of couples and groups of creatures dotted around the edges and centre of the bar, all sitting around clean tables, deep in conversation. There were many Bask Lizards there, a few humans and several Pascinadas. As her head moved around the room and settled on the creature sharing the bar with her to her left, she almost choked on her wine as she realised it was a Bergemumni. Bergamumnis were shaped similar to humans, but with a wet, sticky exterior that exuded an odour that was infamously noxious and the principal reason for them becoming an endangered species. They were also, as any space faring Denuvian Priestess would know, highly influenced and infatuated by the teachings on Pwom, Aria's home planet. She couldn't believe her luck. Assuming this was the break she was looking for, Aria sidled up to the Bergamumni and held out her hand.

"Salutations from the Gods of Pwom, my good heart." She said, almost ceremoniously.

The Bergamumni turned around to face her, immediately recognising the unmistakable voice of a Denuvian from the priesthood...and then screamed when he saw her Movine face.

"Don't be scared, my love." Aria spoke gently and seductively, stroking his forehead as her words smoothly glided out of her mouth.

"You're a Movine!" He exclaimed. "With a Denuvian...voice." He didn't know how to say what was in his mind, whirling around in a confused mess.

Aria realised that her first hurdle was in danger of betraying the stroke of luck she had finding this Denuvian worshipper.

"Okay." She took a slow, calming intake of breath and placed her hands on either side of his head. He was so awestruck by her calming voice that he didn't resist, mesmerised by the suspense of what might happen next. "Listen to me, and breathe deeply." Her voice was gently undulating into a rhythm that was sending him to a meditative state. "Deep, deep breaths..."

The Bergamumni followed her instructions, letting go of the Calpian Leaf Water he was drinking, and letting his arms flop to his sides in submission.

Then suddenly, without a moment of warning, Aria slapped him hard on the side of the face.

"Argh!" He screamed, immediately snapping out of his trance and holding his cheek where Aria had slapped him. As he did this, Aria wiped her hand on the side of the bar to try and remove the gloopy slime from his skin off her sticky hand.

"I am a Denuvian. I have disguised myself as a Movine for reasons that you don't need to know...and I need a pilot." She glared straight at him, invading his personal space in a

155

threatening manner that was extremely effective to a superstitious Bergamumni.

"I am sorry for doubting you." The intimidated sticky creature replied. "I can be your pilot."

Clearly the trance hadn't quite worn off completely.

"I need to get to Corsylia, as soon as possible." Aria continued, still glaring, her head just a few inches from his wet face. "You will be rewarded for your service...but not for a few months...probably."

"The opportunity to serve a Denuvian, even she's a bit Movine, cannot be passed up by any of my brethren, least of all me." He replied, elaborately.

"So that's a yes?" She snapped.

"Yes, we can leave now." The Bergamumni nodded.

They left immediately and within the hour, Aria was back on Corsyllian soil, leaving the Bergamumni with a head massage that he will never forget for the rest of his sticky life. Similarly, Aria was forever scarred by the repulsive level she stooped to, in thanking him for the shuttle back to Corsylia.

Aria knew about Ursulas' reputation on Corsylia. She hadn't met her yet, but Trent had a long history with her, dating back to when he worked with her, running errands and selling arms to nefarious business associates of hers. Trent was good at his job, always great at spotting any threats, with three heads to utilise for lookouts.

Unfortunately for Trent's career on the black market, his relationship with Ursulas got very complicated, very quickly. She disposed of him once she sensed a weak spot in her resolve. He left her dissident and dangerous employment with a huge wealth of stories that would scare the living daylights out of the toughest Gurnad Dragon, this side of the Lantrick System. He often regaled his tales of narrow escapes and unfeasible adventures flouting the law to the rest of the band, especially after their troubles with her Dengen Plant, and Aria had a great memory for details. She knew where Ursulas' main club of operations was, and the back entrance that Trent was so fond of using. For the most part of ten years, Ursulas had stayed within the confines of The Speckled Interruption, a bar that was a great meeting place for dealers, pushers, weapons buyers, prostitutes, black market scientists and small time bandits. Criminals from dozens of different Sectors gathered at the The Speckled Interruption for the chance to find new contacts, for the great atmosphere that was always brimming with cutting edge entertainment on the street level, and the doughnuts that were regarded as impossible to describe by anybody lucky enough to try them on Corsylia. Ursulas was a dazzling seductress too, with translucent skin that perpetually shifted into a myriad of colours at a mesmerising pace, and a single eye in the middle of her angular face that drew you in like a hypnotist's watch and took your focus away from any other

157

stimuli in the room as if your vision was somehow caught in a vice. This natural gift she had for seduction made her a formidable black market trader and fence, knowing hundreds of people that can benefit from any stolen artefact you might have to sell on. She was also brutally ruthless, and had little emotional attachment to her network of robbers and dealers. She found them all disgusting, and deplored their willingness to work for her. This scornful dehumanising of her contacts was exactly the reason for avoiding experiencing her interrogation techniques. Interrogation was never fun, but Ursulas was always on a mission to be as creative as she could with every poor soul that betrayed her.

Using her impressive memory and justifying the patience she demonstrated when listening to Trent's repetitious stories about Ursulas, Aria found The Speckled Interruption in no time at all.

I say that, it was 48 minutes.

So, 48 minutes after she left the space port at the Corsyllian end, and left the Bergamumni reeling with pleasure, Aria walked around the back of the notorious bar and found the back entrance. To the side of the back entrance, on the left of the door, there was a staircase that led to the lower chambers of The Speckled Interruption. These chambers split off into different areas of Ursulas' operations. Aria had a strong feeling that she would be in these chambers, on this lower level somewhere, based on what Trent had said about her working habits. She was convinced that Ursulas was the quickest way to find where Elsa Grabbinot had been keeping Plak, and felt that this was an obvious first call for her investigation. As she approached the door, she looked around and noticed she had complete privacy; this entrance being seldom used by her associates mostly out of respect for Ursulas' authority. Aria tried the door and it was clearly locked. This is not surprising, and Aria had expected this. This is why she brought with her a bag that contained a burrowing creature called a Peeking Scarab. These were determined, curious creatures that, if placed by a wooden surface correctly, would burrow through to the other side purely to satisfy their curiosity. They were often used by carpenters and craftsmen to make their jobs easier. Here, Aria used one effectively to open a locked door. She placed the scarab against the door, just above the lock. After a few seconds of burrowing from the beetle, a hole had been produced on the door that allowed Aria's hand to poke through to the other side and unlatch the lock that was keeping her from going in. A few moments later, Aria was inside the lower chambers of The Speckled Interruption and creeping slowly and quietly through the corridor to inspect the doors ahead of her.

The first door she came across was a thick, wooden door on the left with no noise coming from inside. It seemed eerily quiet but, ultimately, with no evidence of anyone in there, nothing to spark her curiosity. Further along the corridor to the right she could hear voices coming from inside another thick, wooden door. She crept up to the door and placed her head by the side of it, to listen in more intently to what was happening inside the room. She heard a female voice, what seemed like various sounds of electricity and loud, hysterical protestations from a male voice clearly in that room under duress. It was clear, with just a moment in time listening in on the activity in the room that he was being tortured and the female voice was doing the torturing. Knowing her reputation, Aria guessed it was Ursulas, but couldn't hear the details of what was being said. She wanted to get into the room but knew she couldn't just waltz in unannounced. She also knew she couldn't force her way in. She didn't have a weapon on her, which was an enormous oversight that she internally chastised herself for as she thought of a way in.

Her idea was bold, and possibly suicidal, but she thought she could handle it. She knocked on the door, in one of the gaps between the screaming and the torture, and waited. In another gap, she did the same again, feeling more confident about her plan as she waited. After the second knock, a loud noise was heard from the door of several latches being unfastened to allow the door to be opened. A large humanoid brick wall was facing Aria as the door opened in front of her.

160

"Who is it, Nod?" Ursulas shouted. "What do they want?" The recipient of the torture was quietly moaning in the room as she spoke.

"What do you want?" Nod barked at Aria. He turned back to Ursulas. "It's a tall Movine with a false leg at the door."

"Why a false leg?" Ursulas asked.

"I don't know. I didn't ask her."

"No, why are you mentioning a false leg?" Ursulas repeated.

"I don't know...but she doesn't look threatening."

"Ah, I see." Ursulas' voice from the back of the room continued. Aria interrupted her, strolling in with force, knocking Nod out of the way as she walked through the door.

The room was a bare concrete cell, with a humanoid man lying face up on a metal table with pulleys, electrodes and savage looking pointed instruments around him on the table. Ursulas was standing beside the table carrying a whip in one hand and a surgical saw in the other. The walls were an unhealthy green from being dank and neglected. In truth, the room was used a lot, but Ursulas always thought the smell and the Corsyllian rodents that frequented the lower chambers of the club created the atmosphere she preferred. The man on the table stopped groaning for a moment, distracted by the arrival of this female Movine with a false leg. Ursulas placed the saw and whip down on the table, and turned to Aria, with a patient and curious air of surprise.

"What is a Movine with no apparent threat to us coming down to the lower floors of The Speckled Interruption for, today, then?"

Aria put her risky plan into action.

"I am here to represent the 'Herbington Cartel'. They are interested in seeing how you work as they are planning on expanding into this star system and heard of your reputation."

Aria's voice was confident and authoritative, even if the plan was 100% crazy.

"The Herbington Cartel?" Ursulas repeated, shifting her one, central eye to Nod as if asking if he had heard of them.

"Nope, no idea." He shrugged, sensing her question.

"Where do they operate now then?" She asked, suspiciously.

"Mostly the Lantrick System." This was a good moment in improvisation, as Aria being disguised as a Movine, and referencing the system they originate from, was a good link that may have brought more credibility to the story.

"Lantrick System, eh?" Ursulas repeated. She poured herself a glass of Rannick Juice as she spoke, examining this visitor to her torture cell as she poured the drink.

"What do you want to know?"

"I have been asked to observe you, and report back with contacts and details about how you operate."

Ursulas smiled, starting to believe the story and complimented by the interest from the Lantrick System. "It seems, Nod, that my status in the quadrant precedes me!"

"Indeed, ma'am." He replied. "Do you want me to kill her?"

Aria almost jumped at the sudden threat.

"No, not yet." Ursulas calmly replied. "Let's give her what she wants for a moment, while we get what we came for from this little Trannip." She said, pointing at the man on the table, and comparing him to a local rodent that you couldn't trust even after giving it the best cheese on the planet. "Please sit there and watch...and take notes, if that's what you want." Ursulas motioned to the floor beside the wall to Aria's right. Aria double checked she meant sitting on the floor, with her arm, then, on confirmation, sat on the floor. She was uncomfortable, but stunned that her story seemed to work. Ursulas turned her attention back to the man on the table.

"Okay, you pathetic Earth dweller. Are you going to start talking?" She cracked her whip as she demanded information again.

"I have said, time and time again, that I know nothing of what you talk about." The man sounded exhausted, frustrated and almost patronising, while still clearly in pain.

"You are playing a dangerous game, my friend." She suggested.

"I am not playing a game. I came into your bar, unaware of what you do here and just wanted a drink."

"A likely story." She tutted. "Nod, we need to teach this man a lesson."

Nod moved closer to the table: the man on the table began screaming again, and Aria felt the sense that something really horrible was going to happen to him within the next few minutes.

"Take off those stupid looking ears!" She scowled.

Nod, without any display of emotion, and with the clean cut of a lifelong barber, cut off the desperately protesting man's ears. The man screamed the kind of scream that would normally be heard for miles, now wasted just within the walls of this expertly sound proofed cell. He struggled with his manacles as he attempted to cope with the overwhelming pain. Ursulas continued with her interrogation;

"So, you see now how serious I am. Who are you working for, and why have you come to The Speckled Interruption?"

Ursulas was walking around the room as she asked this question again, and strode across the room with the confidence of someone with the power to freely cut someone's ears off without reprimand.

"I can see you've said something to me as you're walking around. I can't see you properly though, and I can't hear you very well." The man on the table shouted, through gritted teeth as he dealt with the pain.

"What?!" Ursulas looked back at him, irritated by his response.

"I can't make out what you're saying." He shouted again. "You cut my bloody ears off!"

She looked at Nod with a roll of her eyes. She kneeled down to his level, and faced his face that was turned to the side to catch what she was doing in the room.

"Can you read my lips?" She asked, slowly, with exaggerated movements from her mouth.

"Yes, I can." He shouted, again, through the pain.

"O...K..." She mouthed, unnaturally.

"Who...are...you...working...for?" She spoke slowly and with wide vowel motions and an overly expressive tongue.

"Argh!" The man screamed. "How many more times can I tell you!" He was screaming at the top of his voice now. "I am just here for a drink!"

"OK, Nod." She turned back to the security guard again. "Take out his eyes."

"WHAT?!!!" The man was screaming louder, and more high pitched than he thought possible. His voice was breaking as he screamed, "I am just here for a drink!"

165

Aria was quietly thinking that Ursulas was completely bonkers, having no context for this interrogation but seeing the most barbaric questioning she had ever witnessed. Nod was reticent and looked at Ursulas with a cautious look of uncertainty.

"What's the matter?" She said, impatiently.

"I don't want to be 'that guy'...but if we take out his ears, and THEN his eyes...we won't be able to ask him questions anymore..."

Ursulas thought about this new conundrum.

"Hmm...I get what you're saying." She pondered.

The man on the table watched, still trying to contain his vocal reactions to the excruciating pain. He could see a discussion between the two of them, but wasn't sure what it was about. He glanced at Aria for a moment, not really clear about her role in all of this, but mouthed the word 'HELP' to her, optimistically. Aria winked at him and nodded to him, as if to reassure him that she had a plan. She was improvising her entire approach to this situation, and being such a lover of Denuvian Jazz, she was reminded of the feeling of creating a sonic masterpiece, but this time through her actions in this torture cell.

"What should we do then?" Ursula continued the discussion with Nod. "Take out his legs?"

"Well, we might want him to show us something...and he won't be able to take us."

"Hmm..." She pondered some more. "What about if we take off his arms?"

"I don't know..." Nod thought. "Again, I don't want to be 'that guy' but...bit harsh isn't it?"

"Oh, this is annoying." Ursulas had a short temper and this stalemate was making her even more irritable. "Can we just put the ears back on and talk to him again?"

"He's a human; you can't just attach them back on with humans." Nod explained.

"Arse." Ursulas said, torn about how far to take this. There was quiet in the room. The unfortunate man's mutterings on the table had become just a very stifled involuntary groan, emitted under his breath. He looked to Aria with his eyes wide, as if asking for help.

"I have an idea." Aria said, breaking the stalemate and giving the two criminals a start as their deep thought was interrupted.

"This is a human, right?"

"Yes, unfortunately." Ursulas replied, turning her big eye straight at the man on the table in a threatening glare.

"Well, I've heard that if you mix their blood with Rannick Juice, it sends them all crazy and they will tell you anything." Aria was making this up, but Movines weren't known for having the confidence to lie, so she was in a good position. She winked at the man on the table as she said this, away from Nod and Ursulas' vision.

"Really?" Ursulas was sceptical. "That sounds ludicrous!" She balked.

"Yeah I know. Have you been on Earth? They're crazy over there."

Aria's words certainly fitted with the humans' reputation. The one human Ursulas knew well was Lazy Riff, and he was the oddest creature she knew.

"Okay, let's try it." Ursulas grabbed some Rannick Juice and indicated to Nod that he should scoop up the blood from the table area, and give it to her. Then she mixed the two elements together, the Rannick Juice and the man's blood, and held it aloft, inspecting its colour.

"Well I have to say, it does look like it's reacting."

Aria had unwittingly set off a chain reaction in the receptacle that Ursulas was holding. Human blood mixed with Rannick Juice could be explosive. Most humans couldn't drink more than a small thimbleful without choking or desperately coughing out a burning sensation in their throat. Aria had attempted to kick-start a scenario where this unknown man on the table would support her story and start acting like the Rannick Juice would have an effect on him, and Ursulas would be persuaded, a little more, that he was telling the truth.

What, in fact, happened, was that his shackles were taken off by Nod, his head lifted up so that he could drink the liquid that had formed in the receptacle, and then the pressure in his stomach began to make his chest expand.

Aria, Ursulas and Nod looked at each other, then looked at the man on the table. He looked at his chest for a moment, and then looked at Aria with an anxious expression on his face, then his entire body exploded in front of the three shocked onlookers, and all over the two that were torturing him. There were tiny bits of him covering them, as they froze in utter shock.

"Well, I didn't expect that." Aria said, calmly.

Penny was in constant psychological contact with Lilly as Lilly was captured by Ray's men, brought in front of him, and sent off to the Orientation sessions. She felt the experience of surprise when she fell through the trapdoors and eventually onto the sliding tunnel that led the band to the streets of Corsylia. She knew Lilly had been taken on the plane, and was willingly going after Carlo DeMarco, with the hope of finally halting the harassment he was giving them to perform for him. Their feelings, thoughts and experiences were utterly tied to each other in every way. It took a steady, continuous concentration to give them a chance to make decisions by themselves, while somehow blocking out the life of the other twin. It was something that marred their early years with stress, depression and constant migraines, but now they are both able to sort through the mire of processing that can separate the two minds, so that they can function productively.

For now, Penny was content to attempt to help out this side of the ongoing feud between Ray and DeMarco. She was aware that Aria had sneaked away to find Plak, and was intent on lending a hand with her mission. Her reasoning was that she was a lot closer, and would probably need the help. She was looking for a Denuvian Priestess, unaware that Aria now looked like a Movine, dealing with the inept dexterity of a false leg.

After a few hours of fruitless snooping and mounting frustration, Penny decided to go to the Sinking Wharf, to stake out Ray's hideout, and hope for some progress there. While she did that, she kept in close telepathic contact with Lilly, asking her to ask the band for advice and to send her ideas if any came up while they journeyed toward DeMarco's hideout. She was clutching at straws and she knew it. A moment of genius from anybody she knew would be most welcome.

Aria was in the strange position of looking like a different species, in front of one of the most notorious and unpredictable criminal chiefs in the area, with a terrible story about a curious gangster from the Lantrick System to base their entire interaction on, while witnessing a tortured man exploding in front of her. Last night she was playing flute with her band.

"So who did you say you were working for, again?" Ursulas turned to Aria, bits of blood, skin, bone and other matter scattered over her face and body as she looked at the Movine in front of her.

Aria didn't have the energy to keep up the pretence.

"Okay, I need to talk straight with you." Aria started. "I am not a Movine."

Ursulas and Nod looked at each other, apprehensive and confused.

"You certainly look like one." Nod said, correctly.

"Yeah, well, I got a Hobligon to change my appearance." She explained.

"Wow." Ursulas said, calmly. "Why did you do that?"

"Is it a sexual thing?" Nod asked, politely.

"Urgh! No!" Aria blurted, appalled at the suggestion.

"Was it to fool us?" Ursulas' tone changed slightly, almost turning her enquiry into a threat.

"No, not at all. I was running from Ray's men."

"Ray?!" Nod shouted.

"Ray?" Ursulas interrupted. "Ray, from The Sinking Wharf? The Frergen beast who loves Raggets?"

"Yeah, that's him...although doesn't everyone like Raggets around here?"

"True...but he eats them like they're going extinct. It's horrific watching him guzzle them poor buggers." Ursulas almost looked sensitive as she said this, blinking her eye in empathy.

"Anyway, that's him." Aria was keen to get back on track. "He's after me...well, all of us, and demanded we did a job for him."

"After all of us?" Ursulas probed. "Who is all of us?"

"Good question. Apparently you know Trent and Lazy Riff?"

"The Brown Yelp Guys!" She smiled as she shouted this. "*Brown Yelp Gang*" She corrected.

Ursulas gave her a look, which was her way of dominating the conversation and rolling her eyes at Aria, without actually rolling her...eye.

"Them." She said, glaring at Aria.

"Yeah, them." Aria glared back, defiantly.

"Aren't those the guys that had that load of Dengen plant and had to scarper?" Nod asked.

"That's right. They ballsed that up." Ursula said, sighing. "I told them to be careful. It was a right mess."

As she turned to face Nod to elaborate on what a mess it was, Aria interrupted;

"Thing is...Ray was looking for me because I ran off, from one of his men." They both turned back to look at her. "I came back for Plak."

"Plak?" Nod repeated.

"He's an *actual* Movine." Ursula explained. "He plays the floaty melodies with the other one...DK?"

"Yeah, DK." Aria agreed "Ursulas...Plak is in trouble."

"What kind of trouble?" Ursulas was genuinely fond of the band and her voice began to show concern.

"Some bounty hunter type woman has him chained up and if we don't come up with the 40,000 credits that Jenken owes DeMarco by the next lunar cycle, he will be killed."

"Oh, okay." Ursulas replied. "Don't hold back."

"How do we know she's telling the truth?" Nod inevitably asked.

"We don't." Ursulas replied, casually. "Why are you here, funny looking, false leg not actually a Movine woman?"

"Oh, my name is Aria. I'm a Denuvian."

"O...K..." Ursulas hadn't come across a lot of Denuvians but thought them to be more rational than someone employing a Hobligon to change their features. "Nice to meet you, Aria."

"I'm actually with Riff." She said, unhelpfully.

"With Riff?" Ursula repeated, looking around the room, confused.

"No, as in *with Riff*" The point was as clear as mud, "as in...a relationship. He's my guy." She said that with a desperate attempt to explain herself, then felt self-conscious at the awkward word she used.

"I'm very pleased for you." Ursulas replied, not quite seeing the relevance. "You haven't answered my question. Why are you here?" She was getting impatient and motioned to Nod to make her some more Rannick Juice.

"I know you have a history with Trent and Riff -"

173

"- not really Riff, but Trent yes," Ursulas interrupted.

"- well, yeah I know you have a history with Trent, and he said you might be able to help us find this bounty hunter and maybe where she is hiding Plak."

"Hmmm..." Ursulas was given a glass of Rannick Juice, she lifted her glass to the table with the remains of the interrogated man on it, almost silently toasting him, then drank the glass of Juice in one gulp.

"So a bounty hunter has your Movine guy hidden somewhere on Corsylia?"

"That's right, yes." Aria replied, smiling with hopefulness.

"Do you know this bounty hunter's name?" Ursula asked, with an almost patronising tone.

"Elsa Grabbinot." Aria replied.

Ursulas and Nod looked at each other and burst into simultaneous, and ear piercing, laughter.

"Elsa Grabbinot?" Nod shouted, almost mocking Aria for saying those words.

"Yeah, did I say something funny?" Aria asked, innocently.

"Elsa Grabbinot is a rank amateur." Ursulas settled down and explained the outburst, smiling smugly.

"She always uses the same place, doesn't she?" Nod asked Ursulas.

"Absolutely." She replied, without a hint of doubt.

Aria's eyes lit up as it looked like the disguise, the story about the crime lord from the Lantrick System, and witnessing the exploding man, was all going to lead somewhere.

Ray's security men (and less humanoid members of his staff) had taken his newly made robot Brown Yelp Gang to their next venue, on the beautifully green, forest planet of Vestrell. He had hired the sound and vision engineering company, 'Les Manfred's Gig Boys', a company known light years from its humble beginnings in Gosport, on New Earth. Their reputation for loud, memorable and sometimes notorious gigs was legendary. Les Manfred, himself, was a short man with wispy hair giving the effect of wings sprouting from his largely bald head, and from the glasses that sat permanently on his ears. He was pleased to get this gig with The Brown Yelp Gang, especially as Ray had decided to tell his men to keep it a secret from Les that it wasn't *actually* the band, but a metallic replica. They had a six gig run, by which time Ray assumed the real band would have had enough time to collect the information they needed to challenge Carlo DeMarco's suspicious activity. The first two gigs would be on Vestrell, and then they'd be flying off to the neighbouring planet, much further from that system's sun, the ice Planet of Aquilos. This would create new problems for the crew and the metal band, but for now, the priority was keeping the fans happy on Vestrell. There had been a major promotional campaign sent out by Jenken over the six

175

months before the gig, as they had enjoyed years of success on the major cities on the planet, but never visited to gig there. So the anticipation was palpable. Ray's recent second publicity campaign to roll out the new theme of robotics and artificial intelligence was a tactical move to prepare the fans for the potential shock.

"WITNESS THE NEW CONCEPT FOR THE LEGENDARY BROWN YELP GANG" the posters and streamed bulletins proclaimed. "A NEW SHOW THAT ROCKS THE FUTURE AND ROLLS THE EVEN FURTHER FUTURE"

Ray was better at threatening people than writing advertising slogans.

The first gig on Vestrell was in the capital city of the biggest continent on the planet, the prosperous, authoritarian city of Lidos. They were treated like royalty when the enormous shuttle with Les Manfred's Gig Boys' gear and the replicas landed. 436 fans, from an impressive range of different species, all gathered at the space depot for the landing and cheered hysterically when the 'band' appeared in front of them.

"This is a good start." Polly, Ray's chief of operations whispered to the Trent replica.

"Affirmative." The Trent replica simply said.

Polly shuddered, wondering how the crowd will take to the 'banter' on stage between the songs...

Throughout the first day, there was no sense that the band could be robot replicas. The crew, and the staff of 'The Seeping Hole', where their first gig was being held, were stunned and impressed by the band's willingness to stay in character throughout the whole day. Ray's men occasionally fabricated a scenario where the band needed some private time together, out of costume, to reduce the risk of discovery but, ultimately, they were presenting a facade of an insanely committed band to their new concept. The music coming from the band was all electronic and processed through presets and digital circuitry, so the sound check was done quicker than any other sound check in Brown Yelp history. There was no guitarist saying they couldn't hear anything. There were no sudden leads or pickups failing. There was no drummer spending twenty minutes rubbing his chest with Haciid Oil to massage the skin through the gig. There were no moments where the lead singer argued with himself in a hostile display of proof that there were three sides to every story. It was simply a case of the sound engineers mixing the sound correctly, and the robots on stage running through a few songs to acclimatise themselves to the venue. It was a small venue, with a high ceiling. Elaborate paintings of the construction of Vestrell's cities laced the ceiling that acted as a beautiful distraction to the audience, as they walked in ready to welcome The Brown Yelp Gang for the first time. The replica band had the luxury of not experiencing nerves, as they had the luxury of having no feelings whatsoever. They analysed the last few tours and calculated the set that was most likely to be successful, and decided to start the gig with 'Show me where you put it'. The audience went wild.

This was the song, more than any other song in this electronically calculated set, that wasn't as affected by the new digital reworking of the songs. The opening riff was a staccato style guitar phrase that was easily replicated by the robot Riff on his Corsyllian keytar. This riff alone set the audience off into a cacophony of screaming and yelling phrases like "We love you Riff!" and "Movines Rule!" It was, truly, a shame that those involuntary bursts of affection were light years from their targets.

Chapter Eight

The tall, thin pilot successfully achieved the seemingly
impossible, hovering above DeMarco's main base of
operations and releasing the Mikkle Bird with the band
astride it, for them to eventually land safely on its roof.
Then, with the same level of stealth befitting one of Ray's
right hand men, Deet and Teddy landed on Praxim 7 soil,
ready to find their own way into the compound. The main
base of operations for DeMarco's nefarious business deals
was on the quiet, backwater swamp town of Blurgh, a town
that was so far away from the main capital City of Praxim 7,
that it was almost lawless. There was the occasional casual
patrol from the air, which hardly ever led to an in-depth
search of the area. DeMarco's activities were well known
around the planet and the nearby systems, but the Praxim
7 authorities were intimidated by him, and felt that their
resources were better used for less challenging criminals.
So Blurgh was consistently left to its own devices, and
consequently left in the grip of DeMarco's whims and
urges.

DeMarco's main base of operations was a complex cul-de-
sac of buildings that were dominated by the tallest, thickest
shaped building that usually contained DeMarco and his
various henchmen. The courtyard was busy during the day,

with an array of business deals and threatened errand boys scampering around the pathways between the buildings. At night, it was much quieter, with only the occasional security guard patrolling the grounds, often without incident, waving across the courtyard to the few other security guards absentmindedly strolling through DeMarco's grounds. Having arrived at night, Trent, Jenken, Lilly, DK and Riff had the luxury of settling into their new environment without an immediate battle on their hands. The Mikkle Bird had strict instructions to fly back to Corsylia once the band had been dropped off on the roof of DeMarco's main base. They all sat crouched on the roof, watching the Mikkle Bird fly away and disappear into the mist of the clouds above.

"There goes our ticket out of here." Riff said, facetiously.

"You joke, Riff, but how do we get back?" DK responded, rationally.

"I think this is one of those situations where opportunities will present themselves to us as we go along." Jenken said, philosophically.

"Or not." Deet said, typically pessimistically.

Jenken looked at him and gave a simple 'hmmph' sound in resigned agreement. They stayed crouched on the roof, as DK asked the question that had been in the back of every mind crouched on the roof since they had left Bragal;

"Jenken," he began, "how are we doing with the money we owe DeMarco?"

"Yeah, "Riff joined in, "and are we going to just go up to him with our money and say 'here you are, dude, here's the dosh'?"

"I just want to knock his block off!" DK whispered through gritted teeth.

"I expect we all do, DK, but I think using that approach would be suicide." Deet replied, condescendingly.

"I'll join in, if we're going for that approach." Lilly added, after the moment had passed.

"Okay, I've been keeping tabs on all of it as we've been going along." Jenken whispered, keeping an eye out for any patrolling security. "So far, we're not there, but not doing too bad."

"What does that mean?" Trent's right head asked.

"In numbers." Deet added.

They all looked at Jenken expectantly.

"Okay, let's see." Jenken said, pulling out a small screen from his left side pocket. He flipped a keypad from the bottom of the screen and began typing in numbers.

"I'm impressed that you kept a log." Deet said, sincerely.

"This is Plak's life at stake; I'm not going to take this lightly." Jenken snapped, quietly.

"Yeah, fair one." Deet replied.

"So," Jenken continued, "from those first two gigs, we have managed to get just under 1,000 credits for our merchandise."

The band nodded their heads in a consensus of satisfaction with this tally.

"Then with the bootleg shirts that Teddy sold, that was an extra thousand credits." Jenken added.

"That's 2 then." Riff declared, unhelpfully.

"Well, I sold the freighter." Jenken turned to them all in turn, smiling.

"Ah, yes, of course." Trent's middle head salivated with anticipation. "That should be good."

"Well not too bad." Jenken replied. "We got 24,000 for that lovely little ship."

They all responded with quiet variations of 'wow' and 'no way' while either dropping their jaw, sucking up the air to express their surprise, or just simply widening their eyes in disbelief.

"That's 26 then." Riff replied, clarifying their position again.

"...and then there's the special box set that Trent released." They all looked at Trent when Jenken said this.

"You're a sly one, mate." Riff nudged him, still speaking just above a whisper.

"Well, it's just sitting there otherwise." Trent replied, smiling smugly.

"What did you put on it?" DK asked.

"Demos, drunk stuff, random shit basically." Trent answered, honestly.

"Nice!" Riff said, resisting the urge to high five him above DeMarco's main base.

"Did you put 'How is this going to fit me now that I'm a Lizard?'" Lilly asked, joining in on the fun.

There was a slight pause as the band frowned and looked at each other, confused.

"Was that actually by The Trustables?" Deet asked anyone who might know the answer.

"Yes, it was!" Riff said, almost blowing their cover with his enthusiasm.

"Different band, Lilly." Trent said, flatly, to the bald girl beside him.

"Well, what has that stuff sold so far anyway?" DK asked Jenken, breaking the tension.

"Okay, get this," he replied, increasing the suspense. "So far, over just one day, that box set, only available as an electronic stream straight from the archives..."

"Yes?" DK was bursting with frustration.

"...has given us an extra 13,000 credits!" Jenken's voice remained quiet, but his tone was brimming with excitement in sharing the news.

"13,000 credits for me singing on the loo?!" Trent exclaimed.

"Yep. You could simply fart and they'd buy it in droves." Jenken replied.

"That's on the second batch." Trent answered, without any hint of pretence.

"That's great news, though, Jenken." Deet said, unusually positive about their predicament.

"That's not all." Jenken added.

"Aw, I like this." DK was smiling joyously as he thought about his musical partner trapped in the warehouse somewhere, helpless.

"Our fees for the first two gigs were 10,000 credits; first one being 2,000 and obviously the one for Ray being 8,000."

"Hence us being here doing this for him." Deet scoffed.

"Absolutely." Jenken nodded in agreement.

"So, wait a minute." DK was adding it all up in his head as Jenken was breaking it down. "That means we have reached 49,000 doesn't it?"

"It certainly does, my friend." Jenken smiled, knowing how much this would mean to DK. "It's all in my account, waiting to go to whatever dodgy account DeMarco wants to put it in. We can give him that 40,000 whenever he wants it."

"That's amazing." Lilly said, staring at the band she had worshipped from afar for so long, now enamoured by how quickly they recovered the money.

"What about the campaign for the new album?" Trent asked.

"What new album?" Riff interjected, with a confused tone.

"It wasn't a new album, but we were going to say it was a new album." Trent explained.

"That's a bit weird isn't it?" Riff said, oblivious to the conversation at The Atomic Wombat.

"That was put on the information stream straight away and that's been gaining momentum too." Jenken said, still whispering to them all.

"Go on, spill it." DK said, now so excited he wanted to blow a brassy burst from his snout to the observing skies.

"Okay, well so far we have had 12 hundred donors, and most of them have been very generous. In the 18 hours that this new album has been on the information stream waiting for donations, it has reached..."

"Come on, Jenken, we're not game show contestants." Deet groaned, impatiently.

"...5,600 credits."

They all sat on the roof, quietly, smiling in contentment that the seemingly insurmountable goal of 40,000 credits was achieved well before the end of the lunar cycle, and without too much illegal activity. The moment of reflection was long and laboured, with Trent and Riff occasionally looking at each other and sniggering, in their relief. The vulnerable position that they had been put in was apparent to them as they waited for the satisfaction to sink in. Being dropped above the main base of operations and moving so sneakily around the base was not the ideal way to be noticed by DeMarco's security. They needed a way down so that they could approach the base with a more congenial entrance.

"We need to get to DeMarco without him thinking we're up to something." Jenken stated, to all of his companions on the roof.

"Agreed." Trent agreed.

"Yes." Riff said, also agreeing.

"How do we do that then?" Lilly asked, innocently.

They all looked around the roof, uninspired and...stuck.

Ursulas was more than happy to help Aria with her plan. It wasn't the connection with Trent, although that did help. The main motivation for her was her intense dislike of Carlo DeMarco. He had been consistently overruling her at every stage of development in her business, and demanded thousands of credits in protection money from her during the early years of The Speckled Interruption. He had a knack of taking money off of you, persuading you that it was somehow a sound investment, then almost convincing you that you shouldn't be trying to make money in the first place. It was a clever way of metaphorically holding his rivals heads under water while they drowned in his audacity, his self-confidence and his lack of empathy for anybody with a pulse. Ursulas had years of resentment and outrage to work through, and assisting Aria in retrieving her band member from DeMarco's convoluted kidnapping threat was just the tip of the iceberg. Once this was done, she was keen to see how else she could help.

Elsa Grabbinot was a creature of habit. She was an extremely successful bounty hunter, but that was mainly because she wasn't challenged very often. The code of ethics that operated in Corsylia meant that as long as she didn't abuse her bounties and remained on the right side of decency, the awareness of her hideouts among the Corsyllian underworld was not an issue. Ursulas knew that she wouldn't be keeping Plak in her home, which just left the warehouse that she used to keep the goods she picked up along the way. Her bounties were often kept in this warehouse overnight, while she planned her next move. In this case, she had taken a job that required many nights of captivity in her warehouse, which was unusual for her, but DeMarco's demands were often met without question. Her warehouse was a fifteen minute ride on Nod's Hover-Car, which, even with the high saturation of Corsyllian traffic, was still the best way to travel in Corsylia. The Hover-Cars were great vehicles for sneaking around Corsylia as their engines were silent and their doors were sealed with felt padding that allowed for passengers to leave the vehicle with very little sound emanating from the car. As they stood together in front of the warehouse, Aria spoke quietly to Ursulas;

"I appreciate the help, Ursulas. I cannot thank you enough actually, for bringing me here."

"That's not a problem." Ursulas replied.

"Thank you." Aria repeated. "Thing is," she continued, "I really want to kick this woman's arse myself."

There was a slight pause.

"...if that's ok?" Aria added, humbly. Ursulas sniggered, under her breath.

"Knock yourself out." She replied. "I will be at the back of the warehouse, in case she escapes."

"Agreed. Thank you." Aria repeated.

"Nod, you go with me." Ursulas instructed.

She gave Aria one last salute with her left arm, then walked to the back of the warehouse with Nod. Aria looked at the front of the warehouse, now on her own, but confident that she could take on Elsa Grabbinot. She approached the main, front door of the warehouse and listened in, with her head against the door to the side. The sounds inside were muffled, as the door and walls of the warehouse were made of sheets of metal that blocked out part of the sounds of the surrounding street. Aria could hear a woman's voice speaking, but couldn't make out what was being said. The occasional rattling of chains was heard, and a low mumble that could have been Plak, although it was impossible to tell from outside the warehouse. She decided to throw caution to the wind and confront this situation head on.

"Elsa Grabbinot!" Aria shouted, in the direction of the closed, metal door in front of her.

There was silence.

"Elsa Grabbinot!" She repeated. The sound of chains and the movement of furniture was all that came back to her as a reply.

"Elsa!" Aria said one last time. "I am here to see my friend." She said, laying her cards clearly on the table.

"Well, not just to see him, but to see him set free."

There was another silence that felt, to Aria, like a lifetime.

"You're not having him." Elsa's voice finally created a two way conversation through the walls of the warehouse.

"Ahh." Aria sighed. "There you are."

"Who are you?" Elsa shouted, still happy to communicate from inside those metal walls.

"I am Aria, flute player for The Brown Yelp Gang and a decorated priestess on Pwom."

"Hello." Elsa replied, glibly.

"Have you harmed him?" Aria asked, still shouting through the walls.

"Nope. That's not my thing." Elsa shouted back.

"Are you in there, Plak?" Aria raised her voice louder, as if it was necessary to reach the other person in the room.

"He can't hear you." Elsa shouted back.

"Why not? What have you done to him?"

"Nothing. He's asleep."

"Did you drug him?" Aria was still shouting.

"No need. He gets bored and sleeps."

Elsa wasn't lying. Plak had developed a default sleeping position while being captive.

"So what's the plan?" Elsa shouted, teasing Aria with a move to develop the stalemate.

"I'm coming in to get Plak." Aria stated, plainly.

"I wouldn't do that." Elsa threatened.

"Why not?" Aria shouted back, indifferent to the threatening tone.

"The place is booby trapped."

"Really?" Aria said, not quite believing her.

"Absolutely, you won't get very far."

"Prove it." Aria shouted, defiantly.

Elsa was insulted by the suggestion that she was pretending that the warehouse was booby trapped. Her ego forced her to immediately prove the existence of the booby traps she had placed around the entrance to the warehouse.

"Listen to this!" Elsa shouted, as she threw a large coil of metal chains across the room to the traps by the door. Instantly the traps all activated and sprung up around the door, as the chains made contact. As they all exploded in their reaction to the chains, Aria decided to make her move and heaved the door open with one all-powerful shove from her left shoulder. Moments later she was in the warehouse staring at the sleeping Plak, and the menacing presence of Elsa standing between her and her chained up band mate, armed with a pulse rifle.

"I guess you know enough about ego to know how to manipulate me." Elsa sighed, as she watched the door open and Aria step through. She felt the embarrassment of the first defeat in this encounter.

"I just want Plak out of here and back with the band." Aria said, now walking forward, toward the armed bounty hunter.

Elsa raised her pulse rifle at Aria, expecting her to stop in her tracks.

"I'm happy to shoot you, Movine." Elsa shouted.

"I'm not a -"Aria sighed, "oh, never mind."

With that sigh of resignation about her altered appearance, she ran at Elsa with an impressive speed, considering her false leg was hampering her movement. Elsa fired three shots at Aria as she ran at her, and two of those shots hit Aria; one that hit her left shoulder and sent her staggering back a little, and one on the false Movine snout, that had, as a result, become half a snout. When she was close enough, Aria leaped forward toward Elsa, twisting her body in the air so that her legs were first to impact the recoiling bounty hunter. Elsa's body was fiercely knocked to the ground but she instantly rolled away and stood up again as if it was all one harmless bounce. She had let go of the pulse rifle in the fall and was facing Aria now with her arms outstretched, ready for hand to hand combat.

"You think you're going to beat me, lady?" Elsa said, confidently.

"Oh, if you know anything about me, you'd be shaking in your knee high boots Ms Grabbinot."

"Come and get me." Elsa teased, with her arms poised, ready for contact.

Aria noticed metal pipes across the ceiling of the warehouse and ran at Elsa, jumping onto one of those pipes as she ran and flinging herself toward Elsa's head again. Elsa looked for the pulse rifle, that was a few feet away, to her right. Before she could reach it, Aria was on top of her again, with her legs wrapped around her neck in a vice like grip. They both fell to the floor, and writhed around with both of them grabbing each other to get the upper hand. Aria was feeling the pain from the shot to the shoulder, but her adrenalin and training at the priesthood kept her a formidable challenge to Elsa. Still gripped by Aria's legs, Elsa pulled up her legs to grip Aria's head in a similar way. Both were now tightening their hold and moving around the floor like a high concept dance piece about fraught relationships. The warehouse was full of obstructions, and it was one of those obstructions, a wooden pallet lying across a pile of tyres, that broke their hold on each other. In the struggle, Aria's back slammed into the pallet on one of the sharp edges, causing her to loosen her grip on Elsa. Elsa took advantage of this and swiftly stood up, kicking Aria in the shoulder where she had been shot.

Aria screamed in pain, gritted her teeth and stood up again. They were both now looking dishevelled and filthy, the floor of the warehouse being unkempt and dirty.

"You're not going to win. I have gigs to do." Aria huffed, between catching her breath.

"I'm all good. Try again, Denuvian." Elsa said, with the bravado of someone with no pressing engagements to worry about. Elsa moved her fingers in a beckoning manner, almost smiling provocatively.

Aria simply began to channel her will of prayer.

"Staktik laktipna laktipna laatneen." Aria chanted.

Then she chanted the same again. Elsa looked on, confused and static, waiting for something to happen.

"Blah blah blah." Elsa said, mockingly.

Aria continued to chant the will of prayer. As she reached the sixteenth chant, her voice started to rise in pitch and in volume. By the twenty third chant, her voice had become a scream. Elsa looked on almost bored, but fixated by the spectacle in front of her.

So fixated, in fact, that she failed to notice that Aria had performed the 'Transcendental Axis Leap' ritual with her meditative chanting, and successfully created bilocation, making her body physically present in two places. Aria's dislocated body flew at the unsuspecting Elsa and kicked her directly in the head and immediately knocked her unconscious.

Aria thanked her gods and found some rope from the mess on the warehouse floor and tied her up. Ursulas and Nod had been watching from the other end of the warehouse, and slowly and methodically clapped, almost patronising her.

"Who would have thought religion would create such a great weapon to use in a fight." Ursulas said, smiling, as she walked toward Aria's position.

"It's usually all about looking at yourself and understanding the world around you. This time it was about kicking her arse."

"Well, whatever it's for, I'm impressed." Ursulas conceded.

"Can you teach me?" The great, hulking form of Nod barked behind them both.

"If you have about 20 years and a new set of trousers to spare." Aria replied.

"Is this your guy?" Ursulas pointed to the wall on her left, where Plak was sleeping, chained to the wall.

"That's him."

"Thought so. I remember the album covers." She smiled, ultimately still a fan of The Brown Yelp Gang.

"We better wake him up hadn't we?" Nod suggested.

"Absolutely." Aria agreed.

With that, Nod picked him up and shook him in a violent, seemingly uncaring, way like a rag doll.

"WAKE UP!!" He shouted, a few inches from his face.

Plak woke up.

"I guess that would do it." Aria raised her eyebrows, admiring the subtlety.

"What? Who's? Wha? What? Aria?" Plak tried to orient himself to the sudden appearance of these three people, as Nod bit his chains off and picked Plak's body out of the coils of metal that had surrounded him. There was enough of Aria in her disguised appearance for an immediate reaction from her bandmate.

"How are you doing buddy?" Aria said, relieved to see him awake and alive.

"Oh, not bad." He replied. "It's been an eventful few days!"

"I can see." Aria answered, not aware of anything he might have done besides stay locked up, chained to the wall.

"I'm in love!" Plak shouted to the world, lifting his head to aim his words to the ceiling, and saying it louder than he had ever shouted anything.

"Wow." Ursulas smirked. "I didn't see that coming."

"In love?" Aria asked.

"Oh, Aria. It's a beautiful thing." Plak had now stepped out from where he had been sleeping beside the wall, and was wandering around the warehouse, spinning with his arms outstretched. "Love is like a gentle brush of wonder sinking into your skin like a star about to explode in your face."

He was gushing with love. Nod found it distasteful. Ursulas found it hilarious, and Aria found it odd and disturbing.

"What the hell has been happening since you've been here?" Aria asked.

"I met someone."

"How did you meet someone?"

"She looked after me, so that I wasn't lonely."

"What?" Aria was raising her voice, confused and worried about his state of mind. "What kind of kidnapping is this?"

"Elsa was always a considerate thief and bounty collector." Ursulas interrupted. "I'm not surprised. Once she set up a counselling service for all those that she had maimed or slightly injured in previous operations."

"She's a lovely little lady." Nod swooned, looking at the unconscious body of Elsa a few feet away from him.

"Ah yeah, lovely. She threatened to kill my friend, here." Aria protested.

"I actually don't think she would have done." Plak argued.

"Oh, really?" Aria was losing her patience with his lack of gratitude.

"Well, that doesn't matter now cos she's dead." Plak bluntly stated.

"She's not dead, I just knocked her out." Aria corrected.

"Okay, fair enough."

"So who is this person that looked after you?" Ursulas asked, intrigued and still amused.

"Not a person as such, not a human person anyway. The most beautiful Bask Lizard I have ever seen, with a voice you could eat for lunch and still be on your feet."

"Still be on your feet?" Aria thought the metaphor was clumsy at best.

"Yeah, it's a phrase...from somewhere." He clarified.

196

"Plaaaaaak?" A Bask voice was heard from the entrance to the warehouse that Aria used to start the fracas with Elsa.

"Ah, and there is that lovely voice now!" Plak said, with an excited, thrilled tone. He looked over Aria's head and beyond their area of the warehouse to try and spot her as she came in.

"Where's my chewy boy?" Nesta said, as she walked through the warehouse to where the others were.

"Chewy?!" Aria found this term of endearment repugnant and scowled at Plak as she heard it.

"She's my little sexy serpent woman." Plak was lost in a fog of anticipation after hearing her voice again.

"Give me strength!" Aria huffed, not impressed at all by this apparent infatuation.

Moments later, Nesta appeared with her ukulele, ready to sing with him again and relieve Elsa to go out and do whatever Elsa needed to do. She stopped in her tracks, several feet away from the gathering in front of her, once she had processed the sight of Elsa on the floor unconscious, Plak untied and standing freely beside her, and three complete strangers all looking at her with frowns on their faces.

"Hello?" Nesta attempted.

"Yes, that's a good start." Ursulas nodded. "Hello to you too. So you're the snaky sexpot that this snouty sexpot has been ranting about?"

"What?" Nesta was still confused and anxious.

197

"Don't worry about them, Nesta." Plak suggested. "They're jealous."

"Excuse me?" Aria interjected. "Jealous of what, exactly?"

"True love!" Plak swooned again, saying those words with an exaggerated high pitched lilt that brought out a disapproving groan from the others.

Nesta was reassured by his declaration of love and continued to walk toward the gathering, stopping at Plak's open arms to give him an affectionate hug.

"I've missed you." She said, smiling at him.

"Me too." He replied to her, gazing at her huge, yellow pupils. "It must have been about four hours!"

"It was actually only two, but time is a cruel mistress when you're in love!" Nesta's words floated through the air like Plak's declarations of love earlier.

"Can someone just shoot the pair of them?" Aria said, killing the mood completely.

"Aw, it's cute really." Ursulas quipped, the romantic deep inside her sneaking out for a quick comment before hiding back behind her ruthless gangster persona.

"Well, sorry to break up this little love nest, but we have to get you back Plak." Aria spoke efficiently and with authority.

"What?" Plak turned from Nesta's gaze, as if he had no idea where 'back' was.

"We need to get you back..." She repeated "...to the band."

The penny dropped; Plak remembered his life before Nesta for a moment and realised why there were three people rescuing him.

"The band!" He nodded. "Of course."

"Yeah, they're all worried about you. Especially DK."

"Ah, DK." Plak smiled, remembering his partner and good friend.

"Plak, it's only been days that you've been locked up in here. You're acting like it's been years!" Aria was getting impatient now and visibly irritated.

"When you're trapped in the wondrous spell of true love, time and memory become brothers in arms, fighting for life amongst a barrage of physical pleasure and spiritual bliss."

"Oh, for all the gods' sakes!" Aria snapped, not amused at all.

Nesta giggled, loving the expression of their deep and instant love that was tripping out of Plak's delirious brain.

"Isn't he gorgeous?" Nesta said, to Nod.

"Yes, he's gorgeous." Nod agreed, somehow swept up in the moment.

Ursulas gave him a look of surprise. Nod shrugged in surprise back.

"How is everyone?" Plak asked, slowly returning to the physical world that his rescuers lived in.

"They're OK. The situation with the debt has got more complicated, but I'll explain later."

"Complicated? How?" Plak was concerned by this.

"Erm..." Aria didn't necessarily want to give him the whole story straight away but thought it best to at least summarise; "Well, we've ended up agreeing to work for Ray, the guy who runs everything in Bragal, in a bid to topple Carlo DeMarco's grip on...everything."

"Working for Ray, the big fat amphibian thing that shoots anything that questions him?"

"That's the one." Aria replied. "He's kind of forced us to work for him."

"Figures." Ursulas added, with disdain.

"You're with us aren't you?" Aria turned her attention to Ursulas for a moment after her comment.

"Oh yes, of course." She replied. "I will always do what I do voluntarily though." She added, smugly.

"Well, we're just a rock band, so we don't always hold the best hand." Aria turned back to Plak. "So, clearly you haven't got anything to pack up to leave, so let's just go." There was a moment of stillness from Plak, and then he dropped the bombshell.

"I am not going with you, Aria."

"You what, now?" Aria gaped at him in shock.

"I'm staying here with Nesta." He looked at his new love as he said this, beaming from one side of his face to the other in overwhelming passion.

"You can't." Aria was desperately trying to articulate what was in her head.

"I can do what I want!" Plak protested.

"He can do what he wants!" Ursulas agreed.

"Shut up, Ursulas, you are not involved with this." Aria snapped.

"Technically she is, as she brought you here." Nod argued, gently.

"Well you're not in the band!" She snapped again.

"I am done with the Brown Yelp Gang, Aria." Plak said, apologetically.

"What about the rest of us?" Aria had changed her tone to a more helpless whine.

"You'll be fine." Plak said, cheerily. "You've done gigs while I've been in here."

"We have...but we were treading water until you came back, Plak." Aria pleaded.

"I'm sorry, but my mind is made up." Plak spoke firmly to all of them gathered together.

Elsa began to revive and lift herself off the floor. Plak noticed this and instantly crouched down and whipped her with his snout, sending her back into the unconscious world of sleep.

"Are you giving up music?" Aria had now accepted his point, and was just curious now about his plans.

"Oh no, of course not." Plak was emphatic. "We will be forming a duo and performing across the system as - "

"- NESTA AND PLAK!" Nesta interrupted.

"PLAK AND NESTA!" Plak corrected, moving his right arm in an arc as if to indicate the words being written across a sign above a venue door.

"Ouch." Ursulas chuckled as she could see the ego's already clashing.

"Well, I guess I'm pleased for you, my friend." Aria had calmed down and was keen to wish him luck.

"Thank you, Aria." Plak half bowed. "I will keep in touch."

"Oh yeah, you better."

"Maybe there'll be a support slot for us on another tour?" Plak smiled, serious about the suggestion.

"Of course!" Aria replied, not having any power in the band to influence this.

"Thanks for rescuing me."

"That's OK, my friend." Aria smiled. "I think we may have the debt in hand anyway, or at least a big chunk of it, so DeMarco may not have killed you."

"Oh, right!" Plak was pleasantly surprised at the band's resolve.

"Jenken sold the freighter."

"Whoah," Plak was visibly stunned. "He loved that ship."

"Well, we love you, Mr Toots Blower." This was one of the band's nicknames for him that didn't come up very often, thankfully.

"Keep the faith brother." Aria held out her hands to shake them, as was the Denuvian way of saying goodbye.

Plak grabbed both of her hands in his hands and they shook, three times, as is the custom on Pwom. Aria gave a respectful nod to Nesta, and looked at Ursulas and Nod. "I guess we need to leave these two love birds to it, and get to Praxim 7 to help out the band."

"I hear you." Ursulas replied.

"Can we take Elsa with us?" Nod asked, in a distasteful way that brought a new level of awkward to the building.

"What do you want her for?" Ursulas asked, and then thought again. "Actually, don't answer."

Chapter Nine

Ray was happily sitting alone in his office, guzzling Raggets at his desk with the usual mess of saliva, Ragget blood and pond water creating the fetid mess around him as he ate. It was a day of reckoning for one of his agents who were sent out to investigate DeMarco's plans before Ray decided to use The Brown Yelp Gang. The agent was a small creature with ten bendy limbs, opposable thumbs and four other digits on each of those limbs and a legendary sense of smell from their drooping snouts that would give any Movine a run for their money. He was a Hassienda, a rodent who was also from the Lantrick system; small enough to subtly observe but mobile enough on their distinctive hover platforms, to move around quickly if needed. As he hovered into The Sinking Wharf on his platform, he was feeling a little sheepish as he didn't have a lot to share with Ray. One of Ray's Bask Lizard guards had directed him to the room; there was a deathly silence. Ray had stopped ramming Raggets into his mouth when the Hassienda had entered the room, and waited eagerly for the update.

"Well?" Ray barked, sharply.

"Um...I...have...got...some information." The Hassienda was quaking as he spoke. The silence in between his words felt like years in length, as the room closed in around him.

"Come on then, spit it out!" Ray was utterly impatient about all things tied with business, and these small moments of trepidation from his agents incensed him into an intolerant fever. With a long, audible sigh, Ray punched some triggers on his keypad and an enormous claw grabbed the Hassienda by the layer of fat on his tiny neck and pulled him off his hover platform, leaving him dangling in mid-air, in front of Ray.

"You have been working with me for 10 months now, Rigly." Ray's voice remained threatening as he glared at the suspended Rigly. "You need to give me the information I need, or I will feed you to..."

Ray thought for a moment, and then made a decision.

"...myself."

"It was hard to gain access to the documents, and the lower levels." Rigly was spluttering in a panic. He wasn't particularly having a great year but getting eaten by Ray would be the last straw.

"Why was it so hard, Rigly, my boy?" Ray's friendly language was not delivered with a friendly tone.

"DeMarco is obsessed with musicians. It's all he thinks about."

Ray let out a belly laugh that shook the foundations of the building.

"...erm...as I was saying..." Rigly was a little more nervous, not truly understanding where the laugh came from "...he seems to give all kinds of access to his guests, especially if they are musicians. I managed to get around a lot of his base of operations without being detected, but struggled to find out the details of his plan."

"Did you not think of masquerading as a musician?" Ray suggested, antagonistically.

"Ray, you know that Hassienda's are not taken seriously as musicians." He had a point. "What was that guy that came out of the blue a few solar cycles back? Walked on stilts and wore a massive hairpiece."

"Ah yes." Ray knew the reference. "He put out all those power ballads."

"That's the one. He gave himself a special name because he was the first Hassienda to cross over to another system."

"Yeah, he was..." Ray thought back "...he was called 'The Eternal Voice'. That was it."

"Yeah, that was it."

"What happened to him?"

"That's my point. He was shot and killed."

"Oh, not so 'Eternal' then."

"No, exactly." Rigly was getting passionate now, swinging from the giant claw. "He had tons of hate mail because he was a Hassienda. Then somebody killed him. Since then, no Hassienda has performed outside of the Lantrick system."

"Hmmm..." Ray pondered the little guy's defence. "Okay, what have you got?"

"Well I know he's planning something." Rigly began.

"Well I KNOW THAT!" Ray's voice boomed across the office.

"Something that involves weapons..."

"Yes?" Ray was leaning forward now, intrigued.

"...some kind of music festival..."

"Yes..." Ray knew this already.

"...and some kind of big robot thing."

"What?" Ray had heard something new now and wanted the details. "A robot thing? Tell me more."

"That's it, I didn't find out much more than that. He's having it built down in the lower levels of his main base of operations. He's planning some kind of takeover of the system I think."

"The whole solar system?" Ray couldn't quite believe the audacity of the idea.

"Apparently it's all linked to his music ambitions. He thinks he shouldn't have to pay for any music so thinks if he owns everything and everyone, then he can get whatever he wants, whenever he wants."

"He's going to put on some kind of multi-planet war, so that he can listen to music he likes?" Ray spat the words out, appalled at the ludicrous nature of the plan.

"Apparently, I was told, he lives for music and apparently, so I was told, he never gets enough of it."

"Right..."

"- and goes on and on about it being free everywhere."

"Music?" Ray was trying to keep up with this character profile.

"Yeah, he reckons it should be like air."

"Air?"

"Yeah, like...free."

"Wow." Ray looked down at the mess on his desk. All of the Raggets had been violently eaten and all that was left on his bowl was the blood and sauce, dripping off the sides of the table. "I knew he loved putting on music gigs and promoting bands, but this is an odd reason to begin a war with everyone in the system!" Ray was practically talking to himself, surveying the bowl and surrounding areas of the table for more Raggets. His saliva flew out of his mouth in several directions as he muttered these words to himself.

"To be honest, I think he'll be doing all that for other reasons besides the music thing."

Ray looked up, as if noticing Rigly for the first time.

"I just kept hearing that it was a big motivation for him. This music being free everywhere thing." Rigly added, nervously.

"Okay."Ray wasn't exactly satisfied but he knew he wasn't getting anything more out of his Hassienda agent. "Thank you for this small bit of information. I will relay that to the people that replace you."

Seconds later, the giant claw had sent Rigly flying toward Ray's huge, slimy, open mouth. He had swallowed him whole, with much less mess than any one of the Raggets that he loved so much.

Almost immediately after Rigly disappeared down Ray's throat and began to be digested, one of his security guards entered the room, as if waiting outside for the right moment. Ray looked up, visibly disturbed by the interruption.

"What do you want?" Ray shouted at him, angrily.

"Sorry to disturb you, Sir." The guard was scared, as most of them were when they were in Ray's vicinity.

"What is it?"

"There's a complication with the Brown Yelp Gang replicas."

Ray's tone changed, to concern. He was still aggressive, but it was aggressive concern.

"What is the problem? Have they shorted out?"

"No, nothing like that, sir."

"Have they rebelled?"

"No, sir...although apparently the replica of Trent is asking for more money."

"Fine. Give him more money." Ray dismissed the request with a wave of his fat, stubby hand.

"...oh and the replica of Riff is demanding robot groupies."

"What?" Ray was getting irritated again. "What does he want groupies for? He has no urges."

"Apparently he is saying that he can replicate Riff's behaviour on stage better if he replicates his antics offstage too."

"Sounds like an excuse to bang another robot?!" Ray shouted. "Tell him to do the Aria robot."

"Will do, sir."

"Okay, so is that it?"

"No, not at all. That wasn't why I came to see you." The guard said, apologetically.

"Well, what is it?" Ray's tone was a mix of sighing and threatening that he had perfected over the years of criminal dominance.

"It's the latest gig. The fourth gig of their tour."

"Yes, it's another one on that forest planet, right?" Ray was aware of the details but didn't see the issue yet.

"This wasn't an ordinary gig, sir."

"What do you mean?"

"This one is the other side of the planet, where the tribal societies are. There is no electricity. Apparently the band was going to do the fourth gig on the tour as fully acoustic. No amplification at all."

"Right." The issue hadn't burrowed itself clearly into Ray's brain yet.

"Well, sir. The replicas cannot perform without electricity. They are robots. They have to be plugged in, and all of their gear and instruments are digital workstations."

"Oh, bottom dwelling hair munchers." Ray didn't curse like that very often. Clearly he could see the issue now.

"Can they get charged up for the day and sent over?"

"I'm afraid the charge doesn't last the length of sound checking and gigging and all that." The guard was starting to relax now, as Ray's voice had calmed to a more conversational tone.

"So there is literally no electricity there, whatsoever?" Ray checked again.

"It's the Forest People of Camu." The guard explained. "Almost the whole of the southern hemisphere of Vestrell is covered in expansive forests and lakes and mountains and...more forests."

The guard was running out of steam, but his point had been made.

"It's fine, I get it. I've seen the images on the stream."

"Right, so, what can we do about it, sir?" The guard was humble for all of the regular reasons, as well as the fact that he was at a loss for finding a solution.

Ray sat staring at the guard, silently and motionlessly thinking about how to solve the problem. The guard had seen this before, so he wasn't alarmed. By the third minute of blankly being stared at, the guard was starting to wonder if Ray was having a reaction to a dodgy Ragget, or if the Hassienda he had just eaten was diseased. Then suddenly, in a way that made the guard jump out of his skin for a moment, Ray shouted his solution to anyone that could hear him.

"ELECTROCYTE FISH."

The guard's eyebrows leapt to the top of his forehead when he realised what Ray was saying.

"Get me hundreds of them. Pack them all safely in water containers. Hundreds of Electrocyte Fish"

"Are you sure, Sir?" The guard was reticent.

"Absolutely." Ray was animated by a swell of enthusiasm that spouted from his posturing ego. "We are bringing electricity to the lowest bowels of Vestrell." Ray started to laugh one of his enormous belly laughs that felt like a minor earthquake from inside the building. "Tell Les Manfred's Gig Boys that they have a slightly different set up for this gig. The tribes of the tree continent on Vestrell will never forget this!"

Ray's wet, bulbous face was alight with ambitious pride, now focused on bringing electricity to a population that didn't know what it was and hadn't felt the need for it before.

"No, I guess not, Sir. It will certainly be a memorable evening." The guard walked out of the office, on a mission to get everything prepared for an all electric, all digitally enhanced music performance to a tribal people with no experience with electricity. This was going to take some preparation.

Penny had been staking out The Sinking Wharf, hoping that Aria would return to Ray's office whether or not she had found Plak. Her plan was to act as a conduit for everyone, relaying updates to her sister through their telepathic neural pathways. She was right, of course, but the initial encounter was a little confused and awkward. As Aria, Ursulas and Nod turned into the pathway from the road running the other way, Aria spotted Penny, and immediately called out to her;

"Lilly!" She shouted. "Lilly, it's me, Aria!"

Penny clearly recognised her sister's name being called out, but wasn't sure who this Movine was with the collapsed snout calling her sister's name. She watched in silence as the three figures got closer. She was intrigued by the translucent kaleidoscope of colours emanating from the tall woman's skin, and surmised quickly that the thick set man behind her was under her authority somehow. She couldn't work out what the deal was with the Movine though...

"Lilly!" Aria called again, this time, not particularly loud as they were getting close to The Sinking Wharf, where Penny was loitering. Other passersby were distracted by the noise that Aria was making, and occasionally whispered criticisms to the person they were walking with.

As they reached a close enough distance for Penny not to have to shout to be heard, she gave Aria some vital information. There was something about her appearance

213

that was reminding her of someone, but she couldn't quite figure out who that was yet.

"I'm not Lilly." She said.

"You're not Lilly? Aria was confused.

"No, Lilly is on Praxim 7 with the rest of The Brown Yelp Gang." She said, nonchalantly.

"So, are you her sister? The twin?" Aria was piecing things together at a painfully slow speed.

"Who is this?" Ursulas interrupted, hoping to be given the chance to catch up with what had been going on. Aria turned to Ursulas and Nod.

"This is a telepath twin. Apparently there's not many around, but she is one of them."

"Hello." Penny added, smiling at them.

"A telepath?" Nod said, eyes widening in fascination.

"No, I can't blow things up with my mind." Penny said, anticipating the first question.

"Oh." Nod looked bitterly disappointed.

"So, how does it work then?" Ursulas responded, enquiring for more than just information about what she couldn't do.

"I guess it's mostly about me and my sister." Penny continued. "We feel each other's feelings, speak to each other when we're miles apart and can know what's happening in each other's lives."

"Fascinating." Ursulas smiled, finding one of the seats being offered outside The Sinking Wharf to sit on for the conversation to continue.

"So do you know what's happening with the rest of the guys?" Aria asked, sitting herself down close to Ursulas.

"Yeah, sure...or at least I did anyway." Penny replied.

"Hold on."

Penny, just like Lilly when she created the ambient music from the green room a few days earlier, closed her eyes and started to concentrate. Nod, Ursulas and Aria respectfully watched in awe as they imagined her mind travelling across light years to connect to her sister's mind for a meet up and a chat. After almost a minute of silent concentration, Penny opened her eyes and looked at the three gawping faces surrounding her. She smiled at them, politely.

"Okay, I can first tell you that they are all right." Penny began.

"Oh, that's wonderful."Aria answered, grinning. "Tell Riff I love him." She realised immediately that was an ill-informed interjection and added a quick, "sorry", awkwardly smiling at her companions.

"Erm...it appears that they have all split up. Lilly is with Trent, Jenken, DK and Riff. Lilly told me that Deet and Teddy have been dropped off somewhere else nearby because Teddy couldn't leave the shuttle in the way that the others left."

215

"Wow, that's incredible." Aria answered, blown away by Penny's natural brain activity.

"Yeah, I agree. So, you have always been able to do that?" Ursulas asked, naturally thinking about how she could exploit the sisters' abilities for her own ends.

"Since I can remember." Penny replied. "It was very confusing for us when we were little. We didn't understand why we knew everything that was happening to each other, and couldn't explain the intense feelings we were getting."

"Yeah, I imagine it was very weird." Nod said, empathetically.

"It was traumatic, to be honest." Penny replied. "We're OK now. It's good to know we have each other's backs."

"That's what Lilly said when she met us."

"Alike minds think alike." Penny replied, almost winking.

"So, anyway, what are you doing here, outside The Sinking Wharf?" Aria asked.

"Waiting for Aria. I know she's gone off to look for Plak."

"Oh, I see why you're confused." Aria remembered her disguise. "I can't wait to get rid of this Movine disguise."

"Is that you, Aria?" Penny asked, now hoping for some progress to tell Lilly about.

"It is." Aria replied. "Sad news about Plak though."

"Is he dead?" Penny put her hand to her mouth in shock. She hadn't met them formerly but both sisters were long term fans of the band.

"No, he's not dead."

Penny breathed a sigh of relief.

"He has, unfortunately, left the band though." Aria continued.

"Left the band?" Penny was stunned.

"Yeah, we did rescue him, and he was grateful, but now he's buggered off with a lizard woman." Ursulas was straight to the point.

"A lizard woman? Do you mean a Bask Lizard?"

"Yeah, a Bask Lizard." Ursulas clarified, despite feeling that it was unnecessary.

"OK, so Plak is safe, and you're now ready to get back to the matter with the debt?" Penny was catching up quickly.

"Absolutely. I wanted to come here first to find out what was happening a Ray's end. That whole robot replica thing was a bit worrying. It would be good to find out how that has gone so far."

"Robot replica thing?" Ursulas didn't know about this development.

"Yeah, he's made some other versions of us, while we investigate the big DeMarco guy." Aria explained, in a voice that couldn't hide the disapproval behind the words.

"You live very odd lives, you lot." Ursulas jeered.

'Vestrell is in for a treat' Ray thought, as he sent out the relevant messages to get this second gig on the forest planet all set up and ready to go. His security crew, now moonlighting as stage and road crew, had managed to locate and contain 436 Electrocyte Fish. These fish would be the key to running power for the PA and stage for the replica Brown Yelp Gang gig. Most of their flat, circular bodies were filled with millions of tiny cells that fired off a powerful electric charge through their central nervous system and through their bodies, eventually escaping from the fish through their triangular mouth. Hundreds of these fish would be hooked up to a stabiliser that would ensure the electrical current was consistent and always powered on. Then that current would be hooked up to the various electrical power cables that the stage and PA needed. It was ambitious, and would change the culture of the tribal people of Vestrell forever. Ray was an ambitious businessman that would never let anything get in his way, even centuries of tradition and a people's connection with nature. The gig was happening, and there would be power. The information stream was full of advertisements and publicity for the gig; this time there was a focus on a patronising idea of giving electricity to the savage people of Vestrell. It was typically unflattering and simplistic;

'COME AND SEE THE BROWN YELP GANG FOR THE FIRST MUSIC GIG IN VESTRELL HISTORY TO BE GIVEN TO THE IDIOT TRIBES OF VESTRELL!!

THE BROWN YELP GANG WILL BE PROVIDING SONGS, LIGHTS, MUSIC AND ELECTRICITY!!

218

COME YE ONE AND ALL FROM ALL CORNERS OF VESTRELL FOR THE GIG OF THE CENTURY"

This was a shocking publicity tactic that was brazenly insulting to the indigenous people of Vestrell, but the band needed an audience and Ray wrote the publicity himself, as he did with the previous gig; arguably a man with a rare quality of indifference to any offence he may cause.

Ray had been particularly clever in working out the most suitable support act for this gig. Thinking of the rustic setting for the gig, he booked a great up and coming band of nature loving hippies from Corsylia called 'Ambient Dreams'. They were very popular in Corsylia among the rich members of Corsyllian society that wanted to end space travel and get back to foraging for food and burning the neighbours houses, like 'the good old days'. Ambient Dreams were a nine piece band that consisted of forest animals from the woodlands of Corsylia that had been trained to make melodic noises by their manager, Silas Craneswater-Finch. He had the brilliant idea of creating a band of tuneful animals that would remind the 'ignorant public' as he affectionately called them, to think about nature more.

So, the preparations for setting up the electricity conduits and the regulation from the stabiliser had produced the correct amount of electricity for the sound check to go ahead without a hitch. The beautiful, chaotic noise of Ambient Dreams was successfully captured by the PA and

219

the replica band for the headline set were suitably satisfied with the results of their tech rehearsal on stage. Once the bands had finished sound checking, both retreated to their makeshift dressing rooms that Ray had hired to be set up in the forest. The walls were rickety and unstable, but they had dressing rooms. The standard rider that Ambient Dreams always requested had been laid out in troughs, trays and buckets along the walls of the dressing room, with a specific temperature being regulated through the room for their comfort. Beyond the requirements of the two bands playing that night, Ray had brought more real estate to this side of the planet than anyone ever had in the known history of the planet. He knew this, and was quite pleased with himself.

As the hours slipped by, the audience began to gather for the gig. The forest was invaded by a cavalcade of aliens and Vestrell natives from all sides of the planet, and all areas of the Corsyl system. Every type of species that Les Manfred's Gig Boys had ever seen and every shape and gender of those species were lining up to see this gig. This was a big deal; news had gone viral across the system that this side of the planet was going to experience its first ever dose of electricity. For this auspicious occasion, Ray rewrote some of the programming of the replica band, in honour of them making history.

Ambient Dreams walked, flew and swung on stage to a rapturous applause. The sound of hundreds of thousands of creatures surrounding them in the forest filled the air. They were all vying for a good view, either on land or hanging off the nearby trees. The Ambient Dreams couldn't believe it. Before this gig, they hadn't played outside of Corsylia.

The lead 'vocalist' was a six foot, four legged fox native to Corsylia, who walked up to his microphone and barked and howled for about 30 seconds. Not many of the audience would have understood him, but roughly translated, the Corsyllian fox had said,

"Hey man. We've never played a gig outside Corsylia, and we're scared shitless!"

The rest of the band and a select few of the audience sniggered in response to the humble, but endearingly honest, entrance from the band leader. Then the music played.

It was wild, it was beautiful and it was a wonder to hear. Every note and harmony had soul, coming from a life experience of the animals performing it. Rhythms were multi-layered and blended into the narrative of the melodies. It was an absolute triumph and the crew from Les Manfred's company were all glued to their seats enjoying the spectacle. What most people didn't realise, of course, was that what they were hearing, and enjoying, was the perfect blend of the noise of the forest on stage, and the noise of the *actual* forest they were performing in; there was no way to discern what ambient noise was coming from the band, and what the PA was picking up from the natural surroundings. The crowd didn't mind, or notice, so the support slot ended with a standing ovation that was hundreds of thousands of persons strong.

After a short break for setting up the headline band, the replica Brown Yelp Gang climbed onto the stage from the makeshift steps they had built from the forest debris. The replica Deet waddled straight up to the front mic and uncharacteristically chose to get the crowd going himself. "How are you all doing?!" He shouted, with the booming sound of his voice being sent across the forest with absolute clarity, and a little bit of reverb.

The enormous crowd went crazy with excitement. They were also very excited to see Deet addressing the crowd like this, utterly blind to the fake nature of the band in front of them.

"I see you've brought a lovely, sunny night with you!" The replica Deet shouted, unaware that the raining season on Vestrell was literally 30 days of constant rain, and not at this time of the solar cycle. The crowd were so excited that they cheered anyway, despite the unlikelihood of rain. The rest of the replica band joined Deet on stage, and started getting their fake instruments ready. Then the crowd immediately recognised the first few words of the first song;

"Show me where you put it!
Show me where you put it!

222

Show me where you put it, I've been looking for hours.

Show me where you put it!

Show me where you put it!

Show me where you put it! I'm in need of it now!"

This was one of the most anticipated songs that the crowd were hoping to hear.   It was one of their early big hits, and still resonated with audiences years after the song's release. The eternal search for the thing that someone had moved is universal and ultimately, timeless.

News spread that The Brown Yelp Gang had done what no other band had ever done before; played an electric rock gig in the tribal forests of Vestrell. Their name was everywhere. The media on the planets of the Corsyllian system, and the planets beyond into the neighbouring systems were all putting up variations of 'The Brown Yelp Gang Plug Into The Trees of Vestrell', as the biggest news story of the week. On one planet this was bigger news than the royal baby, and for this particular moment in that planet's history this was a shocking indication of the band's impact, as this royal baby was born with extra limbs. On another planet, in the neighbouring star system, an International World War was declared, but announced after the news of The Brown Yelp Gang's triumph on Vestrell.

Trent, DK and Riff had decided to split up with Lilly and Jenken and communicate with the tiny adhesive communicators that Ray had made for them, to be stuck on their left hand. Jenken had the idea of confronting DeMarco head on, from a simple knock on the front door. He figured that he had the money he owed, so it could be a reasonably simple conversation.

"If anyone sees anything, get on this," Jenken lifted his hand to indicate the communicators as he whispered this, "and tell everyone what you know. We need to stick together, but not be together."

"Agreed." Riff replied. "Stick together, don't be together."

"Don't stick together, don't be together." Trent's middle head gave a thumbs up as he said this, followed by the heads on the side looking at the middle head, frowning.

"No?" Trent said, quietly.

"Stick together..." Jenken said again, "...don't be together."

"- and let everyone know anything that you know." Riff added.

"Indeed." Jenken replied.

"So, who is going where?" Trent asked quietly, reasonably.

"If myself and Lilly go towards the back there, down that flight of stairs, we can then nip down to the front to see if they would let me see him legitimately." Jenken pointed to a stairwell that hooked onto the back of the building and led to the ground floor below. "Then you guys take the stairs inside from over there." He pointed to a doorway

224

that was clearly the usual method of reaching the roof from inside.

"Yeah, brilliant." Riff replied, still whispering. "- and don't stick together."

"Yeah, but stay with Trent and DK."Jenken clarified, turning back to Riff.

"Oh OK." Riff nodded, wishing he could just go back to Corsylia and play guitar.

"Shall we meet back here?"Trent asked.

"Well, I don't know what will happen from my conversation but we'll keep this roof as the meet up point whenever we get back together."Jenken answered.

"I don't think we should linger too long down there. Let's just say an hour or so?" DK suggested.

"Guys, I might be able to do some good up here." Lilly said, addressing them all at once. "If I really concentrate, I may be able to project myself with you and..." her voice struggled for specifics..."move things if I have to?"

"I thought you could just speak to your sister or something?" DK said softly, shocked at this revelation.

"Well, I don't know if I can do it, but I'd like to try." Lilly replied, smiling.

"Okay, Lilly, I'll go and meet with DeMarco on my own. You stay here. You guys go down there and see what you can find." Jenken said.

"Good luck Jenken." Trent said, putting his hand on his manager's shoulder.

"Yeah, good luck, mate." Riff echoed Trent's words.

"See you soon, Jenken." DK added.

"Aw, you guys are adorable." Lilly joked.

"I will keep my channel open when I'm in front of DeMarco so you can hear what he's saying." Jenken suggested.

"Great idea." Riff replied.

It clearly wasn't a good idea, as a criminal opportunist like DeMarco wouldn't be happy to see a communication device broadcasting the conversation to an unknown location. Unfortunately The Brown Yelp Gang had never done anything like this before, and it was starting to show. What they were good at was performing, and they were being outshone by digital copies of themselves, that were starting to enjoy the gigging a little too much.

Chapter Ten

◆ ◆ ◆ ◆ ◆ ◆ ◆ ◆ ◆ ◆

Available now on the information stream, hot off the
desks of Vestrell!!
The First time The Brown Yelp Gang has released a
live bootleg.
Thirteen new recordings from the record breaking,
ground breaking, silence breaking show in the forests
of Vestrell!!
Such classic hits as
'Show me where you put it',
'Fallet Fish',
'I can shoe you in next week'
and of course, the biggest hit of them all,
 'How is your hair'.

For three weeks the bootleg album will be available for
just 30 credits, all payable to this link below:
Brown Yalp Gang Inc.
Click on the link above and get this special
commemorative bootleg now, before it's too late and
you're dead.

◆ ◆ ◆ ◆ ◆ ◆ ◆ ◆ ◆ ◆

"What the hell is this?" Trent almost blew their position, as they crept down the stairwell to the lower levels of the main base of DeMarco's operations.

Trent had taken out his entertainment screen to check the time, and noticed an advertisement, plastered all over the information stream. He nudged Riff and DK.

"Look at this!" He was whispering but couldn't conceal his outrage. The other two crept up next to him to see what he was looking at. "It's a new release from us!"

"That's not from us." DK argued.

"Well it's the Brown bloody Yelp Gang!" Trent was still whispering but his rage was building.

"It's not, mate." Riff pointed to the screen. "Look, it says Brown Yalp Gang."

"What?" Trent snapped, not in the mood for nonsense.

"It's just a band that has a similar name, like the bands 'Scream' and 'Steam'."

"No, look at the songs, they're our songs!" Trent was stabbing the screen as he said it, as if it was the screen's fault.

"That must be the replica band that Ray built." DK said, correctly.

"What?" Trent's fragile temperament was boiling away beyond the ability to see the logic behind DK's words.

"He made a band didn't he? A band of robots." DK continued. "It must be them."

"Cheeky bastards." Riff said, catching up.

"That's outrageous." Trent whispered. "They can't do that. They're our songs!"

"Do you think Ray has done this to make more money out of us?"DK asked, also whispering.

"Well, he can't though, can he?"

"Nah, this is bullshit." Trent slammed the screen shut and hid it back in his back pocket. "When I get out of this whole thing, I'm going to disconnect their cables, and send them off to the junkyard."

"Me too." Riff said, showing his feelings of brotherhood.

"Well, let's see if we can get somewhere with this first." DK added. "We're supposed to be looking for clues about what DeMarco is putting all that money into."

"Yeah, fine. I'm not a happy Calpian though." Trent snorted. All three heads mumbled to themselves in frustration and repressed anger over the bootleg album that the replica band had released.

"Me too." Riff added, despite not being a Calpian.

They crept down the stairs as silently as they could, going particularly slow to make the snooping as uneventful as possible. Trent was at the front, holding his high heeled shoes with his left hand and holding the wall with his other, keeping an eye on any movement below them. DK was behind him, also holding his shoes. Riff was at the back, moving slower than the others, wielding a 10 inch long lead pipe in one hand, which he had found on the roof. He had left his shoes on the roof, so he didn't have to hold them.

As they reached the bottom of the first group of steps that led to the roof, they could see a corridor in front of them, and another group of stairs leading further down to a level below that. Trent whispered behind him to keep going to the next level of steps, and they both nodded in agreement. The corridor they passed was empty of activity; just a number of doors along the corridor that they weren't interested in investigating. They had a hunch that the biggest secrets would be on the lowest levels of DeMarco's base. As they walked slowly and quietly down the second set of steps, a voice was heard through a loudspeaker system running across the base.

"Good Afternoon, lovely, happy workers." It was a female voice, speaking with a jolly, animated tone. "This is your friendly assistant, Brenda, with your reminder of the schedule for the day. You should have finished your first shift in about ten minutes. You can move along to the catering floor for your lunch. Remember, eat well and you'll work well. Work well and we stay on schedule for the big festival. Carlo is watching you all."

The three snoopers stayed frozen at the spot as the voice from the loudspeaker spoke. They looked at each other as they listened, trying to ascertain how to use this development to their advantage.

"Shall we see what food they've got?" Riff whispered.

"No, you idiot." Trent snapped, still whispering. "That's not what we should be doing."

"You're unbelievable." DK joined in.

"All right. Ease up." Riff put his hands up in defence, attempting to block their frowns with his lead pipe.

"Did you eat on the shuttle?" Trent asked, sounding like a parent.

"Yes, of course I did." Riff looked at the floor as he replied.

"Let's worry about the food once we've found something." DK said, still whispering.

"Yeah, it's all good. It sounded from that woman like they'd have some nice stuff there...wherever the catering floor was..."

They stopped talking and returned their attention to the next level of steps. This led them to a closed double door, and another level of steps going down to their right. There was still no activity on the stairwell, and little noise coming from the door ahead of them.

"This is too easy." DK said quietly, anxious of the unexpected success they were having.

"We haven't gone anywhere yet." Trent whispered back.

"I need a pee." Riff said, starting to worry about whether he'd get a chance to deal with it.

"What?" Trent turned around.

"I said, I need a pee." Riff was shrugging, aware of the awkward situation. "If we see somewhere..."

"Yeah, fine, if we see somewhere." Trent shook his head in disbelief.

"Let's keep going down." DK said, saying what the others were thinking.

They proceeded down further to the third level below the ground. That level began with a large double door with a handle on each door and a circular window into the enormous room beyond the door. They noticed the window immediately and crouched down in an instant, to prevent their presence from being detected. Still crouching, Trent looked to their right and noticed there were no more descending steps; the stairwell had reached its final floor.

"Look, we're right at the bottom." Trent nudged the others.

"Okay, this could be it." DK said, anxiously.

"I hope they've got somewhere I can pee." Riff whispered, preoccupied with his bladder issues. "Maybe I'm getting old..." Riff was whispering to himself now. "...I'm sure I went in the shuttle. It's only been a few hours, I'm sure. I don't know, but I definitely need a pee now..."

He looked up and they were both looking at him, scowling, as if waiting for him to finish.

"Right." DK said. "I'm going to look through the window, and you guys stay there for a second. Trent, your heads will be more conspicuous so I'll see what I can see through the window."

"Makes sense." Trent said. His other heads mumbled in agreement.

DK stood up, still stooping so that only a little of his head was visible on the other side of the window, and peered through to see what was on the other side. Beyond the door was an enormous room that spread out far and wide. The room's dimensions defied his expectations, as the high ceiling betrayed what DK thought had been the amount of steps he had passed. There were people everywhere; more specifically, Bask Lizards in dark green uniforms and bright green bowler hats. DK stood just in view of the room and watched for a moment.

"What's in it?" Trent whispered.

"Hold on." DK waved at them both with his left hand as he watched.

This door seemed to be set at one end of the room. All of the uniformed lizards seemed to be walking to that end to pack things in large wooden boxes, or to take something out of the boxes. Some of those boxes had what looked like various different bits of shaped metal, as if they were parts of a bigger construction. Other boxes had tools in them. DK recognised some of the tools and knew that this floor must be full of mechanical engineers.

"They're building something down here." DK turned back to the others to give them a barely audible update.

"What are they building?" Riff asked.

"I don't know. I can't see it." DK answered, quietly. "It's over there." DK pointed to his far right.

"This could be it." Trent said, coldly.

"Yeah, I think it is. It's a big operation down here." DK said, turning back to the room to work out what to do next. It was a good job he did, as he immediately saw one of those uniformed Bask Lizards walking toward the door, in a deliberate motion, clearly on his way to fulfil a job he was doing. DK swung back to his friends.

"There's someone coming!"

"Oh shit!" Riff got up and started to walk back up the stairs.

Trent followed him. DK looked at them, and looked back at the room, and then thought confusion was the best answer for this situation.

"Give me the pipe, Riff." DK shouted to Riff. "Quickly!" Riff threw the pipe at him, assuming he was going to whack the engineer with the pipe as he came through. He was wrong. DK, once he had a firm grip on the pipe, walloped his own face with the pipe as hard as he could. Blood streamed from his snout as he screamed in agony and rolled around the floor, dropping the pipe as he held his face as it throbbed...and bled. Trent wasn't sure what he'd done or why, and stood at the stairwell immobilised by his crushing indecision. Riff realised that DK's screaming would have brought attention to their covert activity, and thought 'in for a penny, in for a pound'. He ran through the double doors and started shouting to anyone that would hear that his Movine friend had hurt himself on the stairwell. Trent realised that he was better off running up to the next floor, so there was less to explain, and swiftly ran to the closed door on the floor above, utterly confused by his friends' behaviour. Four Bask engineers ran past Riff to find out what was going on in the corridor. They didn't quite understand why there was a random Movine in the base, but ultimately, they could only know by taking a look. Riff was left gawping at the expansive space in front of him, as he tried to take in the full view of this spectacular room. There were platforms lined along the walls where engineers stood; platforms that ended inches away from the colossal machine that dominated the middle of the room. On the far wall, a long panel of switches and levers connected to the machine in the middle of the room was bleeping away and flashing its lights at Riff's wide eyes. It was clear that this was the expensive investment that DeMarco was putting his money into. Riff lifted his left hand to speak through his communicator.

"Don't look for me, guys. I'll see you later."

- and with that, Riff was running further into the room, looking for somewhere to hide quickly before he was noticed. The four engineers that ran through the double doors to DK were the ones that would have noticed Riff run through and hide. The ones that were working on the machine in the middle of the room were happy to leave the security to the other engineers, unaware that it wasn't going well.

Riff found a box that was large enough to house his long, thin body. His mission was to find out what that machine was, and to find somewhere to pee.

DK had heard Riff's voice as he was writhing around, holding his nose. He noticed Trent had disappeared ('thanks mate!') and heard the words 'see you later' from Riff. Figuring that this was far too dangerous to do on his own, DK got up quickly and stared at the Bask engineers in front of him, still holding his nose.

"I'm lost." He said, psychologically crossing his fingers.

"You're lost?!" The engineer closest to him said, finding it hard to understand why he was there. "Why are you here?"

"Are you the medic?" Another engineer asked, calmly.

"Eh?" The first engineer said.

"Panik's had his arm trapped in the stabiliser." A third engineer added. "We called a medic. It's a right mess."

"Yeah, that's right. I'm the medic." DK's tone made it quite obvious that he was making this up, but their expertise was clearly in engineering and not in spotting trespassers.

"Ah, great." The first engineer turned back to DK, after learning of this new problem from his colleagues. "Follow me, then."

DK was led through the double doors and into the main room. He lifted his head in awe as he soaked up the high ceiling of the room, and almost gulped when he saw the enormous machine in the middle of the room. He looked for his friends but didn't see them anywhere. ('bastards')

The four engineers led DK to the back of the room, passing the machine that dominated the room without glancing at it; they were used to its presence and had worked on it every day. DK was desperately trying not to look too surprised by the scale of what they were working on. The noise in the room of metal on metal and the sparks and the bleeping from the row of lights at the back was also making DK nervous and disorientated. He put the thoughts of his band mates abandoning him to the back of his mind and concentrated on being a medic.

Moments later, they were leaning over Panik's injured body, now released from the stabiliser by the other engineers. He was holding up his arm and shouting at his colleagues in front of him.

"Argh!!" He shouted.

DK glanced at the other engineers briefly, and then looked down at Panik, crouching beside him to get a good look. Panik stared at the Movine a little shocked at this being the medic.

"Hmm..." DK pondered, poking the arm. "I can see what the problem is."

The other engineers looked on, fascinated by the medic at work.

"Yeah..." DK continued. "He definitely trapped his arm in the stabiliser." He turned to the other engineers; "Have you got his arm out of the stabiliser?"

They were a little confused by the seemingly obvious answer.

"Erm...yes." The first engineer said, pointing to Panik's arm.

"Good...good." DK continued to look like he was examining the screaming, bleeding engineer below him. "I know what he needs." He said, and punched Panik in the face, knocking him out instantly.

"He needs sleep."

"Thank you so much." The first engineer was immediately shaking DK's hand in gratitude, beaming with relief that the accident had been 'dealt with' successfully. DK couldn't believe his luck that the improvised diagnosis and recommendation for sleep had worked so well.

"I'll take you back to the lobby, Dr...?"

DK hesitated when he noticed the next challenge...making up a name.

"Dr...Dr." He accidentally said.

"Dr Dr?" The engineer frowned.

"Yes. With a family name like that I was bound to go into medicine wasn't I!" DK said, brushing off the strange name he had picked.

"I guess so..." The engineer replied, taking DK's word for it.

As the first engineer led DK to the stairwell, DK looked around and tried to take in as much as he could from around the room. He could see the machine was some kind of horizontal humanoid machine that he estimated at about 50 feet long. If he had a strong knowledge of Earth literature, he would have made a mental note of how much it looked like Gulliver strapped to the land by the little people of Lilliput. In this case, the straps were wires leading to the machines against the wall, bleeping and flashing their electronic thumbs up that everything was working fine. He didn't notice Riff, who was still hiding in the metal box, unaware that his Movine band mate had walked this far into the complex. As DK and the first engineer reached the bottom of the stairwell, DK looked behind him and attempted to lose the friendly, helpful engineer with him;

"I'm OK from here. I've been here many times and know it like the back of my hand." DK said, nodding as he said it, willing the engineer to return to his work.

"OK, that's fine, Dr Dr." The engineer replied. "Thank you for your assistance."

"It was my pleasure." DK said, and turned away to walk up the stairs.

The engineer returned to the main engineering room. DK picked up his pace walking up the stairs, keen to get to the roof to breathe at a normal rate, and to put an end to his impressions of medical personnel.

Lilly was on the roof, wrestling with feelings of frustration and inadequacy as she imagined what her new friends may be experiencing in the main building. She had tried for what seemed like hours to influence their situation with her telepathic abilities. She was in close contact with Penny, but she was unable to move anything beyond what was on the roof. She feared that her powerful mind was unable to manipulate any matter that she couldn't see. Penny consoled her from her position in Bragal, but ultimately, Lilly was left waiting for the others to return, aggravated and restless.

Jenken was at the front of the building as Trent and the others were descending the second stairwell. He had the easiest job as far as how he was going to enter the base of operations, but the hardest job as he was confronting Carlo DeMarco. This gave Jenken a sense of foreboding that was more intense than the first time The Brown Yelp Gang had played to over a million 'people' on the 'Lake of Unsettling Stomachs'. That was a great gig, but Jenken thought he was going to pass out from the nerves. This time, he was facing the door of the main base, and bracing himself for his first encounter. There was a keypad lit up to his right as he faced the door. Jenken stared at it, not knowing what to do. Then he noticed a button that appeared to be the main focus of the keypad, set apart from the numbering system

240

on the pad. Not sure what it would lead to, Jenken pressed the button that looked like the game changer. Immediately there was a low hum heard outside that echoed through the corridors of the ground level of the base.

A few moments later, a Bask Lizard dressed in the uniform that Riff and DK had witnessed, opened the door and shocked Jenken with his genial manner.

"Ah, Jenken Janes." He began. "Mr DeMarco is expecting you."

"Really? Jenken queried. "He's expecting me?"

"Yes."

"What, now?"

"Well not necessarily now." The engineer explained "...but he is expecting you."

"Ah, okay." Jenken nodded, now more confident about this new and awkward exchange.

Jenken was led through the initial corridor and to the right, as the corridor turned suddenly into a new, almost identical corridor. The floors, walls and ceilings were spotlessly clean; a creamy white glaze giving the walls a clinical look. The grey floors had a bounce to them, like a malleable plastic was under your feet. He followed the mostly silent engineer through another four corridors that looked exactly like the first two, baffling the band manager as to the layout of the rooms and the directions they were taking. For what seemed like hours, Jenken walked obediently through the winding corridors of the base until they both came across a large, light green door locked by another keypad that had a similar design to the one on the main front door. The engineer punched in a code and the door opened, revealing a wide space that was filled with countless machines similar to the ones that Riff and DK had found. There were several uniformed Bask engineers dotted around the room and the head of operations, Carlo DeMarco, facing them sternly as they walked in.

Carlo DeMarco was staring at these new arrivals from a table, where he sat, grinning from ear to ear.

"Janes, my boy." DeMarco greeted Jenken with a loud, cheery, hugely self-confident voice. "Glad you made it. I knew you'd be here soon." His voice was either intimidating or terrifying depending on your relationship with him.

"Mr DeMarco. Nice to see you again." Jenken lied.

"Come here. Sit with me." DeMarco gestured to the chair opposite him, next to the table. "Time to have some fun!" Jenken gulped as he said this. DeMarco lived his life based on a constant need to prove his bravado, his power and his great constitution. He was also as consistent as clockwork with his meetings; anyone who was starting an encounter with DeMarco would be expecting to go through some kind of macho ritual. If anyone refused, they were usually shot for their insolence and insulting reluctance to amuse DeMarco.

So, Jenken sat at the chair, awaiting the first ordeal of this encounter with DeMarco. He wasn't waiting long, as DeMarco immediately clapped his hands loudly, which was followed by the sound of a gong from somewhere indefinable in the room. The other engineers in the room stopped working, and directed their attention to DeMarco and his new challenger, Jenken Janes. From the right side of the room a male figure appeared with an unnaturally wide smile and a smooth, almost melodic voice that addressed the engineers in the room. He was wearing a beautifully tailored bright blue suit with a white fedora hat slightly tilted on his head.

"Okay, okay, people." The blue suited man waved his arms around for added theatrical effect. "We have a new challenger for the coveted position of 'Most important person in the universe!'

' *Wow, DeMarco doesn't do things by halves* ' Jenken thought to himself.

"The first round of this crucial contest, is a test of constitution."

Jenken looked around the room, eager to notice clues as to what this test of constitution was going to be. Seconds later, a large torso with a tiny head and legs waddled into the room. It had two impressive horns on either side of its head, a grimace that would wipe the paint off a battleship cruiser and a right hand fist that swelled like a relentless beating heart.

243

"Jenken Janes." The smiley man continued. "- and Carlo DeMarco, meet Florence, the meanest man-goat this side of the Kallanite system." There was an instant surge of 'ooh' from the engineers, who had all gathered around the table to see the battle being played out before them. "Your task is to stay conscious after six blows to the head from Florence's mighty hand." The gasp from the spectating engineers was fake, but effective. Jenken was regretting walking into the main base now and wishing he was back in Corsylia, locating mandolin strings or filing Trent's teeth before a gig.

Florence hit Jenken first, with a powerful blow to his head. Jenken didn't see it coming, and wasn't mentally prepared for the assault. His head naturally got knocked back from the force of the blow. Jenken shook his head, as if shaking off the pain he was desperately trying to suppress. "Impressive, Mr Janes." DeMarco said, and promptly got his punch to the head, equalising the first round of this 'game'. Then, as warned by the bubbly announcer, Jenken was given a second knock to the head, this one leaving a cut on the side of his lip. Jenken used his tongue to lick part of the blood away while staying steadfast in his chair. The second blow to DeMarco's head didn't produce a cut, but did produce a number of guttural sounds like 'Argh!' and 'Gahh' from the equally steadfast DeMarco. The third blow continued this ritual of both competing individuals remaining committed to the pain through gritted teeth. The engineers were all fired up now and started taking bets on who they thought was going to win. Their reactions began to get deafeningly loud by the time Florence had dealt his fifth blow to their heads. Jenken's brain was swimming now, and the throbbing pain was becoming all consuming. DeMarco was starting to see double, but was grinning with a masochistic glee that certainly gave him the advantage here. The sixth, and last blow, for both people facing each other at the table, met with a more vocal reaction from the ones being punched, as well as a more hysterical burst of excitement from the engineers betting against each other. As the excitement simmered down, and the engineers' noise ground to a murmur, DeMarco spat the blood out of his mouth and addressed the crowd;

"That was round one. It seems Mr Janes has a sturdy constitution." There was no irony or hint of jealousy in DeMarco's tone. He enjoyed the challenge, hence why every encounter was similar to this.

These last words were followed by a stillness in the room which was eerie and suspenseful; the atmosphere in the room becoming thick with expectation.

"Bring it on, Mr DeMarco." Jenken lied. "These tests you offer are fantastic character building moments that I live for."

"I don't believe you." DeMarco said and instantly produced a short laser pistol from the back of his trousers, pointing it at Jenken, menacingly.

"Is this round two?" Jenken asked, shakily.

"Indeed it is, my old friend." DeMarco looked demented, but nobody batted an eyelid as they were used to it. "Now, dodge these bullets."

DeMarco fired shots at Jenken, deliberately aiming slightly away from Jenken's jittery body, as he had no plans to kill him; just scare him. Jenken swerved and ducked accordingly, managing to get through a few minutes of being shot at without actually being harmed.

"Very good, Mr Janes." DeMarco said, clearly enjoying himself.

"Do I get a go?" Jenken asked, as the shooting stopped.

"How insolent!" DeMarco replied, and shot at him, this time aiming at his left knee.

Jenken howled in pain as his left knee started to bleed from the shot.

"Now for 'Round Three' and my favourite round," DeMarco grinned, still looking unhinged.

The announcer from Round One appeared again, this time in a bright yellow suit and a black fedora hat, smiling at the engineers that were surrounding the competitors. Jenken looked on, hoping to survive this last round so that he could speak to DeMarco, while closing his eyes to concentrate on dealing with the pain from his knee and the sting from the repeated blows to his head. Through squinted eyes and baited breath, he awaited the details of the last round.

"I will give you one word. The first person to add the opposite word to mine, without the use of your arms, will get a point.

Jenken gave an involuntary sigh of relief as he realised this round wouldn't be violent.

"The person who hasn't responded gets hit by this!" The announcer produced a mace from somewhere behind him.

Jenken cursed under his breath. "Then I will give an acronym, and the first person to tell me what it stands for, gets a point."

Jenken raised his eyebrows in anticipation for the next bit of information.

"...and the one who hasn't given me the meaning is hit by this!" The mace was raised again, this time evoking an enthusiastic cheer from the engineers, who had begun betting again.

"Mr DeMarco, can we just talk?" Jenken knew it was probably pointless but he felt that he had to try.

"Shut that brain of yours up now and concentrate on the game!" DeMarco bellowed, without a hint of empathy.

Jenken immediately returned to his subdued, humble state.

"Of course." He said, resigned to this ridiculous test of...something.

"Okay, here is the word..!" The smiley announcer shouted from the left side of the table.

The engineers all hushed in anticipation.

"PASSING!" He shouted, to the 'contestants'.

There was a short pause...

"Not passing!" DeMarco shouted, confidently.

"YES!" The announcer shouted back.

"Are you serious?" Jenken was livid. "That's ridiculous!"

"Ridiculous is what ridiculous does." The announcer crouched down to Jenken's chair and gave him this 'pearl of wisdom' directly to his battered face.

"Yeah, whatever..." Jenken was losing the will to fight this nonsense. He was busy feeling sorry for himself as the mace struck him across the head, giving him a new colour to his already decorative face.

"Last round..." the announcer warned "...this time it's an acronym. What does this stand for?"

There was another hush of stillness in the room. The engineers glared at the contestants as the last question was given to DeMarco and Jenken Janes.

"C.D.I.A.G.L."

Whispers spread across the room as the engineers attempted to solve this new riddle. DeMarco looked directly at Jenken, challenging him to think of what the acronym represented. Jenken hadn't heard this particular acronym before, and was usually confident in identifying companies or slogans from just the initials. He was stumped.

The atmosphere in the room became extremely tense, as precious moments ticked past and nothing was coming to mind for Jenken to respond to the challenge. Finally, after what seemed like an eternity, DeMarco broke the silence.

"I know what it is." He stated.

There was a gasp from his engineers.

"We have an answer from Mr DeMarco." The announcer replied with a theatrical wave of his arms, almost as if he wasn't being employed by him.

DeMarco left a pause in the air, for extra dramatic effect.

"Is it..." The gasp occurred again "...Carlo DeMarco is a great leader?"

"YES!!" The announcer shouted, as if there were some form of victory being witnessed.

"This is an outrageous fix!" Jenken objected, just before feeling the second mace to the head.

This time he was knocked unconscious from the powerful, merciless whack to the head.

Jenken Janes slowly lifted his head, regaining consciousness and feeling a thunderous throb running through it as his eyesight recovered its clarity. He quickly realised he was in another room, away from the crowd of engineers that had gathered around the absurd games DeMarco had initiated, and surveying 4 plain, grey walls. He looked around the room and sat on a metallic functional chair, surprisingly not tied to it, but in an otherwise empty room with just one door providing an exit. During the seconds that followed Jenken's reawakening, DeMarco walked in through the plain, grey door in front of Jenken's chair. DeMarco was followed in by one of the Bask engineers from the other room.

"Hello again." DeMarco greeted Jenken, pleasantly. "Are you sore?"

"I am actually." Jenken snapped. "I have known you for many years Mr DeMarco and deserve a better welcome than that."

"A better welcome?" DeMarco chuckled, setting off sycophantic laughter from the Bask engineer behind him. "People often die from my little parlour games. They don't have the stamina."

Jenken gulped.

"Fine." He wasn't interested in pursuing that line of attack. "Can we get back to the business of why I came here?"

"Jenken Janes. You cannot walk in here and demand an audience with me."

"I am not demanding anything!" Jenken protested.

"Have you seen my new pieces of art?" DeMarco enthusiastically snapped, suddenly leaping closer to Jenken's chair. "Have you seen them?"

"Erm...no." Jenken wanted to say yes, just to avoid seeing them, but he was too anxious about his lie being spotted to maintain that tone.

DeMarco turned his head to the Bask engineer behind him;

"Get me the orange one, the blue one and the green one."

DeMarco barely turned his head back to address the engineer, but the engineer immediately ran back out of the room to get hold of the artwork DeMarco was so enthused about.

"It's wonderful isn't it." DeMarco gushed. "I can say anything and they just do it."

Jenken was unsure how to respond to that so gave a slight nod and a raised eyebrow in acknowledgement.

"Watch this." DeMarco said and grabbed a small speaker from the left, inner pocket lining of his jacket. With a wink and a smile, he switched a lever on the speaker and held it to his mouth, still looking at Jenken for his reaction.

"Listen up, everyone. I want you all to shout, as loud as you can, DeMarco! DeMarco! DeMarco! He is so fine, he is my leader." DeMarco then raised his index finger in the air, in anticipation, and then those exact words were heard from a mass of Bask voices from further down the corridor. Jenken nodded again, giving DeMarco a thumbs up, which wasn't quite what DeMarco wanted, but was at least a mark of approval. DeMarco stared at Jenken for a short while longer. The tension in the small, grey, bare room grew as the silence engulfed the cold air and left it gasping for a sound to rescue it. DeMarco screwed up his face in frustration, almost as if there was something missing in the conversation, despite the shallow tone and simplistic direction it had taken.

"I'll show you how much they fear me." DeMarco was determined to impress Jenken. He lifted the speaker to his mouth again. "Run against the wall as hard as you can. I want to hear your bodies smash against the wall and some of your bones crunching."

Jenken looked at him in revulsion as, true to form, the sound was heard from further down the corridor of hundreds of Bask bodies smashing against the wall violently.

"Mr DeMarco, I already know that you are a formidable business man with several cards up your sleeve. There's no need to show me all of this."

As he said these last few words, the Bask engineer that initially followed DeMarco in returned to the room with the three paintings; the orange one, the blue one and the green one. They were all exactly the same; a bad caricature of DeMarco's head laughing, in the centre, surrounded by blocks of paint in the painting's colour, either orange, blue or green respectively. They weren't the worst pictures Jenken had seen, but then he had seen Movines from the Lantrick system 'paint' in a way that caused a civil war on Movine 3 that lasted 23 years, so this is faint praise. Jenken was fully aware of the right response of course, and dutifully gave his verdict to move the encounter along; "They look wonderful, Mr DeMarco." His voice sounded sincere despite no sincerity whatsoever. "Did you *really* paint these yourself?"

"I did." He replied, beaming. "Well, I did the first one."
His tone changed to something more subdued. "I say
that..." He hesitated "...I did the background sections of
the other two."

"Well, I love them."

- and without a moment to draw a breath –

"- so can we talk about the money I owe you?" Jenken was
trying to sound calm, but was tired, anxious, distrusting and
feeling extremely vulnerable.

DeMarco smiled for a brief moment again.

"Absolutely, old friend." DeMarco's manner was appearing
lighter and more amenable than before. "First though, I
want to show you something." His enthusiasm quashed
Jenken's low expectations with ease, as they walked out of
the room and DeMarco led them to a lift. He turned back
to Jenken again.

"When I show you this, you will wish you were 50 years
younger and living on my planet."

"Bold statement." Jenken replied, almost immediately
thinking, *'what the hell am I doing, giving Carlo DeMarco
backchat?'*

"Bold statement maybe." DeMarco conceded.

They both stepped into the lift, with DeMarco punching in
the keys for the highest floor of his base.

"This will make your toes split into six sections."

Jenken looked at DeMarco confused about the statement about his toes and quietly waited for the lift to reach the higher floor.

Incidentally, as he was doing this, unbeknownst to DeMarco and Jenken, Trent, Riff and DK were on the other side of the building, sneaking past that level, eager to reach the bottom.

As the lift opened up its sliding double door to the highest floor of the base, DeMarco outstretched his arm with a grin, offering Jenken the first move out of the lift.

"I am fine, you go first." Jenken said, anxiously.

DeMarco sniggered and danced out of the lift. A few feet away from the lift was another double door, this time with a large circular window across its centre. DeMarco stood beside the window and ushered Jenken over to look into the adjacent room, through this window. Jenken looked, trying not to be distracted by the gleeful look on DeMarco's unhinged face.

"Beautiful isn't it." DeMarco whispered to Jenken, as they both stared inside.

"What am I looking at?" Jenken whispered back.

Inside the long, narrow room were rows upon rows of beds, each with a small child sitting on the end of it, their legs dangling over the edge. Beside each of those children, on a stool next to the bed was a humanoid musician, each of them wielding a variety of different instruments, evidently speaking to the children and occasionally giving the child the possession of the instrument.

"They're teaching them."

"Riiiiight." Jenken was unsure of the significance of this room to the grand scheme of things, and the grand theatre of DeMarco's criminal underworld.

"This is why I do all that I do." He was still smiling at Jenken, and still whispering.

"What is why?"

"This. What you're looking at. That is why."

"What?" Jenken was getting impatient.

"They are my musicians. They belong to me."

Jenken listened, trying to work out how far DeMarco was going with possession of these children.

"They will play music for me and will be the future of music in the new world!"

"Who are these children?" Jenken asked, not convinced that he wanted to know the answer.

"Various street kids. They didn't have a home or a purpose until I gave them one." He looked as proud as his words suggested. "They owe me their lives, but I just want their music."

"You can't just claim their lives." Jenken forgot for a moment who he was talking to...

"I certainly can, Mr Janes!" His whisper threatened to blow into a shout as his gritted teeth held the words back. "Once I have set off the great remix, with my new machine, I will lay the foundations for a new world, where music is heard everywhere, for free."

"Great remix?" Jenken was getting concerned but was aware of how much he was learning from DeMarco's boastful revelations.

"Ah yes. The great remix. I will be flattening the city and starting again."

Chapter Eleven

Teddy and Deet were dropped off a few hundred yards away from the base, in a field behind the suburban section of Blurgh. They felt safe enough, but a little vulnerable being separated from the rest of the band. Teddy had warmed to Deet immediately when she first joined the band, because he was the most proactive in settling her in. In comparison, Riff didn't notice she had joined for the first few weeks of rehearsals. Teddy and Deet stared at the town in front of them. Behind them was swamp land, with the sound of the local insects' stridulation bringing a peaceful pulse to the swamp's ambience. In front of them was the town's main area of activity. Residential houses blended with traders, taverns and craftsmen under the gleaming moon of Praxim 7. Above the town's residential skyline, DeMarco's base of operations towered above, like a warning to the town and a stark reminder to the two members of the band that their mission could lead to a confrontation with this narcissistic behemoth dominating the town. The night was giving them shelter and a chance to plan ahead.

"I think we need to take advantage of being separated and find information from somewhere outside the main base." Deet suggested.

"Affirmative. There is a good chance we can collect additional information from a worker from the base, while the others go for the direct route."

"Exactly, Teddy." Deet smiled. "Let's casually walk into that road over there and see what we find."

Deet pointed to an opening into the cobbled lane where the swamp grassland transformed into a paved pathway. They walked slowly, and relatively quietly, taking advantage of the darkness to survey the area as they walked. Behind them the swamp continued to gently make its presence known with the calm flow of the water and the chirping of the native insects. A few minutes later, the restful noise of the inactive swamp was behind them and the noise of the town, and the more urban smells of Blurgh's town centre filled their senses. They walked along the path and came to a wider opening that spread out into a road, bringing with it the occasional sounds of footsteps along the cobblestone and the distracting sounds of revelry coming from their right. Deet nudged Teddy as he heard this revelry and nodded in that direction.

"Could be interesting." Deet winked.

"Could be dangerous."

"Could be interesting and dangerous, but useful."

"Could be interesting, dangerous, useful and expensive."

Teddy was clearly cautious.

"Could be interesting, dangerous, useful, expensive and exactly the reason that we're here."

Deet walked further down the pathway to the right, with Teddy reluctantly following behind. Soon enough, the revelry revealed itself to be coming from a tavern that seemed to be the last part of Blurgh to be awake and active this time of night. They could hear shouting, laughing, a general murmur of collective chatting and music coming from the tavern. Teddy looked up to see the name of the tavern above them;

"The Swamp Beast." She read, with the tone of ominous curiosity. Deet looked at her, knowing exactly what she was thinking.

"Hey, Teddy. Just because this place is called The Swamp Beast, it doesn't mean there actually is a swamp beast in that swamp!" He gestured to the swamp behind them as he spoke.

"Well I guess we can worry about that later, if it happens." Teddy said, uncharacteristically dismissive.

"My thoughts exactly." Deet agreed. "Let's see what's in here."

He slapped Teddy on the back, and immediately shook his hand as the pain from slapping her metal casing flowed through his hand. Then he turned his attention to the tavern and made his way in.

As they walked in, they were hit by how busy the tavern was, and how every corner of the room was full of gambling activity, loud, boisterous carousing, obvious and mutual flirting and the occasional more secretive, whispered conversation at the back of the room. The music they could hear from outside was live music, coming from a trio of performers. They looked humanoid and possibly originally from Earth, and therefore totally out of place in this tavern which was almost exclusively populated by Bask Lizards. Deet looked back to Teddy and then nodded toward the bar. They both found a spot by the bar that wasn't occupied by a Bask Lizard and turned their attention to the Lizard barman facing them.

"Are you musicians?" The bartender asked them, without a hint of a greeting.

"Erm...yes." Deet replied, unsure of where that was leading.

"I see." The bartender's tone remained forceful and almost confrontational.

"Is that a problem?" Teddy asked, with a mechanical objectivity that the barman took as bravado.

"Not at all. We often have musicians in, especially this close to The Great Big Beat Festival." His tone remained the same, and Deet and Teddy realised it was simply his natural manner.

"Ahh yes, The Great Big Beat Festival." Deet said, picking up on a thread he thought could be useful. "Who runs that?"

"What?" The bartender looked at Deet with a sideways double take. "You don't know who runs the festival?" His bewilderment was obvious in his face and his tone.

"We've travelled quite far, from the Lantrick system, because of hearing about the festival. It's getting a lot of publicity. Everyone is talking about it."

"Yeah, hence the name." The bartender interrupted.

"Well, yeah, a great deal of publicity. We wanted to see if we could get a slot." Deet put his left hand on Teddy's metal shoulder as he spoke.

"You wanna play the festival?" The bartender said, provocatively.

"Yeah, how do we get a slot?" Deet asked.

"You're in luck." He replied, coldly. "See those guys over there?" The bartender pointed to the trio performing their loose, improvised 'elastic' music by the back wall.

"Yeah, what are they playing?" Deet asked, screwing his face into a scornful show of distaste.

"It's new elastic music from the Braxton system." He was watching the band as he spoke. "It's weirdly hypnotic, but utterly bonkers."

"Is it popular around here?" Teddy asked, adding digital notes to her database as they continued their investigation.

"Oh yes." The bartender answered, still sounding like he was verbally attacking them. "They're a big feature of the festival. They can play for hours without a point."

"So they have a long set?" Deet asked.

"Of course. Each of their songs lasts about an hour, so they can't play for less than 4 hours without their fans rioting."

"What are they called?"

"Dramatic Spleen."

"Urgh!" Deet replied, shocked by the name.

"Before their lead drummer killed himself, they were called, 'Dramatic Spleen in Sauce'.

"Nice." Deet continued to be disgusted.

"Well, they sound great." The bartender continued to speak to them while watching the band.

"I guess." Deet replied. "If you like hearing five different songs played at the same time."

"Anyway, what can I get you?" The bartender turned back to face them.

"Have you got Leaf Water?"

"Leaf Water?? Are you a Calpian or something?" The bartender could see that Deet was from Hurl, but was being facetious.

"Yeah, it might be a weird request, but one of my close friends is a Calpian, and I miss him."

"I get that. It kind of tastes like an actual Calpian doesn't it!" The bartender released a subtle smirk at this comment.

"Well I don't want to lick him or anything, but yeah, I guess it does."

"I can get you that. What about your metal friend here?"

"I just need recharging."

"Can't help you there, doll." The bartender shrugged, earnestly.

"No problem, it's not desperate."

"Good to know." The bartender turned away from the two new arrivals and prepared the Leaf Water, the Calpian delicacy that would ultimately give Deet the sensation that Trent was in the room. As he handed Deet the Leaf Water, Deet continued his line of enquiry about the festival.

"So, who do we talk to about playing at the festival then?"

"You need to speak to Dramatic Spleen. They run one of the stages." His tone was becoming warmer and slightly more welcoming.

"Fortuitous!" Teddy remarked, pleased to have made such progress during their first encounter in Blurgh.

"You'll have to play obviously." The bartender added.

"OK." Deet said, happy to duet with his robot companion. He looked at Teddy, who winked at him.

"They're approaching their first break. They've been playing for an hour so far."

"Still their first song?" Deet asked.

"Absolutely." The bartender replied. "They had a support band but that isn't going well."

"Who was it?"

"It was Nicholos Cosmos"

"NICHOLOS COSMOS?!! AROUND HERE?" Deet was suitably impressed.

"I wouldn't get too excited. He won't be playing."

"What happened."

"Too much Pulling Water."

"Oh..." Deet could see where this was going.

"He's on the roof at the moment busy being stunned at how beautiful the universe is."

"What a shame, I'd love to see his set."

"Me too. He still performs 'I gave you my heart and you turned it into a paper aeroplane and threw it into an incoming train and then just left it there as if it was a bit of smelly glue'. I love that one."

"Yeah, that's a classic. I remember the cover was just Nicholos sitting on a sofa made from parts of his own body."

"Indeed." The bartender's tone was lightening a little. "It wasn't actually his body though, it was just trick photography."

"Yeah, that makes sense." Deet agreed, earnestly.

"So, anyway, if you want to speak to them after they've finished their first song, they'll be pleased to have a replacement for Nicholos."

"Yeah, how long did you say this song was?" Deet asked.

"About 93 minutes, but only 10 minutes left."

"We'll wait."

The replica band was doing extremely well. The bootleg album they released without the consent or knowledge of the real Brown Yelp Gang outsold everything the band had done in their illustrious career. These digital copies were astounded by how well it was going and were buzzing about their future in the music industry. They had raced to their shuttle to head toward their next gig on Aquilos, after hundreds of fans descended on them at the shuttle port. They panicked and felt mobbed, but they all loved the feeling and certainly weren't expecting it when they first got activated by Ray's scientists to take over the Brown Yelp Gang tour.

"When do we become more important than the first Brown Yelp Gang?" The replica Riff addressed the rest of the band as they approached the ice planet of Aquilos.

"I see your point." The replica Trent replied. "I think it's a good question."

"I think it's a pertinent question." Teddy agreed. "We are now the active, touring version of The Brown Yelp Gang."

This statement was followed by a wave of realisation across the shuttle, as the replica band made some leaps in logic as they redefined their role in Ray's plans, and dismissed the temporary nature of their employment as robot replicas. Aria's replica was first to articulate this new outlook;

"So this is a crazy development. We are the Brown Yelp Gang, if you look at it from the perspective of the people coming to see us at every gig."

"We're not even competing. We are the only ones playing!" DK added, becoming animated from the idea of making this arrangement more permanent.

"Now, this is exciting." Plak replied, getting swept up in the moment with the rest of the band.

"So how do we make sure this becomes the new norm?"
Teddy asked, provocatively.

A moment of silence followed while they considered their
options.

"Do we kill them?" Riff asked, with a reasonable, calm
tone.

"We could, but that might upset the fans." Trent replied.

"What if we killed them without the fans finding out?" Plak
suggested.

"Like, in a dark room or something?" Riff pondered.

"With a silent weapon?" DK joined him.

"That sounds very exciting." Deet replied, still considering
the options. "I just think there is another way."

"Something less violent, less messy." Aria agreed with
Deet.

Silence followed again.

Then the shuttle pilot lifted his head and shouted behind
him, to the band from the front of the shuttle;

"Why don't you just take them to court?" The replica band
all looked to the front of the shuttle. "If you do it through
the court, all legal like...you'll never have to worry about
murder charges, revenge incidents, rabid fans seeking dead
bodies or even guilt – I know you lot are more than just
robots; I think you would be wracked with guilt."

"Take the band to court?" Riff shouted back to the front of
the shuttle.

"For the right to have the name?" DK joined the long distance conversation.

"Yeah, why not?" The shuttle pilot shouted back. "I think you're great."

"Really?" Aria's replica smiled, soaking up the compliment.

"More than the other Brown Yelp Gang?" Deet shouted.

"Oh god, yes." The pilot replied. "That lot are a bunch of lunatics. Can't stand them. They're so full of themselves. They literally think they're the best band in the universe!"

The replica band turned back to their own conversation.

"I think we could do this. We could end up the best band in the universe!" replica Riff concluded.

Trent had made his way up to the highest floor of DeMarco's base of operations and stood by the single door that they passed on their initial descent. This time he could feel the pressure of being separated from the others and felt the need to escape the Bask engineers that appeared below him. He wasn't sure what was on the other side of the door, but he could feel his heart pumping at a breathtaking rate and felt the decision being made for him. Within thirty seconds of his arrival on that floor, Trent darted into the adjacent room through the single anonymous door in front of him. As the door swung back and forth behind him, Trent surveyed the room that he had suddenly appeared in. Lining the walls of the room were the beds that would soon be shown to Jenken in DeMarco's big moment of bragging. Each bed had a child sitting on it. The races and the genders varied but there was a consistency running through this room. Every child had an adult with them, playing an instrument. Some beds had Movines helping Movine children with their snouts. Some beds were occupied by the many tentacled invertebrate race, the Snaffans, with young Snaffans being shown how to utilise all of their limbs effectively. Some had humanoid tutors showing advanced techniques on stringed instruments. Every being on ever bed turned around with a start when Trent leaped into the room. His quick examination of the room gave him the confidence to address anyone that would listen.

"Hello!" He said cheerily.

Trent's left head panicked and supported the middle head with a loud declaration;

"We're not going to kill you."

"Of course we're not!" The right head added, thinking they needed to pull back the connotations of that statement.

"We are here in peace." Trent's middle head calmly smiled.

With another, more detailed, check of what was in front of him, Trent surmised that this was some kind of music tutoring hall, presumably one of the more musical elements of DeMarco's activities. Trent thought about it for a second and realised he could blend in quite nicely, if he was careful.

"I'm actually here because Carlo has asked me to come down and give you some help with your singing."

Trent's other heads agreed, now enthusiastically feeling like they're on safer ground with this tactic. This was met with a human voice from the back;

"Are you the lead singer from The Brown Yelp Gang?"

"Oh!" Trent was immediately glowing from the compliment of being recognised. "I am actually, yes."

"Oh." The unknown face at the back turned away with a disappointed 'humpf' after hearing the confirmation and moved his attention back to his guitar.

All of the other tutors and children in the room turned their attention away from Trent and back to their tutoring session, almost in unison, like a synchronised dance move. Trent mumbled something like 'well I guess we'll have to just mingle with them and look useful' and decided to intervene with a studying Movine near him. He used his experiences with Plak and DK to give them advice that was actually received well, even if it was unexpected. He continued to work his way around the room giving helpful tips on how many hours of practice he would recommend, what to eat to remain healthy for a demanding work schedule, how to ensure that your band stays friends and some unwanted tips on how to orchestrate conversations when you have three heads. None of the tutors or children in the room had three heads, so this was superfluous but inevitable, as Trent was clearly making this all up as he was going along. His pretence that DeMarco had asked him to visit the tutoring chambers to share his knowledge was working well. He was accepted in the room and managed to speak to most of the tutors and students on the right side of the room.

His situation got more complicated when DeMarco's face appeared at the window of the door opposite the one he used to enter the room. He was immobilised in an obvious 'I shouldn't be here' way when his gaze fixed on DeMarco. On seeing Jenken appear next to him, looking through the window for the first time, Trent couldn't help himself; he waved at him enthusiastically. Besides the tutors and students at the back, who hadn't noticed DeMarco's appearance at the window, all other eyes in the room fell on Trent, then to DeMarco's face in the window. Then they looked back at Trent.

DeMarco flung open the door and walked in, with a swagger that inevitably comes from running the base, intimidating the locals and overseeing all criminal activity in Blurgh and beyond. He was followed by Jenken, who waddled in without the swagger, or the confidence, or the upper hand.

"What the hell are you doing here, Trent?" DeMarco shouted out to the three headed singer.

Jenken immediately noticed Trent floundering and jumped in to support.

"He's here with me, Mr DeMarco." Jenken blurted, anxiously.

"Of course he is, he is your singer. I'm not stupid." DeMarco chuckled. "The question is what is he doing here?"

"Oh, he's helping the students out." Jenken was improvising.

"Is he?" DeMarco addressed the room. He received back a semi-enthusiastic murmur that supported Jenken's claim.

"Okay." DeMarco was grinning now. "Thank you for your help, Trent."

"That's not a problem." Trent said, thinking he had got away with it. "Anytime you need a hand, just call me."

"OK, my friend, don't get ahead of yourself." DeMarco shut Trent's ease down with a stern reminder of his place in the room. He then turned back to Jenken;

"Right, Jenken Janes. We have some business to attend to."

"Oh, absolutely." Jenken was keen to get rid of the debt to DeMarco and was happy that it appeared to finally be happening.

"Follow me." DeMarco ordered "...both of you!"

Trent walked out of the door opposite to the one that he had arrived in, as he followed DeMarco and Jenken out of the room and into another doorway to the left.

271

"Take a seat." DeMarco gestured to the chairs that were in the room, propped up against the tables along the left wall. This appeared to be a communications room. There were screens across the wall opposite them and a digital interface that recorded the images on the screen, and also acted as a communications device around the base. A Bask Lizard sat in front of the screens watching the images as they walked in.

"Are they all here?" DeMarco addressed the Bask Lizard in front of him.

"Well you've met Trent. I saw him enter the room earlier, but you came in shortly after that."

"Okay, so we have Trent here and Jenken who came to see me voluntarily. There are others in the band. If you see one of them, let me know."

"Will do."

"Good man." DeMarco turned to Trent and Jenken. "Now you two need to follow me. We have lots to talk about."

Trent's three heads and Jenken's head all gulped, realising that their plan had got more complicated.

"Your communicators are useless here too." DeMarco gestured to the devices on the back of their hands.

"Hello?" Jenken raised his hand to his mouth. "Hello?"

"We sent out a pulse wave that fried your communicators in an instant. You really should get better at being covert." DeMarco was stifling a laugh at this point, thinking he had all of the cards the band was trying to play against him.

272

"We can chat about what you're doing here and what I want from you in my office. Come on."

DeMarco led them out of the room and through another door that led to a stairwell they hadn't seen before. Clearly they had only explored part of the complex.

Fortunately for Riff, the dozens of engineers in the main operations room with the huge machine in it had not seen him and were all too complacent in their work on the machine to notice Riff slowly lifting the lid of the box he was hiding in. The screens in the communications room only showed what was happening in the rooms themselves, DeMarco hadn't decided to put cameras in the stairwell, so Riff would be in a better position if he could join DK out of camera shot. With the precision and cautious movement of a man adept at regularly sneaking away from Aria for a meeting with a groupie, Riff spent a few minutes taking a careful look around the room to find the source of the deafening sound of manufacturing metal and electronics that he could hear from inside the box. He wasn't sure where the other members of the band were, but he was happy that he could see what was happening in that room, as it looked like something DeMarco would need a lot of money to build, and looked particularly threatening. With a resolve to get back to the roof as soon as possible, Riff waited for his moment to leap out of the box and make his way to the stairwell.

Ray was pleased to touch base with Aria and her companions when she eventually got to speak to him. It had taken a while to convince the security guard that she was actually Aria, still suffering from her less than temporary disguise. The unfamiliarity of Ursulas, Nod and Penny didn't help. Aria was forced to give the guard a detailed history of the band and sing every line from her lead song from the fourth album, 'You left me no choice but banana'. With permission from Ray, the guard accompanied them to his office and promptly left, leaving Aria, Ursulas, Nod and Penny facing the repellent sight of Ray scoffing Raggets into his mouth. As was always the case, Ragget blood was all over the desk and saliva and sauce dripped from everywhere in the office; along the floor, all four of the walls and mostly Ray's desk. Ursulas couldn't help but show her disgust on her face. Nod was surprised, but not particularly repulsed. Penny was too intimidated by the entire scenario to see Ray's eating habits as anything but more stress to pile onto her adventure with The Brown Yelp Gang.

"Who's this, then?" Ray broke the silence with an understandable desire for an update.

"Ah, Ray." Aria began. "This is Ursulas, old friend of Trent's and someone directly affected by DeMarco's activity in Corsylia." Aria gestured to Ursulas as she spoke.

"Ursulas. Wow. We finally meet." Ray had heard about Ursulas' activity and high esteem in the metropolitan crime ridden streets of Corsylia. "I have heard a lot about you."

"I've heard a lot about you too, Ray." Ursulas smiled, genuinely pleased to finally meet him too.

"This is Nod, her...guy." Aria stumbled on this as she hadn't been introduced to Nod, formally.

"My guy?" Ursulas chuckled, at the thought that they might be in an intimate relationship. "He certainly isn't my guy." Nod looked disappointed at losing the chance of pretending to be Ursulas' 'guy'. He had always loved her. There had been several times in the past where he had risked his life for her, and it was purely out of love; not what Ursulas regarded as an occupational hazard.

"Pleased to meet you, Nod." Ray slobbered.

Nod nodded, accordingly.

"This is Penny." Aria gestured to Penny, beside her.

"Not Lilly?" Ray asked, predictably.

"No that's my sister." Penny answered.

"Ah, I see." Ray replied, dismissively. "So what's happening with you lot?" Ray's words were accompanied by the slurping sounds of his salivation and messy eating.

"Well, we found Plak." Aria declared, proudly.

"That's good. Where is he then?"

"He decided he wanted to leave the band."

"Wow. That's a new one." More Raggets were mercilessly consumed as he spoke.

"Freaked me out too, but there ya go." Aria was keen to move on. "So now we're here to hopefully get to the others and stop DeMarco from causing any more damage."

"Hmmm..." Ray stared at her as he guzzled the Raggets.

"What?" Aria was confused and impatient.

"You need to know some of the developments in this whole mess."

"Okay."

"- and am I right in thinking that you can tell your sister what you know, from here?"

"That's right, Mr Ray." Penny nodded, humbly.

"Okay, good. Tell your sister this update, so that she can tell the band."

"Absolutely, Mr Ray."

"So, the replica band that I created, so that you could investigate what DeMarco was doing, has been making great waves on the live music scene. Everyone is talking about them."

"Eh?" Aria balked. "They were supposed to be just doing our job."

"Well it turns out they're doing it better than you did." Ray continued to stuff Raggets into his mouth as he cold-bloodedly described the complications. "The word out there is that they're thinking of taking the band to court for possession of the name."

"That's insane!" Aria was incensed.

"It's unusual, I will give you that."

"This is classic." Ursulas smugly chuckled to herself as Ray updated Aria on the replica band activity.

"As for the band themselves, I have no idea what happened after they entered DeMarco's base, because they're communications were jammed once they entered the building."

"So we don't know if they're OK?" Aria sounded worried.

"Nope." Ray was indifferent, and direct.

"We don't know if Riff is OK?" Aria inevitably cared more about her lesser half.

"No, we don't." Ray knew her motivation for the obvious question, so let it go. "So basically, we need to get you to Praxim 7 as soon as possible, so you can get the band out of there, then we find out what they have managed to get from their visit to the base, and then we go from there."

"Where do we go from there?" Aria asked, anxiously.

"Once you get everyone back on a shuttle headed back here, I need you to see Dr Schoenberg."

"Dr Schoenberg? Who's that?"

"Don't worry about the details now, Aria." Ray continued. "If you all see Dr Schoenberg you'll be better equipped to kick DeMarco's balls."

"Ah OK. I look forward to it." Aria smiled; intrigued to meet this doctor that Ray wants them to visit.

"We're ready when you are." Ursulas wasn't interested in wasting time chatting.

"What she said." Nod added.

"I will feel a lot better if I'm with my sister." Penny said, still not quite looking directly at Ray's slobbering face.

In a matter of minutes, Ray had used his considerable resources to get another shuttle ready, and a suitable pilot, for delivering Aria, Ursulas, Nod and Penny to DeMarco's base on Praxim 7. The mission was clear and there was little conversation on the journey from Bragal to Praxim 7. Penny continued to send messages of reassurance to Lilly. Lilly was extremely frustrated, feeling stuck on the roof of the base of operations, and that frustration was making Penny extremely impatient to get to Praxim 7 to support her. The pilot for the shuttle they had was as indifferent to The Brown Yelp Gang as the pilot who was taking the replica band to Aquilos for their next gig;

"Have you heard the bootleg by the 'other' Brown Yelp Gang?" The pilot broke the ice with a conversation none of them wanted.

"No, and I am not interested." Aria snapped.

"Aw, man. You need to listen to it. Those songs have never sounded so great!"

"Not interested!" Aria was raising her voice, but the pilot seemed to be blind to her perspective.

"From the first track on that bootleg, you just get drawn in." The pilot was shouting enthusiastically behind him, as if he didn't have the victims of the bootleg in his shuttle.

"They do that classic, 'In, out, up and over'. It sounds amazing, you can hear the crowd going wild!"

"Not interested!"

"You can bet they were all doing the actions for 'In, out, up and over'. Oh, and they also did 'Throw your hands in your hair' which I've always thought was underrated. Such a classic." His voice was loud enough to be difficult to ignore. "The last track on the bootleg is a glorious reworking of the track -"

Aria was a woman of action. Her Denuvian upbringing gave her the resolve to deal with any problem that came up immediately. After the pilot showed no signs of stopping his adoration of the replica band, she felt she had no choice but to strap a parachute onto his back and throw him out of the shuttle. Ursulas, Nod and Penny looked on, impressed but nervous about not having a pilot.

"Do you know how to get to Praxim 7?" Ursulas asked Aria, calmly.

"Yeah, I don't really know why we had to have a pilot really." Aria shouted as she strapped herself into the pilot's chair and took command of the shuttle controls.

"Nice!" Ursulas laughed out loud at Aria's bravado. "You impress me very much Denuvian Movine lady!"

Penny continued to send Lilly messages that they were on their way. Ursulas and Nod looked around the shuttle for any weaponry or other tools that were put there for them before they left. They were pleased to see a small arsenal in the compartments below the main deck of the shuttle, and promptly emptied the weapons out onto the floor of the main deck, to decide what they could realistically take with them. Every style and scale of weapon was lying on the shuttle floor in front of them, waiting to be utilised by these nefarious criminals. Nod picked some pulse rifles and ammunition as he always felt those long rifles suited his height. Ursulas was more subtle in her choices, and loaded up several small, but powerful pulse pistols and concealed them at several points along her loose leather clothes. They gestured to Penny to have a look, but she politely declined, reminding them that she was a child. They shrugged, not quite relating to their reasoning. Aria could see what they were doing from the cockpit and smiled to herself, confident with the new friends she had made, but also now with the head space to be thoroughly irritated by the Movine disguise that she had been simulating. She made a mental note to deal with that as soon as she had the chance. In the meantime the peril that her friends were in was pounding at the front of her overwhelmed brain. She was determined to get to DeMarco's base in Blurgh at a velocity that defied local speed laws.

Consequently, only less than an hour later, the shuttle was approaching Praxim 7 and they were almost on the swampy ground of Blurgh. Aria had read the pilot's instructions on the control panels in front of her, and headed for the swamp that acted as the landing site for Teddy and Deet. It was now approaching the morning after the band's first arrival, and the night sky was turning lighter as the next day yawned into existence.

"Buckle up again, people." She said, to her companions.

"We're about to land on Praxim 7. We need to get out, get to the others, find out what they know and then kick DeMarco's arse!"

"Whoo!" Penny shouted, in an uncharacteristic response.

"Let's get him – and them!"

Penny was getting used to the notion of conflict, and couldn't wait to see her sister.

Chapter Twelve

Riff was in a difficult position. He knew this. He hadn't felt this worried about being found out since he stuffed five semi-conscious 'Happy Bears' in his coat lining, on a flight to a planet that banned hallucinogenic drugs, and bears. He was satisfied with the information he had gleaned from the huge engineering room, and hoped it would be matched with some other information that the rest of the band had discovered. His mission was to get back to the stairwell without being caught out. The only tool he had with him that could be of any use in this situation was the box he had jumped in. He had spare strings, a capo, an automatic tuner and the beak of a Cooder Crane that he used to play slide guitar. He felt under pressure to get into the stairwell as soon as possible, and decided to go for the 'don't mind me, I'm just an innocent box' play. He took a quick peak in front and around him, for curious engineers. As was consistent with their behaviour since he'd been down there, the engineers were preoccupied by their work and didn't notice his eyes poking out of the dark hole between the box and its lid. Satisfied that he could make the first move, Riff held onto the sides of the box and jumped as high as he could, bringing up the box with him with his hands clutching the sides. As soon as the box landed, he ducked down into the box and waited for a few moments, then poked his head up again to see if any engineering activity had been disturbed. It hadn't. Riff chuckled to himself, thinking 'this is like playing the A major pentatonic scale' and promptly jumped again with his hands gripping the sides of the box again. Ducking down, he waited for another minute or so, and then looked up again. He had travelled a few metres and not drawn any attention to himself at all. The deafening noise of the machine being worked on, the monitors and computer banks against the walls were causing the ideal distraction for him, and the engineers were utterly oblivious to Riff's movements toward the door.

The Bask engineers continued to work with their back to Riff, as he moved slowly and methodically toward his miraculous escape. His cautious, meticulous methods may have taken him over ten minutes to travel fifteen yards, but he was doing it without getting spotted. He was channelling his determination to see his sexy Denuvian priestess Aria again and to get to play the next gig, to give him the motivation to work carefully. As the box reached the door that Riff arrived in, he waited a little longer, aware that this was his last challenge before being on less detectable ground. As he made his last sneaky look around the room from slightly raising the lid of the box, he saw a Bask engineer near him, facing away from him, but close enough to be a threat.

Riff deliberated. This was the last moment that he needed to be in this vast room of mechanical engineering. If he could just get rid of the engineer standing near him, he would be home and dry, on the stairwell and on his way to returning to the roof. He replaced the lid onto the box and sat inside for a moment, humming quietly to give himself a clear head. He was humming the song 'I Bet You'd Even Look Good In A Cocoon', one of his favourite of his own songs. After humming the first two verses to himself, he noticed the engineer close by humming the song too. His pitching was off, and the timing was awkward, but Riff knew it was the same song. He stopped humming, and listened for his position to be revealed, as clearly the humming thing was probably a mistake.

"What's that song?" Riff heard the engineer shout to his colleagues in the middle of the vast laboratory.

"What song?" The reply came from an unknown engineer about thirty metres away.

"I don't know. It just popped into my head." The engineer continued. "Da da da da, da-da da-da da-da da-da dum dum doooooooooo"

The engineer replaced his humming with 'da's and 'dum's to make identifying the song easier.

"What the hell is that?" His colleague shouted back.

"It's a song."

"I don't think it is."

"It's about a monster I think."

"A monster?"

"Yeah, a cuckoo-cadoo."

"A cuckoo-cadoo?" His colleague asked, dumbfounded and unaware of any song that refers to a cuckoo-cadoo.

"It goes..." The engineer thinks for a moment "...I bet you've eaten a cuckoo-cadoo."

"I bet you've eaten a cuckoo-cadoo?" The revulsion coming from the discerning colleague was audible from the scornful tone.

"Yeah, I bet you've eaten a cuckoo-cadoo."

Riff was incensed. He desperately wanted to jump out of his box and shout, violently to the Bask engineer beside him, 'IT'S I BET YOU'D EVEN LOOK GOOD IN A COCOON IDIOT!!!' but he resisted the urge and stayed inside the box, gritting his teeth.

"What's a cuckoo-cadoo?" The colleague from the middle of the room shouted, still understandably confused from the made up word.

"I think it's a slimy amphibian." The engineer near Riff replied.

"No, that's a Ragget."

"No, a different amphibian." The engineer snapped back.

"Oh, okay." The engineer was starting to sound less interested. "Never heard of it."

"Urgh!" The engineer vocalised his frustration. "Someone must know that song. It's going to bug me now." The engineer sounded like he was moving as he said this last statement of irritation.

Riff sensed that he had a window of opportunity to act. He slowly and quietly lifted the lid again, and watched as the Bask engineer walked up to another engineer further along the wall and started singing his warped version of 'I Bet You'd Even Look Good In A Cocoon' to someone else. Riff noticed the look of confusion and annoyance coming from the other engineer as he surreptitiously slipped out of the box, out of the room and into the stairwell. He was out of the extremely stressful arena that could have meant his certain death, or at least a gig cancellation, and into the pathway to the exit. He made a mental note to make the lyrics for the albums more obvious on their merchandise.

The replica band was busy promoting and revelling in the success of their bootleg album, recorded on Vestrell. They were all very excited about the future and utterly convinced that the original Brown Yelp Gang were old news. The journey to the ice planet of Aquilos was taken care of for them by Ray's men. They still had Les Manfred's Gig Boys helping them out, and all of the resources Ray was sending out to them, to ensure a successful pretence. He had sent extra speakers, a bigger mixing desk and boxes of new publicity to distribute around Aquilos once they landed. Ray was aware of the complications with the replica band challenging the original band for the right to use the band name, but didn't think it was his problem.

He always found it easy to disassociate himself from problems that he caused.

"We can get this gig done and then we can send out the message that The Brown Yelp Gang is now an electronic, digital force to be reckoned with!" The replica Deet shouted to the rest of the robot band on the shuttle to Aquilos.

"Affirmative, Deet." Riff said, with the closest thing to a smile that his mechanical metallic panels could muster.

"This is only the beginning." His tone had a heightened, raised pitch that came from the swelling of excitement running through replica Riff's digital pathways.

"This could be the start of something huge!" replica Trent shouted from his reclining chair at the back of the shuttle.

"Oh, I know. We will be the biggest band in the known territories." DK joined in.

"No, I mean bigger than that!" replica Trent continued.

"Think of all the tired, indifferent, clapped out and boring bands there are out there. All guitars and voices, just singing the same old nonsense about 'their feelings'."

The rest of the replica band was hypnotically entranced by the epic vision of the future that the replica Trent was painting to this already excitable band.

"What are you saying, Trent?" The replica Riff said, wanting clarity despite being swept up by where he thought he was going with this speech.

"I am saying that we could be the first robot band to remake all that old music into new sounds...we could be the start of something that turns a dozen bands...or even a hundred bands!"

The replica band all gasped in unison, now seeing robots in every venue, replacing 'ordinary' old fashioned sentient bands.

"Can you imagine?" Trent continued. "All those bands transformed into interesting, synthetic, powerful, modern, fresh music!" His voice had now risen to a loud, high pitched crescendo.

The replica band couldn't help it; they all clapped and cheered, thinking of the A.I. takeover of the music industry from the Lantrick System to the Corsyllian System. Their excitement was interrupted by their shuttle pilot, warning of their imminent arrival on Aquilos.

"We're due to land in just five minutes." The pilot shouted to the replica band behind him. "Get yourself strapped up for the landing. There is apparently a big crowd waiting for you at the shuttle port, but we'll sweep past them and get you to the venue, which is only a short drive from the shuttle port."

"We can talk to them, can't we?" Trent shouted back, grasping at the glory awaiting him at the shuttle port.

"Ray wants you to concentrate on getting the gig sorted. He wants you to meet up with Les Manfred's team and sound check as soon as you get there, and to make sure there are no complications."

Ray's words were the final word on their activity; there was no objection, and the replica band obediently prepared for landing on Aquilos.

Jenken and Trent were tired of DeMarco's games, tired of his continuous demonstrations of his power and were desperately eager to get the matter of Jenken's debt discussed. They had been in his office for almost an hour, and DeMarco had bored them silly with tales of his recent acquisitions and business successes. After watching DeMarco juggle 6 leather balls in the air for a few minutes, Jenken couldn't contain the urge to stop him any longer;

"Mr DeMarco, I want to discuss the debt I owe you."

DeMarco dropped his balls.

"It is precisely why I am here in the first place." Jenken continued. "You have patiently waited for me to come up with the 40,000 credits that I owe you...and I can!"

Jenken's words took an upturn as he smiled at DeMarco with a triumphant grin.

"You can?" DeMarco was visibly stunned.

"I can."

"The whole 40,000?"

"Absolutely." Jenken was grinning so wide, that the grin was at risk of taking off.

"Well, that is impressive." DeMarco sounded sincere, as he sat back down at his desk and put the balls in his drawer.

"I have - "

"We have!" Trent interjected.

"Yes, we have, done various things to get the money together and I can transfer it all to you whenever you want it." Jenken nodded as he finished his statement, full of pride and relief at managing to reach this seemingly unobtainable goal.

"Hmm..." DeMarco thought for a moment. "How did you do it?"

"Various things."Jenken was happy to elaborate. "We released a box set of rarities from Trent here."

"Hello." Trent nodded as a fake greeting.

"So that brought a fair bit in."Jenken continued. "We sold our freighter. That was a bit painful to be fair."

"Impressive." DeMarco commented.

"We also put the merch money from the latest gigs into the debt and did a few things like that."

"So you have the 40,000 credits?" DeMarco looked at Jenken slyly.

"Yes. 100%. 40,000 credits. Absolutely." Jenken smiled at DeMarco, then gave a quick smile to Trent too, his close friend and collaborator on the money raising.

"Well, that's good." DeMarco had to admit. "I didn't expect that."

Jenken and Trent sniggered with pride.

"Thing is, of course." The sniggering turned to silence as an overbearing darkness suddenly appeared in the room. "That 40,000 credit debt doesn't really cover it."

"What?!!" Jenken tried to stifle the outrage, but it ended up sounding like a mixture of anger and upset, that was weaker than Jenken wanted, but probably safer overall.

"That 40,000 credit date was issued years ago."

"Yes. So?" Jenken frowned in fury.

"Well, I would hardly be the most feared business man in this star system if I just let a debt go drifting off to the moon and back without any kind of interest."

"Interest?" Jenken was starting to panic.

"Well, yes. I think you owe me far more than 40,000 credits."

Trent and Jenken were exhausted by the whole process of base infiltration and high risk confrontation. This was the last thing they wanted to hear, but they didn't have the energy or the confidence to object.

"So, what kind of figure are you talking about now?" Jenken sighed as he asked this.

"Well, it's not a number of credits."

The Brown Yelp Gang members looked at DeMarco with a worried silence.

"You'll like what I am about to say." DeMarco teased.

"Is it that everything you've just said is a wind up and it's all good and we can go home?" Jenken was only half joking.

"No, not at all. It's better than that."

"Better than going home?" Trent scoffed, his side heads chuckling at the suggestion that there could be something better.

"Your debt will be cleared once you play at my big festival in a few days." DeMarco punctuated the statement with a smile and a slap on his desk.

"Is this the one that we've been hearing about?" Trent replied. "The Great Big Beat Festival?"

"That's the one." DeMarco answered, with an excited tone to his voice. "The Brown Yelp Gang headlining my big event here on Blurgh!"

"Headlining?" Jenken soaked up the connotations of that request. "Are you saying you haven't got a headliner yet?"

"I did." DeMarco replied. "Sadly he said he had to bow out. Something about their drummer not turning up or something."

"Who was it?"

"It was The Drummers of Clang Tang."

"Ah, I see." Jenken could see the issue. "So you want us to play the headline slot?"

"Yes."

"Next week?"

"Yes, in a few days."

"- and then our debt is cleared?"

"Absolutely." DeMarco considered his last statement. "Well, probably."

They both looked at him, frowning.

"We'll work that out once the festival has happened." DeMarco deployed his hitherto successful technique of brushing over the sensitive questions. "Let's just get The Brown Yelp Gang all here in Blurgh in time for the big festival." His voice was brimming with excitement and pride. "It's going to be the most amazing day. I have something special planned for the moment you finish your last song."

"Oh really?" Jenken replied. "What's that then?"

"No, I cannot tell you." DeMarco's frown spoke volumes. "You will know soon enough."

"Is this to do with your 'Great Remix' thing you were talking about?" Jenken asked, thinking he knew the answer.

"My innocent young band manager, what can I say?" DeMarco's voice was somehow conspiratorial and condescending at the same time. "To do with it? It IS the 'Great Remix' that I was talking about. Blurgh won't know what has hit it." DeMarco started to laugh as he elaborated, overcome with maniacal glee, thinking about his plan. "It will be the start of a new era; a new dawn where everyone has one goal, one life and one true religion...me."

"So you start your big 'taking over the universe' thing at that point?" Jenken didn't show any reaction to the worryingly deranged declaration of doom.

"Absolutely. At the end of my first full day festival. A perfect end to a great day of music."

"I guess so..." Jenken said, looking at Trent, with both of them determined to knock him down to size, as soon as they could.

Deet and Teddy had to wait a good fifteen minutes for the end of Dramatic Spleen's song to finish before they coolly informed the audience that they were going for a short break. It was such a 'now' way of giving them the information, that the audience had no clue what the singer meant, but once the band had walked away and music was piped from their mixing desk, it was more obvious what they meant.

As soon as the trio had unplugged their instruments and headed for the bar, Deet was instantly making his way to block their path, preparing to be as sycophantic as he needed to be to get a slot at the Great Big Beat Festival. He was the first one to break the ice as they approached.

"Great set...or song, guys." Deet held out his hand to shake the long haired, casually dressed lead guitarist as he spoke.

"Thank you, I'm glad you liked it." His voice was sincere and pleasant, graciously taking the compliment through years of practice.

"I love elastic music." Deet continued. "You don't hear it enough."

"Oh, I agree." The guitarist replied. "My name is Burgundy."

Burgundy shook Deet's hand as he introduced the other two members of the band to the falsely impressed Deet. "This here is Mauve, and the drummer there is Crimson." They all nodded to each other and smiled politely, waiting for more compliments. All three were dressed in such similar attire that it could have passed as a uniform. Any such suggestion would, of course, be insulting to them.

"I hear you're in need of a support band tonight?" Deet said, boldly.

"Yes, that's right!" Burgundy became animated when this was said, immediately making the assumption that these two strangers wanted to play.

"Well, it just so happens that myself and my robot companion here..." Teddy bowed to the members of Dramatic Spleen after Deet's arm indicated her presence "...have a band we like to play in. We can play for you now if you like? ...to fill the gap from Nicholos Cosmos disappearing."

"Well, he's not disappeared." Burgundy corrected. "He's up on the roof."

Mauve and Crimson added their mumbles of support for the whereabouts of Nicholos Cosmos.

"OK, I'm up for it. Show us what you've got." Burgundy's words were almost mocking in their cloaked cynicism. They gestured to the stage area, still strewn with Dramatic Spleen gear and instruments. Deet and Teddy looked at each other, smirking with excitement of getting their chance to play so soon after landing on Blurgh. They walked into the stage area and hesitated for a moment, suddenly aware that they hadn't discussed what they were going to play.

"What song shall we do?" Deet asked.

"How many songs have we got?" Teddy replied.

"I don't know, they didn't say."

"No. Maybe it will only be one song."

"We need to make it a good one."

"What about 'Fallet Frenzy'? Would that work?" Teddy felt like she was clutching at straws.

"You'd need to provide most of the music." Deet considered the dozen psychedelic layers on that track.

"Indeed." Teddy fell silent for a moment.

"We could do 'Show me where you put it'? People love that one." Deet's face lit up with enthusiasm.

They both looked around the room at the waiting audience.

"I'm not sure this is the right audience." They had no idea what the Blurgh audience wanted, but being put on the spot makes you say things like that.

"Let's do 'You just blew my face away'! We can make it loud and proud and just throw everything into it!" Teddy was more animated than she had been for days.

Deet agreed. He leant back so that he was facing the ceiling, with his back propped up by the drum set played by the main band. Forgoing all of the regular warm up techniques Deet and any other musician from Hurl would use to centre themselves, Deet smiled at Teddy before she began the opening melody. Teddy looked at the crowd in front of her. She knew they had just been enjoying the elastic music of Dramatic Spleen and were probably open for anything. This gave her the confidence she needed to scream into the microphone, 'People of Blurgh! We are The Brown Yelp Gang and we're here to shave your face off with our sounds!' – and then she began the melody.

A few seconds into the song, they had the crowd in the palm of their hand. Burgundy, Mauve and Crimson all looked at the audience as they listened, gripped by Deet's polyrhythm and Teddy's ability to digitally reproduce the melodies from the rest of the band. The atmosphere in the room was electric. Deet and Teddy noticed how well it was going and fed off the fervour of the Blurgh residents they were playing to, and adding new ad-libs and layers to the song. They both hadn't felt this good in weeks.

"There's nothing like it, when it works is there?" Deet shouted to his band mate on the right.

"Indeed!" Teddy shouted back, between the vocal melodies.

As the song finished, the crowd that had gathered in "The Swamp Beast" to see Dramatic Spleen had all become instant fans of The Brown Yelp Gang, albeit in its atypical duo form. A rapturous applause engulfed the room as the final note from Teddy's breast speakers began to die down. The room was filled with the sounds of cheering, whooping, whistling and the slapping of tables. Deet and Teddy looked on, grins spreading across their faces, finally looking at Burgundy for approval.

All three members of Dramatic Spleen were passionately applauding and cheering, overcome with the power of 'You just blew my face away'; a song that, when sung with the full band behind it, sometimes literally blew an audience's face away. Just peeping its head above the noise of the adulation, Burgundy shouted encouragement to the duo; "Play us another one!"

"Yeah, do another one!" Mauve added.

"Who wants to hear another one?" Crimson's shout was more addressed to the audience.

The audience began chanting 'Hup!' 'Hup! 'Hup!' Hup!', which was the custom in Blurgh for demanding an encore. Deet and Teddy were confused and looked at the audience, then looked back at their hosts.

"They want another one." Burgundy shouted.

Teddy turned to Deet;

"Can we do one of mine?" She asked, almost sheepishly.

"You write songs?" Deet was shocked and intrigued.

"Yeah, always have." Teddy added. "Trent and Riff won't listen to them. It does my circuits in."

"All right." Deet nodded in support. "I haven't heard any of your songs either but I'll join in after the first 8 bars.

"You're a good man, Deet!" Teddy was grinning even more now.

Teddy looked at the crowd and closed her eyes, as the first three note melody loop of 'No one ever wants to listen to my songs' begins. The crowd love it. Deet joins in and even, after the second chorus, is heard joining in with the vocal line of the chorus;

"No one ever wants to listen to my songs

No one ever wants me to play them

No one ever wants me to play one of my songs

What am I? Some kind of dishwasher, dishwasher, dishwasher, dishwasher."

By the fourteenth chorus, even the crowd were singing along, having learned the words by the twelfth occurrence of the painfully bitter refrain. The three members of Dramatic Spleen looked on, smiling, and had already decided that if The Brown Yelp Gang were anywhere near as good as this duo that springs from them, that they'd be a great addition to their stage on the Great Big Beat Festival. As the song died down, the crowd repeated their screams of praise to the Brown Yelp duo, and Burgundy called them back over to the bar again.

"That was gorgeous." Burgundy greeted them back, shaking their hands as they reached the bar.

"Definitely the best duo I have ever seen." Crimson added, smiling at the duo.

"How would you like to be the headliners on our stage?" Burgundy offered.

"Wow, that's great thank you." Deet was amazed at how well their evening was going. "What stage is it?"

"There are three stages at The Great Big Beat Festival." Burgundy replied. "There's the Big Beat Stage that the organiser, Carlo DeMarco runs by himself." Teddy and Deet looked at each other, in a subtle acknowledgement of DeMarco's shadow looming over their actions. "Then there's our stage, The Little Beat Stage, and then there's the third stage, which is situated in the neighbouring town over there." Burgundy gestured to Hallin, the town next to Blurgh. "That stage is called The Distant Beat Stage; you don't want to play on that one." Burgundy winked as he said this, with an almost competitive arrogance.

"That sounds great!" Teddy replied. "So we're headlining The Little Beat Stage?"

"Yep. You'll go down a storm."

"We'll talk about payment later, yeah?" Deet added, knowing that it was a touchy subject.

Burgundy glanced quickly at Mauve and Crimson and self-consciously replied with an approving mumble. Deet and Teddy were being facetious; they knew the way DeMarco worked and didn't expect to get paid.

"Be at the back of the stage by 16 O'clock, and you'll be on shortly after that." Crimson quickly changed the tone of the conversation, reminding the duo of the long days on Blurgh.

"Great. We'll be there. Thanks, it's been lovely meeting you." Deet was shaking their hands as he concluded the conversation. Teddy added her handshake and they both walked toward the door they came in earlier. Before they reached the door, they were met by a small bald man with glasses, wearing a smart, pristine orange suit. He was grinning at the duo as they were walking toward the door.

"Brown Yelp Gang?" The orange suited man said.

"Yes, that's right." Deet replied. "Well, two of them anyway."

"My name is Harold. I've been following the band since it started."

"Oh, nice to meet you, Harold." Deet held out his hand and shook Harold's hand, smiling.

"I just wanted to say that I've been looking out for you in the festival news on the information stream, hoping you'd be playing."

"Well, we are now!" Teddy replied with an excited inflection added to the end of the declaration.

"Aw, that's lovely news." Harold said. "Will you be doing some of the old songs?"

"Of course." Deet answered, nodding. "What songs are your favourites?"

"Songs like 'How is your hair', 'See you in the fridge' and 'Show me where you put it'. Those are my favourites." Harold didn't have to think too hard to remember his favourites.

"No problem, we're likely to do a few of those oldies." Deet beamed.

"Good." Harold answered sternly. "The new album is shit."

- And with that, Harold walked back to his seat, waiting for Dramatic Spleen's next set/song.

Deet and Teddy looked at each other with an awkward look of embarrassment, and left The Swamp Beast, pleased with their progress and eager to join their friends at the base. They didn't make any reference to the damning of their latest album, making a comfortable assumption that it was a rogue fan with nostalgia issues.

They could see the base looming above the town, and could see it was a short walk away from the pub. It was getting late, and they had been in the pub for just under an hour, so they guessed that the rest of the band was in the thick of it. The walk from the pub to the back of the main base was uneventful. Deet and Teddy bounced along the road, buoyed by how well their visit to the pub went, and

302

confident about their band mates' progress. They decided to start from the roof of the base, where they knew they were going to be dropped off, and then decide from there what their next move should be. Their spirits were high, and they were blissfully unaware of Carlo DeMarco's psychotic plans for the town, and the star system.

Chapter Thirteen

Once the replica band had arrived on Aquilos for their third gig masquerading as The Brown Yelp Gang, they were all hyperactively restless about performing. The stakes seemed higher now that their ambitions had risen so much higher than just the initial reason they were constructed. Their programming was clearly too complex, and gave them too much scope to start enjoying the live experience. Wanting it for themselves is more a product of Ray's robot division not thinking ahead, and not reining them in; the fact that Ray was responsible for the mess didn't make him any more proactive about solving it. The gig on Aquilos was an outdoor gig, and the debut gig for a new venue that had just been built as part of the new arena in Aquilos City, the most populated area of Aquilos. It was the most demanding of the replica gigs so far, as it was a full 3 hour set that was being given to them by the Aquilos government. The gig was being paid for by the government, to present the opening of the new arena to its people with a show they will never forget; the legendary Brown Yelp Gang, known throughout several different star systems for their amazing rock extravaganzas. It was the replica band's job to match that reputation, as trillions would be watching their performance; on Aquilos itself, and on the neighbouring planets, a broadcast set up by the Aquilos tourist board programme.

Les Manfred was on the site first, with his men, setting up the rigging and array of speakers for the big gig. It was a physically daunting task for them to set up the 36 six metre speakers across the stage with all of the backdrops and pyrotechnics that Ray had added to the staging. The temperature on Aquilos never went above -27 degrees Celsius, which made the physical conditions for the crew particularly difficult. They were wrapped up in huge coats that covered their shivering bodies well, but the extra necessity to deal with the cold made the crew work slowly and less efficiently. Often they complained that they couldn't feel their hands when they were moving heavy equipment along to different parts of the staging area. Polly, Les Manfred's chief of operations was getting impatient with the high winds that were toppling everything she was placing on the stage, and making it too risky for the band to play. Ray's men reassured her that the band had weighted boots on, to compensate for any issue the wind might cause. This was not true, and was a bad case of the crew improvising a story out of fear that they would let Ray down if the gig was cancelled.

The tickets sold well; there were hundreds of thousands of Aquilos residents coming to the big arena in Aquilos City and expecting the gig of a lifetime. The people of Aquilos were the Yakons, human sized and humanoid shaped creatures that looked like walking carpets with limbs. Their faces were only revealed when their enormous mouths opened, and a huge gaping hole with sharp teeth appeared on the Yakon's head of hair. Their eyes were hidden below the hair that covered their faces, and their noses were so small that it would be difficult to see them even without the hair obstructions. The Yakons knew the band well and the news that they were coming to Aquilos met with a tidal wave of hysteria that the authorities found difficult to contain. Graffiti about The Brown Yelp Gang appeared on all of the crystalline monuments and business structures around the populated areas of Aquilos. Media broadcasts were interrupted by manic Brown Yelp Gang fans invading the commentator's space and overtaking the broadcast with chants like 'See You In The Fridge!' 'See You In the Fridge!'...or...'We're back and we're livid!' 'We're back and we're livid'. The initials 'BYG' were appearing everywhere where it wasn't wanted; on sacred religious artefacts, on the sides of public motor vehicles and etched on the blank spaces of advertising billboards across Aquilos. Brown Yelp hysteria had overwhelmed the ice planet of Aquilos. If the band themselves had been there, they would have been buzzing with anticipation for playing in front of that adoring crowd.

As it was, it was the replica band, and things weren't going well during the sound check. The replicas of Trent, Riff, DK and Plak began to freeze up as they waited for the equipment to be cabled together. It took Les' crew just under an hour to defrost the band before playing, and Polly was threatening to walk out and fly home during this whole process. Once the band were defrosted, the moisture in the air was playing havoc with their circuitry and they were finding it difficult to get any songs ran through without one of them shutting down, or simply cutting out intermittently. Polly had found a way of gluing the microphones, amplifiers and Deet's amplification stool to the stage, to protect them from the wind power pounding the area. After the third time that Ray's men upturned the band and sucked the moisture out of their casings, Les and the rest of his crew were told the truth about the band being replicas. Les and Polly's outrage was quickly placated by the threat of a slow, painful death from Ray's security men. The day hadn't started well, and as the audience began to roll into the venue at the start of the evening, the band hadn't managed a whole song without an incident of freezing, circuits sparking out, fuses blowing, someone getting an electric shock or mini- electric fires breaking out.

The replica band was no longer backstage giddy with excitement; now they were terrified and aware that their dreams of taking over the Brown Yelp back catalogue were just a snowball away from falling apart. As the clock approached the top of the 9th hour of daylight, the lights surrounding the arena went down and the sound of a low

307

drone filled the area. Instantly the crowd's natural ambience was silenced as they all stared at the stage in expectation. A few minutes later, the replica Riff ran onto the stage waving to the audience. The audience went wild. Then he played the first riff to the classic Brown Yelp song, 'Show Me Where You Put It'. The atmosphere was incredible. The rest of the replica band followed Riff and they continued to play one of their most popular songs. The noise of the hundreds of thousands of people in front of them was utterly deafening. They couldn't hear what they were doing on stage. They had to guess what sound they were making from their instruments as all nine of their stage monitors were being drowned out by the screaming and whooping of the crowd. They also couldn't hear each other and they made the unfortunate decision to simply guess what each band member was doing, rather than to try and fix it.

Riff was inevitably out of time when he leaped into one of his blistering solos. DK and Plak were not playing their parts in synch, and Deet was losing time with the rest of the band himself, without being able to hear what they were doing. Trent was ad-libbing across all of their rhythms, and somehow making an impressive job of bridging the rhythms together with his voices. Les and Polly were watching from the side with anxious frowns on their faces, desperately worried about if it was going to get worse and if they should intervene. The bad start got worse as condensation began to form inside the replica of Trent and Riff's bodies, and they instantly short circuited. Within seconds they were both on the floor, staring at the audience with eerily open mouths as if they had suddenly died. The screams and whoops of excitement changed to screams of shock and horror. DK and Plak ran to help their replica band mates, but both suddenly froze on the spot as the crystals inside their metal casings froze solid. Deet stood up when he could see that the rest of the band were in trouble, but even he was struggling, as his internal systems triggered an emergency shutdown, after monitoring no change in the temperature during the considerable time they had been on Aquilos. So Trent and Riff were out of action, staring at the audience from the floor, Plak and DK were standing up but frozen solid and Deet was leaning forward from his stool, switched off and motionless.

Ray and Polly looked on in horror at what they could see in front of them, but simply looked at each other, wary of going on stage and making it look worse. The audience had stopped making any kind of screaming noise at this point, and apart from the odd heckle from a disgruntled Yakon at the back, they stood staring for a moment while stillness filled the stage. The sound of sparks firing off from the wet cables on stage alarmed the tech crew and brought out the occasional gasp from the audience.

"We need to turn off the breaker box." Ray snapped to Polly, in a panic.

"Yep, on it." She muttered, and ran off to the back of the stage to turn off the electrical current running through the stage.

Ray looked at the crowd which was starting to get restless. It wasn't long before they began booing in the direction of the stage and chanting lines like, 'Brown Yelp Needs Brown Help' and a more vicious chant of 'You're All Crap And Have Been For Years'. Then, when a couple of Yakons at the front suspected that these weren't The Brown Yelp Gang, then it was game over for the replicas. The couple at the front started muttering to themselves that this could only happen to machines. Their voices began to get louder as they surmised that if Trent and Riff had been electrocuted it would have looked totally different and they would have been carried off to hospital. The whole thing looked suspicious, and this couple were livid enough to push past the barrier and jump on stage. With the ferocity and spite of a scorned fanatic, they both pulled off the heads of Trent and Riff respectively, causing an enormous gasp of shock from the crowd. The Yakon who had decapitated the Trent replica's heads grabbed Trent's mic and addressed the crowd;

"This whole thing is a sham!" He shouted to the hundreds of thousands of Yakons in front of him. "Where is the band? Where is The Brown Yelp Gang? I didn't pay to see some robots pretending to be the band!"

The booing was now a cacophony of contempt.

310

"Where's the music? Where's the music? Where's the music?" The crowd chanted.

Polly and Les looked on as the crowd continued to chant their dissatisfaction. Then a section of the crowd to the left began repeatedly chanting 'Riff!' 'Riff!' 'Riff!' 'Riff!' on every beat of the overriding chant of 'Where's the music?'. Then, as that counterpoint developed, and both parts got locked in rhythmically, another section of the audience to the right began a slow chant of 'D...K!' 'D...K!' 'D...K' which lasted the same amount of time as the 'Where's the music' chant, but created a different rhythm from it, being made of less syllables. Les noticed this three part rhythmical and instantly turned to Polly with a huge grin; "This sounds amazing, doesn't it?"

"Actually, yes it does!" Polly said, starting to notice the musicality of the chants working together.

"I'm going to record it." Les said and instantly produced his mini-computer from his pocket and activated the microphone application. He recorded three minutes of the chant, knowing it would be good to have a few minutes of it so that he could release it as a single. Then he simply gathered his crew, and instructed them to put the replica bodies in their Green Room to be looked at later, while they disassemble the stage area and pack away their gear from the arena. As they did this, the crowd stopped the chanting and just returned to their booing and added name calling to the arena ambience. They also occasionally threw things at the stage crew as they packed up; bits of wood, concrete and even some merchandise they had bought from the arena before the show started.

It had been a total disaster. Once the crowd had dissipated and left the venue to complain about the gig in the media and on the information stream, Ray instructed his men to reboot the replica band. Eventually, they were all active again, and all thoroughly traumatised by the whole experience.

"I can't believe all that work we've done over the last few days has just blown up in our face!" The replica Riff whined.

"I am gutted. Totally and 100% gutted." Trent echoed Riff's disappointment.

"Who's bright idea wa – t - play on - planet this cold?!" Plak threw his arms in the air in disbelief as his words came out intermittently.

"Clearly someone who wasn't a robot!" Deet replied, understanding that their issue was unique to them.

"I can't belie - all - fected though." Riff was clearly also at risk of short circuiting again.

"The sooner we ge – this – net – better!" Trent shouted, unclearly.

"Utter – llocks." Deet said, heartbroken.

Meanwhile, the real Deet and his legitimate robot band mate Teddy had left The Swamp Beast and successfully reached DeMarco's main base of operations. There were a few guards there, but with a few punches from Teddy's metal fists, they were dealt with very smoothly and quickly. Deet just wanted them to get to the roof, where they knew their friends were at one point, even if they had moved. His plan was that they would decide how to proceed from there. The back stairwell that Jenken used to get to the front was accessible from the left side of the building, so Deet and Teddy ascended the stairs quietly but with a determined stride. It wasn't long before they had climbed the 440 spiral steps that led to the roof. They were exhausted, but safe.

As they looked up, once they were off the stairs and on the roof, they saw leaning against a wall to their right, Lilly, DK and Riff, all lined up together, clearly engrossed in a conversation. As the sound of Deet and Teddy approaching them disturbed their conversation, they lifted their heads up and saw who had arrived on the roof.

"Oh wow, you made it!" Riff said to Deet and Teddy as they approached.

"I am so glad you're still on the roof!" Deet said, relieved that his plan made some sense.

"We've been and come back!" DK said, proudly.

"Well some of us have." Lilly had a tone in her voice of someone that has been bored silly and sitting on their own feeling vulnerable and scared.

"Did you stay sitting there the whole time?" Teddy asked, compassionately, while pointing to where she was sitting.

"They thought it was too dangerous, and I was going to try to do something to help from up here."

"Did you?" Deet asked.

"No, I think I can only work with what I can see." Lilly said, having clearly thought about it for the entire time she had been waiting for DK and Riff to return.

"So where are Trent and Jenken?" Deet asked, still buzzing from seeing everyone.

"We're not sure. We lost Trent when we were almost caught by DeMarco's men."

"Whoah!" Deet gasped.

"Yeah, it was close." DK added. "We don't know what's happened to Jenken either..."

Deet and Teddy looked shocked and upset.

"...although he was just going over there to tell DeMarco that he had his money, so he's probably been fine."

"That's true." Deet agreed. "I bet DeMarco was really happy to get his money back."

They all laughed and sat down on the comforting anonymity of the rooftop. They could all feel each other's relief that they were together and had possibly made some progress. Deet and Teddy brought everyone up to speed on their meeting with Dramatic Spleen, and the audience reaction. They topped their story with the news that they had secured a slot at The Great Big Beat Festival. Riff and

DK told everyone about the huge humanoid machine that they had found on the bottom floor of the base. They began to discuss possibilities of what they could do, when Lilly interrupted them after one of her telepathic trances.

"They're here." She said, dramatically.

"Who's here?" Deet asked.

"Penny, Aria and two other people that I don't think you know."

"Where? On the roof?" DK asked, frowning in surprise.

"No, they are about half an hour away from here by foot. I have let Penny know where we are and how to get up here."

The others murmured their approval.

"Let's wait for them here, and then we can have a better plan of action with all of us together." Lilly suggested.

"All of us except Trent and Jenken!" Riff said, anxiously.

"True...but nearly all of us!" Teddy remarked with her typical optimism.

"We won't have to wait long." Lilly added, thinking about her sister being so close.

The five friends all waited patiently and relatively quietly on the roof for what seemed to them to be hours, but was in fact less than an hour. Their faces lit up and they all stood for attention when Aria, Ursulas, Nod and Penny appeared at the stairs that led down the back of the base. Lilly and Penny ran up to each other and embraced. Riff walked

315

directly toward Aria but slowed down as he got closer and saw that she looked more like a Movine than a Denuvian. "What's happened to you?" Riff said, his head in a spin from seeing the love of his life so...Movine.

"It was a split second decision."Aria replied. "I'm hoping to reverse it, once this is over."

"Yeah, I'm up for that!" Riff agreed.

"Watch it mate, you're insinuating that there's something wrong with my looks." DK was not impressed by the implications of their conversation.

"I'm sorry DK. You are beautiful and there are many beautiful Movines in the Lantrick system, but I am a Denuvian and should really look like one." Aria was affectionate, but blunt.

"Yeah," Riff added needlessly. "I got off with a Denuvian didn't I?"

"Well, whatever you look like, I'm glad you're safe Aria." Deet declared, cutting through the bickering around him.

"Where are Trent and Jenken?" Ursulas asked.

"Who's this?" Deet asked, to anyone that was listening.

"That's Ursulas!" Riff smiled, remembering meeting her to buy the Dengen plant off of her on Corsylia before they got mixed up with Ray and DeMarco.

"Oh, this is the famous Ursulas!" Deet replied, genuinely feeling honoured to meet her.

"- or infamous!" Ursulas added, almost mocking her own notoriety.

"Indeed. It's a pleasure to meet you." Deet bowed as he greeted her directly.

"My pleasure entirely. I have been a fan of Trent's band for years."

"Trent's band?" Riff, DK and Deet shouted this in unison.

"Err...you know what I mean." Ursulas was amused by their offence, but brushed it off with her usual domineering arrogance. "Anyway, where are Trent and Jenken?"

"We don't quite know yet, but we think Jenken will just leave by the front door with a pat on the back from Carlo DeMarco once he tells them that his got his money." DK said chirpily.

"You don't ever clear a debt from Carlo DeMarco." Ursulas said, ominously.

The rest of the band on the roof looked at each other with dread.

"Well, we are hoping that it's OK now, anyway." Deet broke the silence. "That should be something less to worry about."

"Why are you here anyway?" Riff turned to Ursulas.

"Myself and Nod are here," Nod subtly waved at them on cue, "because you're all going after DeMarco. I cannot resist that as he's been making all sorts of demands on me over the last few years and if he's going down, I want to be there helping."

The band all looked surprised and nodded to each other, pleased for the support.

"Glad to have you on board!" Riff replied.

"So what do we do about Trent and Jenken?" Deet said, returning to a more proactive thread in the conversation.

"I say, if Jenken came from the roof, and you say it will be all good from DeMarco's perspective," Ursulas suggested, "then we just wait and he'll come back up here, surely?"

"That was the agreement." Deet replied, supporting the idea. "If we stay here, I think we could end up all together again once they get out."

"Then we have strict instructions from Ray to get back to Bragal to see a guy called Dr Schoenberg." Ursulas added.

"Dr Schoenberg?" Deet repeated.

"Yes, Dr Schoenberg. He's going to help us defeat DeMarco, apparently."

"Nice." Deet replied.

"So we wait?" Riff asked for clarification.

"We wait." Deet said, firmly.

"How long for?" Riff asked for clarification.

"Until Trent and Jenken appear." Deet said, firmly.

"Which is fine." Ursulas added, firmly.

"Absolutely." Riff agreed.

There was a moment of silence.

"Is it just me?" Riff broke the silence, "or is it weird seeing Lilly and Penny together, looking like the exact same person, twice?"

Trent and Jenken were now in DeMarco's hands. They had reluctantly agreed to play at his festival for some kind of fabricated extension of the debt that Jenken owed. Jenken had learned about DeMarco's plan for his 'Great Remix' and was hoping the others had information that would complete the whole picture. Trent was happy to be alive, and was impressed by the power so effortlessly wielded by DeMarco in every encounter he witnessed. His mind was still firmly on the mission, however, and his slight respect for DeMarco's success didn't waiver his resolve. He was hoping for a reunion with the rest of the band as soon as he had left the building. As they were ushered out of the main base by DeMarco's Bask lizard engineers, they waited for the engineer to obliviously walk back into the main base, and then made their u-turn back to the side of the building to find the stairwell at the back; the stairwell that Jenken had originally descended when he arrived.

"I think we're OK now." Jenken whispered to Trent as they walked along the wall toward the stairwell.

Trent went to answer, but his side heads slapped his hands over his mouth, so the intended reply became a nonsensical mumble.

"Fair enough." Jenken said, acknowledging the validity of what the side heads had done.

They crept up the stairwell at the back right hand side of the huge building. It took them a good ten minutes but once they reached the top step they were elated to see DK,

Deet, Riff, Lilly, Teddy, Ursulas, a doppelganger of Lilly's that they assumed was Penny and a couple of figures they didn't recognise. Their waiting friends hadn't noticed them, as they had decided to pass the time on the roof with an intense game of 'identify the lint' which had them totally preoccupied and unaware of Trent and Jenken's arrival on the roof.

Trent and Jenken watched their friends for a few minutes, and then coughed loudly. There was no response. Trent coughed in three part harmony. That got their attention. "OH MY!" DK shouted, louder than the agreed volume, and ran toward Trent.

The rest of the band, and the gangsters that were with them, all stood up immediately, grinning on seeing their particular circle complete. Trent couldn't help but ask Ursulas what she was doing there;

"What are you doing here?" Trent was standing only a few feet away from her.

"She's with us." Deet answered. Trent kept his gaze on Ursulas.

"I'm with you." She replied, still carrying her usual swagger of confidence.

"Why?" Trent asked, not surprisingly.

"Cos DeMarco is a complete wazzock!" She never minced her words. Her sharp tone spoke volumes about her contempt for DeMarco and his practices. "I'm tired of giving him money or listening to him making up favours that I owe him."

"Fair enough." Trent knew her well and was aware of some of the ways DeMarco had manipulated her in the past.

"Well, we're all here, then!" Jenken smiled at them, while whispering these happy words.

"Except Plak." DK said, instantly bringing the tone back to a darker, reflective mood.

"This is true." Aria replied. "He is happy though. He is safe and happy. He wanted to start afresh."

"With some flute playing hippy Bask lizard." Ursulas scoffed. "I bet none of us saw that coming!" Ursulas was enjoying that reminder, having no sentimental connection with Plak, aside from loving the band's music.

"Well, I don't think we should stay up here much longer." Aria interrupted. "We need to get back to Bragal."

"We're going back to Bragal?" Jenken almost raised his voice, in shock.

"Ray wants us to see some guy called Dr Schoenberg."

"Dr Schoenberg?" Trent asked, as if he hadn't heard the words.

"Yeah. Dr Schoenberg. He's going to give us stuff I think." Aria wasn't sure but thought she would give them the extra information anyway.

"How are we going to get back to Bragal?" Jenken asked, to anyone that was listening.

"We left our shuttle back at the swamp. It's not far from here, it won't take us long." Aria had a determined, professional proactive tone to her voice as she said this.

"About half an hour." Teddy said, having done that journey earlier in the night.

"I think there's a risk we may be seen going in the direction of the swamp, guys." Riff said, quite correctly.

"That's a fair point, Riff." Jenken was concerned, and desperately concentrating his thoughts on not being spotted.

"I have an answer though." Riff said. They all looked at him, expectantly. "I got out of that base with some careful use of a box that I was in. I literally jumped a few feet at a time, and if anyone turned around, they just saw a box, on its own, just minding its own business."

Riff was exhilarated by the thought that the band might use his idea and grinned at them proudly while they processed his reaction.

"We need a load of metal boxes then...which we don't have." Deet was happy to destroy Riff's moment.

"There's a line of metal bins by the wall." Trent supported his closest band mate with more material for their planning.

"Yeah, we saw them as we came up." Jenken had returned to the 'trying to get other people that aren't excited at all, excited' tone of voice.

"What do you think guys?" Riff looked to the others.
"Shall we try it?"

"I think we should stick together now, whether we try it or not." Aria suggested. They all nodded and mumbled in agreement.

"Let's try it." Deet let out his assertive demand for the next stage of their escape with no objection from the others. They carefully and quietly exited the main base via the stairwell at the back, and promptly slipped inside the metal bins, to initiate their disguised escape. DeMarco kept such a tight grip on the reins in that base of operations that nobody had the thought or chance to distract themselves from their work, and therefore didn't suspect a thing when eleven bins slowly moved a few inches at a time, toward the other side of the road and in the direction of the swamp. Progress was slow but uninterrupted. Teddy's suggestion of thirty minutes was extended by attempts at extreme stealth. All eleven bins were safely rooted in the boggy swamp water, as the eleven occupants rose out of the bins and stepped onto the murky, fetid swamp. Hiding in plain sight was the shuttle that Aria had landed earlier. They all stared at the shuttle, grinning, relieved to be leaving Praxis 7, but aware that they'd be back soon enough. Aria opted to pilot the shuttle on the back journey and the rest of them found a seat to sit in and strapped themselves in.

"Let's find out who this Dr Schoenberg is!" Aria shouted, as the shuttle rose above the ground and flew out of Praxim

7's atmosphere and toward Bragal. They all replied with variations of agreement and motivational cheering. They knew they had just beaten the odds and had survived a far more complex and dangerous situation than any live gig or studio recording they had experienced.

While they were on the shuttle's return journey, Jenken logged onto the information stream, to see how the box set was doing, and was captivated by the sensational story of The 'fake' Brown Yelp Gang. It was all over the information stream. Commentators making reports about it, fans discussing their dismay at The Brown Yelp Gang being fake, celebrity pundits giving out opinions about what The Brown Yelp Gang were doing while this fake band were in operation, and other musicians from other bands giving long accounts and tributes of the band's influence on them.

"Guys, this is priceless." Jenken looked around to get their attention.

The rest of the occupants of the shuttle, besides Riff, all gathered around Jenken's communications tablet, and stared in awe at the fake band's undoing. Riff had immediately slipped into his own reality, separated from his band mates as he played air guitar to the music that was floating around his mind. The occasional snigger, gasp of surprise, outright laughter and knowing smile passed through the people gathered around Jenken's device. Riff was curious, having spotted a few sniggers and gasps as he played air guitar. He stopped for a moment and looked directly at Trent.

"What's happening over there that's got you all fixed on that thing?" Riff gestured to the device Jenken was holding.

"It's the fake Brown Yelp Gang."

"Fake Brown Yelp Gang?" Riff's memory was selective at best; Trent didn't bother explaining.

"They've screwed up now." He was beaming with relief and an overall feeling of superiority, over the robot replicas.

"What did they do?" Riff asked, shouting across the shuttle. "Did they do a drum solo or something?" Riff smiled as he asked this facetious question.

"They played on Aquilos!" Trent replied, also shouting across the shuttle.

"They played on Aquilos?" Aria shouted back, from the pilot's chair in the cockpit.

"Yes!" All three Trent heads shouted for maximum volume.

"That's an ice planet isn't it?" Riff frowned.

"Yep. I reckon they short circuited!" Trent was almost singing his words as he tried to suppress his joy. "They're no threat now."

"This could be bad for us." Jenken said, rarely acting like a manager. "We need to get in front of a camera and upload something to the information stream."

"Yeah." They all agreed.

"As soon as possible." Jenken added.

"His soon is passable?" Riff looked confused and a little lost.

"Yes. As soon as possible." Jenken repeated.

"Who's soon?" Riff asked, still confused.

They all deliberately ignored him.

SECOND SET

SECOND SET

Chapter Fourteen

Mike Finnegan spent his life collecting music and anything related to music. His 58 years on Earth were spent going to record fairs, festivals, band in store appearances and countless gigs. All of his money was spent on music; he regularly took a shuttle away from his home on New Earth, to travel to several different star systems, to find his favourite bands. Elastic music had become a curiosity for him, but it didn't really get big on New Earth, so Mike went as far as the Zappanite System to hear it performed live. He collected anything and everything, from the latest music software that downloaded directly to your feet to intensify the dancing, to the flaky nostrils of the celebrated late singer, Shermanly Berman. Despite his enormous collection of every genre and sub-genre of music from a dozen different star systems, The Brown Yelp Gang were his favourites. He had downloaded Trent's box set of rarities the moment it was on the market, and listened to every track at double the speed so that he could hear it quicker. You couldn't fault his dedication and love for the band.

This is why it was odd that he couldn't see the indications in his new favourite Brown Yelp release, "BYG at Vestrell City", that these were imposters; robot replicas that sounded like...robot replicas. It could be that his hysterical enthusiasm was a blind spot when it came to The Brown Yelp Gang. Whatever the reason, Mike Finnegan lapped up this new release and played it until his ears were ensnared into a relentlessly intense loop of involuntary music imagery that knocked him unconscious for hours. When he came to, he declared to the nobody that was in his room, that 'THIS IS THE BEST THING THE BROWN YELP GANG HAVE EVER DONE!' with a frenzied scream. His 83 year old mother panicked from the ground floor and ran up to his room immediately; "Are you okay, Mike?" She peered her head around the room to see him staring at the ceiling with wild eyes. "Mother, I have been touched by the light." He said, barely managing to articulate his feelings about the new album. "Oh, OK. That's nice." Mike's mother was happily reassured with the comment that she didn't need to investigate. She retreated and closed the door behind her as she went back downstairs.

Mike looked at his music memorabilia as it stared back at him along the walls and across the floor of his room. He was grinning from one side of his face to the other, mumbling 'They've done it again' to himself as he mentally reassessed each Brown Yelp album from best to worst in his head.

The next day he found out they were robots and was utterly speechless.

Dr Schoenberg lived in a 40 foot tall, artificially reinforced concrete castle, towering above the City walls of Bragal's neighbouring town of Dippel. He wasn't bothered by the townsfolk of Dippel, or the larger area of Corsyllia in general, but was occasionally interrupted by Ray's 'goons' as he called them, who were now frequent visitors giving him new instructions from Ray, his latest benefactor for his unnatural experiments. Before Ray had managed to snare Dr Schoenberg in his clutches, the unhinged scientist was exclusively creating different crossbreeds of species from different worlds in his laboratory. Now he feels like he spends more precious time creating new types of weapons for Ray's whimsical fancy. Over the last few months, Ray had been giving Schoenberg instructions on some weapons he wanted for a particular project he was working on. The appearance of The Brown Yelp Gang walking toward the castle portcullis gave Dr Schoenberg clarity on the nature of those new weapons and why he was asked to make them.

"This looks epic!" DK stared up at the walls of the castle, in awe of the majesty of scale soaring above him.

"It's a bloody castle! An actual, bloody castle!" Riff echoed DK's astonishment.

They all paused for a moment on the town side of the castle portcullis. Even Ursulas, who was the most cynical among them, found it awe-inspiring. They watched in silence as birds flew off the highest turrets and small rodents scurried across the castle grounds beyond the portcullis.

"So this Dr Sternblood lives here?" Riff turned to the others, as if he wasn't quite sure why he was there.

"Schoenberg, mate." Trent corrected.

"Schoenberg?" Riff looked at him for clarification.

"Yeah."

"Is that the same as the..." Riff tried to recall where he had the heard the name before.

"The wine on Dodecaphonia VI." Ursulas interrupted. "Same name."

"Urgh!" Deet yelled. "That wine is disgusting."

"Yeah, makes my eyes water." DK added.

"Stays in your taste buds for months!" Ursulas agreed.

"Well, we're not going to see the wine; we're going to see some kind of doctor here." Jenken attempted to refocus the group.

"I guess he's going to give us some kind of medical help?" DK pondered.

"Whatever he's going to do, it's only 3 days until the big Festival that we're playing at." Teddy was straight to the point and practical as ever.

"So do we just walk into the courtyard?" Trent asked, unfamiliar with castle etiquette. "Is there a doorbell?"

"Apparently centuries ago people used to get in by hurling flaming objects at the walls with trebuchets, battering the portcullis with a huge battering ram and scaling the walls to get over the sides of the castle." Jenken replied.

"I don't want to do that!" Riff frowned.

"That looks like an important door there." Deet had found a large wooden door to the left as you walked through the courtyard and was pointing to it as he spoke.

"Nice spotting Deet!" Jenken smiled, and began to walk through the portcullis entrance and to the left, toward the door.

"This is quite something." Aria gasped as she looked around the beautiful, ornate courtyard.

"It really is quite calming." Ursulas replied, softly, as if enchanted by the flora around her and the sounds of the birds singing across the castle walls.

"Don't stay here long then," Nod replied. "You'll go all soft."

"Aw, she's a softie really." Trent said, then immediately regretted it when Ursulas punched his genital area mercilessly and suddenly without cause.

The rest of the company waited for Trent to stand up again, his eyes leaking through the pain, but his tongue successfully silenced. Then, once they were all on their feet and ready to face whatever was in the castle, Jenken grabbed the over scaled metal ring attached to the door knocker on the door in front of them and knocked three times. They waited a moment to see if there was any response, and when there didn't seem to be one, Jenken tried again, this time with more force given to the knocks. A distant voice sounded like it came from inside the house, shouting "all right, all right, no need to get like that, I'm on my way!"

The band all looked at each other, pleased to hear a response but still with no idea who or what might be on the other side of the door. Several latches were heard being unbolted from the other side of the door, as the Brown Yelp collective waited patiently outside. It seemed to take far longer than it needed to, then the door slowly swung open and standing before them, or rather stooping before them was a small man with bulbous head and thin strands of hair drooping past his shoulders, looking up at them from his diminutive position. His eyes bulged in a seemingly unnatural way as his head darted back and forth across the people in front of him.

"Who are you?" He snapped, abruptly.

"Oh, we have been sent by Ray, from Bragal." Jenken began, while the other members of his company stared awkwardly at the stooping man.

"Ray?" The man queried, almost to himself.

"We are The Brown Yelp Gang!" Riff declared, expecting a look of joy from the man at the door, but receiving instead a cold stare of indifference.

"We were told to come here to see Dr Schoenberg." Aria added, hoping to move their conversation forward.

"The doctor is in." The man at the door replied.

"What is your name, sir?" DK asked, trying to be polite.

"I am your humble servant, Stravinsky." The man bowed as he said this.

"Good day to you, Stravinsky. It is so very nice to meet you." DK replied, being overly formal and laying on a thick accent that no-one could particularly place to an era or planet. His band mates stared at him as if he was having an asthma attack. DK shrugged and smiled at Stravinsky, maintaining the polite pleasantries.

"You too, I guess." Stravinsky replied. "I will see if the master will see you. Please take a seat here while I check." Stravinsky gestured to a circle of large, leather chairs to the right of the door. Stravinsky shuffled off to the left, walking with a limp and what appeared to be a permanent arched back.

The band took up Stravinsky's offer and found a seat amongst the leather chairs in front of them. They all sank into them, smiling with an optimism that betrayed the meandering way they reached this point in their tour. They didn't say anything as they were on high alert for greeting this doctor that Ray had sent them to find. Riff hummed some guitar melodies in his head, but this was at an extremely low volume level. The others didn't object or interfere; they were aware that Riff would have been struggling to stay seated without a guitar in his hand.

After about eight minutes of quiet waiting, a tall thin man with dishevelled, grey hair sprouting from a shiny bald head and round rimmed glasses appeared from the left corridor. Stravinsky was behind him, looking up at the tall, thin man with reverence.

"So, you're The Brown Yelp Gang then?" The tall man said, wiping his hands on the side of his long, white coat as he spoke.

"We are." Jenken said, pleased to be making progress at last.

"I am Dr Schoenberg." The tall man said, moving closer to the band and extending his right arm out to shake their hands.

They all politely shook his hand, smiling and silently nodding in respect to their host.

"Would you all like a drink?" Dr Schoenberg asked, softly. They all nodded, humbly.

"Rannick Juice?" The doctor offered.

"That would be marvellous." Jenken replied. He then looked around him and his companions all nodded to him. "For everyone please."

"Of course. Once you've had a bit of Rannick Juice, I will show you to my lab."

"Can I ask what you do, here?" Jenken was straight to the point. "We were sent here by Ray, but we don't know why yet."

"You're doing some kind of job for him, yes?" He knew the answer.

"Yes, that's right."

"I can help you with this job." The doctor spoke with his head bowed slightly and his eyes peering over his glasses.

"That's lovely, thank you." Jenken continued. "What kind of help?"

"You are a nervous bunch aren't you?" The doctor sniggered. "Follow me through here."

He led them to the left, and down the corridor that he had appeared from, with Stravinsky shuffling along behind the band. After walking for about sixty yards, they reached an elevator. Dr Schoenberg halted for a moment, and turned around to the Brown Yelp collective;

"I am about to take you to my secret laboratory. The things you see there are not to be discussed with anyone, even if you get caught dosed up to your eyeballs in Pulling Water, or dangling off a flat planet with the threat of being thrown off." There was a slight pause, as the companions attempted to process what the doctor had said.

"Understood?" His tone was firm but polite.

"Of course." They all mumbled in agreement to Jenken's words of compliance.

"Okay." The doctor replied. "Here we go then. You're going to love this."

The doctor then stepped into the elevator and beckoned the others in with his right arm. The Brown Yelp collective, and Stravinsky behind them, all crammed inside the elevator, jostling for room in a space built for smaller numbers. The elevator immediately dropped down into the lower chasms of the deep shaft that led to the doctor's laboratory. As they descended, a low hum was heard, which had almost every head in the elevator turning round to find the source. The band rolled their eyes in amusement as they realised Riff was humming the melody of 'Down, down into your crevice' as the elevator burrowed further into the depths of the castle grounds. Two hundred feet below the surface of Corsylia, the elevator came to an abrupt halt, and the doctor stepped out into his laboratory. The Brown Yelp collective did not see the landing coming, so stood up from their fall, dusted themselves down and stepped out of the elevator and into the laboratory. They were surrounded by heating apparatus, unfinished experiments, crates and boxes of scientific instruments and equipment and, eerily, dozens of naked dead bodies. These bodies varied in species and state of decay. Each one of them repelled the more innocent Brown Yelp collective, and sometimes slowed their journey through the laboratory when their curiosity got the better of them. They hurried past the bodies and looked to the doctor, who had entered a code on a keypad besides another door, which he promptly opened. He then switched on the lights to the room, and extended his arms in a theatrical gesture to add drama to their already dramatic day.

"Welcome to my lab!" Dr Schoenberg was clearly excited to show them his work. "Here you will get what you need in your conflict with Carlo DeMarco."

The band all muttered interest in Schoenberg's knowledge of their mission.

"Ray has told me everything." Schoenberg stated. "So I am going to give you instruments that will give you great power."

"Sounds interesting." Riff was the first to respond.

"Lazy Riff. Have a look at this." Doctor Schoenberg opened up a crate near him and lifted a guitar out from inside it. He threw Riff the guitar gently but with enough force that Riff panicked for a moment as it glided through the air. He was used to treating guitars like religious objects, so his heart skipped a beat as he concentrated on catching the unfamiliar guitar. Being an expert on anything guitar related, Riff inspected it carefully to try to recognise the company that made it, or the model or any clue to any special feature it might have; he was happy to admit that he'd never seen a guitar that would have been used to defeat a gangster so he was approaching this situation with an open mind. As he turned the guitar over and looked at the underside of the body work, he attached the untied part of the strap to the guitar and placed it around his neck.

"Looking good, Riff." DK said, beginning to get excited about this encounter.

Riff played the first chords of 'How is your hair' on the unusually light guitar and looked up, smiling to the doctor.

"Yeah, nice guitar."

"It's not even plugged in, Riff." Dr Schoenberg could sense that Riff was nervous. "Let me help you with that."

Schoenberg plugged the guitar into an amplifier that was beside the crate filled with guitars.

"Now play it!" Schoenberg was grinning.

"Whoah, that's nice!" Riff said as he played a quick medley of his favourite Brown Yelp songs, then nodded to Schoenberg; "This is a lovely guitar. It plays well and feels very comfortable."

"That's not all it can do." Schoenberg replied, grinning even more. "Go on, squeeze the guitar." Schoenberg added. "As hard as you can."

Riff squeezed the guitar, as instructed. A small missile immediately flew out of the guitar from the top of the headstock at an astonishing speed and hit Dr Schoenberg's ceramic Ragget collection. They all exploded with dramatic disarray, sharp edges shooting past the band like daggers being thrown directly at them and with no trace of the Ragget shape left in any of the figurines.

"Oh, drat." Schoenberg cursed. "I should have moved them."

"Whoah! This is cosmic!" Riff was dumbfounded and stared in awe at the headstock of his new guitar, where the missiles were shot from. The rest of the band stared with him, and looked back at Dr Schoenberg.

"So, we're going to be carrying weapons when we play the big gig?" Aria asked, trying to hide her growing excitement.

"If you've got a big gig, yes." Schoenberg stated. "I don't know what you're using them for, but Ray told me to prepare you for using them." He was talking straight, and with the gravitas that comes from being threatened by Ray's 'goons'. He reached behind him and grabbed what looked like a flute from another crate.

"Here, Aria." He answered her question by addressing her with her new instrument. "Grab this." He threw the flute at her gently, so that she could catch it easily.

Aria inspected the flute, with typical fascination, but glanced back with widened eyes of expectation at the doctor after believing it to be just a flute.

"How did you know I am Aria?" She asked, still painfully aware that she didn't look like a Denuvian priestess and looked more like a Movine musician.

"I watched you all come in through my x-ray detector across the portcullis. That showed me exactly what or who you were." Schoenberg was particularly proud of this device that he had spread across the entrance to the castle.

"So you saw me naked?" Aria was a little offended.

"No, not at all. I did know straight away that you were only a Movine in disguise. I noticed your Denuvian abundance of ribs and the Denuvian way your bones fan out at the top to give you those broad shoulders."

"Impressive." Aria replied, genuinely impressed.

"Play me a melody from 'I shouldn't have said it with an accent', and make sure the other end is pointing upwards as you play."

Aria gave him a look of disbelief then crouched down, pressed the plate against her bottom, adjusted the angle of the rest of the flute so it was pointing away from the others, and squeezed air into the sound hole. She loved playing the melody of 'I shouldn't have said it with an accent' and often closed her eyes as she relished the beauty of the melody for the song. This time she closed her eyes and played the melody smiling as she blew. She blissfully missed the rockets shooting out from the foot joint end of the flute, and the subsequent damage to the castle wall. The rest of the band were speechless, having never seen a flute breach a wall like that. Aria, opening her eyes and looking to her right to the rockets' devastation, was apologetic and humbled.

"I am so sorry about your wall. I just played the song."

"It is fine, Aria. You weren't to know. Repairing the castle walls is something I actually quite enjoy, and me and Stravinsky here," he gestured to his hunched assistant Stravinsky, "get a lot done in a day, so it's fine." Schoenberg was sincere and still smiling.

"Next, I will introduce Trent to his new microphones." Schoenberg was on a roll now, delving into other crates around him to find the next piece of weaponry for the band. "You're going to like this, my Calpian warbler." Schoenberg teased, not particularly politely.

Trent's three heads couldn't help themselves. They all howled, as if calling to the night, overcome with excitement. Schoenberg dived into a different crate and scattered hundreds of pieces of polystyrene packaging foam across the room as he felt inside it. A few seconds later he had produced a microphone from the crate and handed it to the expectant lead singer.

"These are special microphones." Schoenberg began. "As you see, they look very similar to the microphones you are used to using, but with a slightly longer tube where you hold it." The doctor pointed to the microphone as he spoke. "The beauty here is that these microphones will act as fantastic blowguns for short range missiles that will travel beyond 70 miles per hour at their unfortunate target." Trent took hold of the mic and inspected it; much the way that Aria had with the flute a few moments before. He then adjusted his heads, as he typically would, to share the mic, and sang into the spherical grille of the mic as it he had a Brown Yelp fan in front of him. It felt very comfortable, and Trent was confident that it worked, if attached to an XLR lead and fed into a mixing desk for amplification. As it was, it wasn't attached to anything, and no amplification occurred. Trent looked at Schoenberg with a quizzical eye.

"You need to flip it up in the air and imagine it's a blowdart, with poisonous darts inside to fire through the end of the tube."

Trent looked at Schoenberg again, with hesitation.

"It's a cordless mic. It works without an XLR lead. Please flip the mic over and blow into it."

Trent lifted the smallest end of the microphone away from anybody in front of him, and blew into the metal grille on the performance end of the mic. At an astonishing speed, darts flew out of the tube of the mic and embedded into the castle wall in front of them. As the darts pierced the wall, Schoenberg elaborated on what he had given Trent; "Trent, these microphones will be a great asset in your arsenal. You will do great damage with these weapons. Once that penetration had occurred, and you are ready for the last moment in your attack, then the poison filters through the flesh of the victim and corrupts the blood with a powerful poison that kills the victim in seconds."

This was very different to their usual shopping trip to update their gear.

"WOW!" The right head replied. "So we have these instruments with us at all times?"

"Do you sleep with your instruments?" Schoenberg genuinely didn't know the correct answer to this query on etiquette.

"Of course!" Riff shouted, now recovered from the shock of his new missile launching guitar.

"Well, then you will have your instruments with you at all times."

"Fair enough. Thank you Doc." Riff smiled.

"Have we got new weapons?" DK asked, politely and breathlessly.

"Hmmm..." the man said, mysteriously. "The last remaining members of The Brown Yelp Gang are all performers that use their own bodies as weapons."

They all nodded in agreement.

"Deet, you have your amazing Hurl anatomy, and beat the inside of the lining of your stomach better than any percussionist I know. DK, your snout has produced some of my favourite melodies over the years. Both of you are absolutely stunning on stage, manipulating your bodies to great effect during the songs. I could not issue you with more upgraded weapons, as your instrument is your body. So what I have done instead is to give you all an appointment tomorrow morning. The plan of action tomorrow will be to get rid of Aria's Movine features, work through any cosmetic surgery requests you might have and give your musical bodies an overhaul."

"What kind of overhaul?" Deet had thoughts of nightmarish nips and tucks being given to his body, especially with the eerie atmosphere in the castle.

"Don't panic, Mr Deet." Schoenberg was genuinely comforting. "You won't feel the after effects of the overhaul, and will, at some point, realise that your body has been enhanced."

DK and Deet's eyebrows leapt up in shock.

"So we're staying overnight?" Jenken interjected.

"Oh yes, I cannot allow you to leave without my special treat."

The band looked at each other, internally rolling their eyes at another delay that they cannot influence.

"Ooh, a special treat!" Trent's heads shouted in unison, faking a burst of excitement.

"For now, I would like you, Trent, Riff and Aria, to follow Stravinsky here to the first floor where he will show you your sleeping quarters." Schoenberg was looking directly at them as he spoke. "Spend some time getting used to these instruments before you settle for your night's sleep."

Stravinsky grinned and shuffled off toward a flight of stairs at the back, beckoning Trent, Aria and Riff to follow him.

"For you," Schoenberg continued, turning to DK and Deet, "I need you to stay here and prepare yourself for your enhancement tomorrow."

"What kind of preparations do we need to make?" Deet asked, a little anxiously.

"I need you to play these audio files of Hurl drumming and centre yourself into a meditative state." Schoenberg gave Deet a data card with the audio files on it.

"Oh, that sounds easy," replied the one native of Hurl.

"Your bodies will be easier to stretch and mould if your soul is more floppy."

"Of course." Deet bowed, instinctively.

"A floppy soul is ripe for moulding." DK couldn't help but quote the elders of Hurl.

"Indeed. So please concentrate on that through the night and we'll have you primed and ready for action tomorrow." Schoenberg was almost buoyant in his tone, secretly excited to work on their bodies in the morning.

Stravinsky had shuffled back into the room again, after showing the others their sleeping quarters. He beckoned DK and Deet to follow him, and took them to a peaceful area at the back left of the room that was filled with sensory devices that acted as natural psychotropic enhancements.

Then Dr Schoenberg looked at Lilly and Penny.

"You two are extremely special." He began. "When Ray told me about you two, I was so excited to meet you."

"Urgh, that's creepy." Lilly said with disgust.

"Yeah, you know we're young girls right?" Penny added. They both simultaneously and with mirrored movement faked a vomiting action.

"I want to work on your minds." Schoenberg said, ominously.

"You better not harm these girls." Ursulas interrupted his creepy delight in what he was going to do with the girls.

"Yeah, I'll rip this place apart if they get harmed." Nod added a direct threat to add weight to their show of force.

"You don't need to worry." Schoenberg wasn't fazed by their bravado. "They will be safe. The procedure will be painless and the effect will be temporary."

"Hmmm...." Ursulas stared at him distrustingly, having inadvertently developed a hitherto hidden maternal streak. "Their telepathic powers and ability to control the objects in a room will become quite a spectacle."

Lilly and Penny looked at each other, and then looked at Ursulas and Nod, then back at Dr Schoenberg.

"I just need you two to sit up there, so we can start the operations..." Schoenberg gestured to the tables in the centre of the room, surrounded by medical instruments and glaring directional lights hovering over the tables.

"What are we supposed to do?" Ursulas asked, impatiently and still with little trust.

"You two can..." Schoenberg thought for a moment "...go through that door there behind you and make these girls something to eat." He waved his arm to indicate the door behind them. "Tomorrow is a big day for them both."

The next morning, DeMarco was on the site of The Great Big Beat Festival for an update from his extensive team erecting the stages and overseeing the other parts of the festival being set up. This was a special event for DeMarco, as this wasn't just a music festival, but the moment when he takes over Praxim 7 and begins his rule of the star system. He had been buzzing with excitement for weeks, running through scenarios in his head and ordering his security guards to re-enact the takeover while he relishes the moment. They weren't particularly feeling it, and wouldn't be getting awards for their acting, but they complied anyway, as what DeMarco wanted was always obeyed unconditionally by his guards.

He had planned out the festival meticulously; ironing out the details with his team from the Praxim tourist and bakery board. Parking for the shuttles and public transport vehicles coming through the festival was all done on one section at the back of the site. Multi-storey platforms were erected so that the shuttles would use up the same space as the ground vehicles. Toilets were more complicated as different species had different requirements. Most of the humanoid visitors would be fine with toilets like the New Earth style facilities. Others, however, like the 'Flushing Cascader" tribe from the far side of Praxim 7 would simply flood a conventional latrine, so DeMarco fitted special facilities in the toilet so that they could aim at the steaming evaporation chambers sizzling away at the right of the main food stalls. The food stalls had every conceivable type of food that any of the visiting species would like. DeMarco never shied away from controversy, and some of the food stalls had species being cooked that were also visiting customers. He was resolutely indifferent to the complaints he would get from the offended clientele. For him, it was all about variety, and suiting all his visitors' tastes.

Ultimately, this time, the minor details of his event were a little academic as he was intending to massacre his visitors and trash the whole site as a demonstration of his new weapon. The festival was really just a chance to begin his despotic reign over Praxim 7. His team knew this, but always had pride in their work...and besides, the big climax of the festival wouldn't work if there was any suspicion of a bloodbath.

The three experimental musicians from Dramatic Spleen were DeMarco's main collaborators for setting up the stages and running the day on a minute-by-minute basis. They had no idea of his overall plan for world domination, and simply couldn't wait to get on stage just before the main act, The Brown Yelp Gang. They had set their gear up and were running sound checks, for the fun of it, even though it was still 2 days to go before the gates were open and the visitors were welcomed on site. They were a little distracted by the armed Bask lizard guards that were stationed around the site, especially so long before the event started, but trusted DeMarco in a way that smacked of either ignorant sycophancy, or blind optimism. Either way, they weren't suspicious of any foul play that might occur, and were more concerned about any surprises in the weather.

This was partly due to the peculiar weather of Praxim 7. For most of the 485 days of the solar cycle the weather on Praxim 7 was predictable. Whatever the atmospheric conditions were as the day started were, more often than not, conditions for the weather for most of the day. There were, however, the occasional exceptional day, usually during the hottest days, when sudden bursts of acid rain would fall from the sky at a rapid velocity that made it difficult to avoid, and would cause several deaths every year on Praxim 7. These days were nicknamed 'Stay at home days', as most people ran home as soon as there was a hint of a sudden downpour. Lobbyists have campaigned for years to get the administration of Praxim 7 to look into links between industrial activity and the acid rain anomalies, a conflict of interest results in a ruling that only when half of the population of Praxim 7 are killed by the rain, will they look into it. Business experts agree that it needs to be affecting a substantial proportion of the population before it becomes a serious issue. For festival organisers, it is standard procedure to erect canopies across the site that can withstand the acid, in case of this sulphuric attack happening during the event. Dramatic Spleen were excellent organisers and efficiently set the stage rigging up, as well as the acid canopies that acted as a domed shelter from bursts of acid.

The Brown Yelp Gang still had a couple of days to ready themselves for the festival. The morning after they arrived at the castle, Stravinsky prepared the doctor's laboratory as the sun came up and woke up Lilly and Penny, instructing them to freshen up and be at the lab within the hour. Trent and Aria caught wind of this through overhearing the voices in the corridors of the castle. Riff, DK and Deet were fast asleep and usually would be on a non-gig day until halfway through the afternoon. True to their trusting natures, Lilly and Penny got out of their ornate, comfortable beds and went to the bathroom facility together.

"You seem worried, Penny." Lilly said, reading her emotions as if they're her own.

"You can't fool me, Lilly." Penny replied. "I know you're as worried as I am. We don't know this guy and he's going to – what did he say?"

"Enhance us?" Lilly said quizzically.

"Something like that!" There was a tone of suspicious disbelief in Penny's voice.

"I wouldn't mind extra arms!" Lilly said, smiling.

"I wouldn't mind some hair." They both laughed, knowing hair extensions are a silly indulgence that only the Draphine Warriors of Muru-Ka-Ka get away with now. They finished up washing and waking themselves, and then proceeded toward the laboratory on the ground floor. As they left their room, they were met by Trent and Aria in the hallway.

"Morning, girls." Aria smiled at them, affectionately.

"Hello, Aria." They creepily said in unison. Aria's face prompted them to say, "we shouldn't have done that should we?"

"At least when he does it," Aria pointed to Trent beside her, "it's because there's one mind spreading out into three places."

"Yeah, sorry, it's probably a bit weird." Lilly said, smiling.

"Sorry." Penny added, separately.

"We're going to sit in and watch what this doctor does." Trent explained. "It's great what he's done with our new instruments, but we don't want him doing anything dangerous to you two."

"Thank you." Lilly expressed her and her sister's gratitude and then turned back toward the stairs that led to the laboratory.

As they reached the ground floor, Stravinsky was waiting for them at the foot of the stairs.

"The master is waiting for you, now." His greeting was followed by him needlessly escorting them to the laboratory, a few feet away.

"Thank you, Stravinsky." Dr Schoenberg said, condescendingly as they approached. "Now let's strap these girls in and get their brains fizzing!"

The girls looked at each other in dread, but dutifully complied. Trent and Aria looked on from the side.

"Aria, once we have got these girls primed and ready, I will get rid of that ridiculous Movine disguise and make you pretty again." Schoenberg was saying this while moving wires from one machine to another, and flipping switches on the machines that formed a semi-circle around the girls' tables.

"That would be nice." Aria said, fiddling with her still clipped snout.

"So!" Schoenberg shouted. "Let's begin!"

- And as he shouted, he produced a huge mallet from under the girls' tables and whacked them both on the head with one almighty blow that knocked them unconscious.

Aria and Trent looked at him with shocked faces.

"Standard procedure, my friends, standard procedure." Schoenberg then began to attach probes to both the girls' foreheads. As he turned to face the seemingly incomprehensible lights and dials of his machines, the girls started to give out short, subtle spasms that Aria noticed straight away.

"Is that normal?" She asked.

Schoenberg turned around and smiled. "Standard procedure." He replied.

"O...kay..." Aria was not quite comfortable watching this. Dr Schoenberg turned back to his machines, and as the girls started screaming at the top of their voices, Aria had to speak up;

"Seriously, Mr Schoenberg, this looks wrong!" She shouted.

"It's Dr Schoenberg!" He screamed back, angrily.

"What do you call this operation you're doing on these poor girls?!" She shouted back.

"Standard procedure, Aria. Standard procedure."

The 'operation' continued in that vein for the next hour. Something worrying appeared in the girls' behaviour, Aria screamed at the doctor to stop and he simply replied that it was 'standard procedure'. Trent looked on, almost saying something and then staying quiet when Aria got there first.

After a couple of hours of mind expanding experimentation hooked to Schoenberg's machines, the doctor declared that the operation was over.

"The girls will need some rest." He said, directly to Trent and Aria. "Leave them here, and come back as the evening gets dark. That should be a sufficient amount of time for them to be back on their feet."

Aria nodded, exhausted by the whole experience. Trent sauntered over to the girls and checked their pulses, to satisfy his concern that they were still alive.

They were.

Just.

Chapter Fifteen

Praxim 7 was not often visited by tourists. It wasn't the smell, although that didn't help. It wasn't its reputation for being hazardous to navigate around, or difficult to develop relationships in. The people of Praxim 7 were infamous for being selfish, ignorant and quick tempered...but it wasn't that. It was mostly the distance between Praxim 7 and the nearest planet in the Corsyllian system; 568 million miles away. That's a long way by anyone's stretch of the imagination. So Praxim 7 enjoyed a consistent sense of isolation, with a huge gulf between the planet and the busy traffic found tearing around the skies of Corsylia.

High above Corsylia, the heightened activity above the atmosphere had left space debris that could easily be mistaken for large celestial objects; but were just mess left drifting in space by Corsyllian commercial shuttle, merchant and pirate pilots. There was nothing like that around the orbit of Praxim 7; its isolation had protected it from extensive littering.

So, it was a colossal shock to the Praxim 7 administration when thousands of ships descended on Blurgh, a sleepy town usually ignored on the planet, in the 36 hours leading up to the music festival. Carlo DeMarco had done a great job in selling it to the neighbouring planets. Say what you like about his psychotic attitude to sentient life, but he certainly knew how to market a gig. The frequent appearance of the words "Great Big Beat Festival at Blurgh, on Praxim 7" had paid off. The slogan that was attached to the marketing campaign; 'You will die with your ears blown off from this permanent party!' could have had something to do with it too, but also could have put people off. Either way, the administration leaped into action and sent dozens of law enforcement officials to the festival site, to potentially be a deterrent for anyone tempted to disturb the peace of Praxim 7. DeMarco found this deeply irritating, but also had enormous faith that his 'Great Remix' would be successful, despite possibly getting unwanted interference from the law.

So, on the evening of the night before, DeMarco gave his permission for the hundreds of thousands of visitors to be let onto the site. The site was ready, and the market and food stalls were already making a mint in profit before any music had been played on the stages. The music would be blasting out from the huge array of speakers on both of the two stages on site, from the midpoint of the next morning. The third stage was so far away from the site that nobody really noticed it was there, or made any effort to find out. The night before the festival started was all about the visitors settling in, spending money on food and getting to know the people listed as performers in the programme, available online on the information stream. DeMarco smiled as he walked around the site; it wasn't the pleasure of seeing lots of 'people' enjoying themselves, it was more the morbid pleasure he had in knowing that he would be slaughtering many of the people he passed once 'The Great Remix' began. He was a nasty piece of work, and it was about time somebody stood up to him and challenged his authoritarian arrogance.

The Brown Yelp Gang had gathered for their early afternoon dinner at Dr Schoenberg's castle. Lilly and Penny were up and mingling with the others, while concentrating on suppressing the power they had been granted by Schoenberg's machine. Dr Schoenberg had boasted that Aria's operation was going to be a short, easy one, and Aria did come out the other end with exactly the same, naturally Denuvian features as before and with no scarring at all. She was genuinely grateful to him, after she had started to believe that whatever the Hobligon had done was permanent. Aria was late to the gathering of Dr Schoenberg's guests at the long, oblong dining table, as she needed to meditate after the adrenalin rush of giving her body to Schoenberg's surgical promises. When she did appear, Riff couldn't contain his relief for seeing the love of his life looking like a Denuvian priestess again, and not a Movine with a long snout.

"You look amazing!" Riff fawned.

"Thank you, darling." Aria swayed, with Riff's words added to her already exhilaration of being 'fixed' so well.

"Wow, you did a great job on Aria, doctor." Jenken said, his eyes bulging with shock.

"Alright mate, calm down. She's not just something to look at." Riff said, chivalrously.

Aria raised her eyebrows in astonishment.

"Fair one, Riff. I was just saying..." Jenken put his hands out to reassure Riff that there was no objectification happening. Aria silently grinned at the altercation.

So the table was set, Stravinsky brought out each individual's food one by one, bowing and fawning whenever he placed the food in front of them.

"Stravinsky, you don't need to bow so much to us." Jenken said, kindly and politely.

"Oh, master, I am not worthy to even listen to what you're saying."

"Seriously, we are not that important. We're a big deal on some planets, but in this castle we're just some people who came here because we were told to!"

"Oh, master, I am not worthy to even listen to what you're saying." Stravinsky said again.

Clearly, he wasn't listening.

"So," Schoenberg addressed his new friends, "you're all set to face DeMarco's security forces?"

"Yeah, but a massive thanks to you for helping." Jenken said, smiling at the doctor.

"It's not them I'm worried about; it's the big robot man thing that I saw on the lowest floor of his base." DK declared, ominously.

"You told me about this last night." Schoenberg added, sympathetically. "You'll be fine. You have the weapons I gave you, which will give you an advantage."

"Advantage is a strong word." Deet replied, with his typical cynicism.

"We don't really know what this machine is capable of; we just know it's linked to this thing that DeMarco called 'The Great Remix'." Jenken added his knowledge to the conversation.

"He's going to release that robot onto anyone that's at the festival once we've done our set." Trent had a hint of concern in his voice.

"That will be an awesome finish to our set!" Riff declared, not really thinking of the death toll.

"People are going to die, Riff. We have to work quickly once we see it starting." Aria was, as always, wise and forthright in demonstrating her moral compass.

"I guess so..." Riff conceded "...but we should definitely do something like that at a gig. Full death and misery stuff." The band members sitting around him didn't react. It was always better that way.

"That should be our cue to go." Jenken said.

"Eat something first. I can imagine the prices at DeMarco's festival will be astronomical!" Schoenberg insisted.

"You're right." Jenken replied. He had been to many festivals before and undertaken many fruitless searches for cheap food.

They all enjoyed a quiet moment as they ate their food. After they had gulped down what Schoenberg had given them, they collected their things, which now included the weaponised instruments. Trent's microphone, Riff's missile launching guitar and Aria's lethal projectile shooting flute were all significant advantages in their bid to topple DeMarco. Ursulas and Nod had kept the weapons with them that they had acquired on the shuttle, and were confident that would be enough for them. Deet and DK had been worked over by Schoenberg and Stravinsky in the early morning, and both of them were overflowing with feelings of power and natural enhancement. They had no clue what Schoenberg had done but enjoyed the mystery of that, and didn't enquire too much. They brought all of their things to the front of the hallway, by the main door of the castle, and waited. Schoenberg had organised a Mikkle Bird to come to the castle and then take them to the festival site. They would be there about seven hours early, which would give them the chance to watch some of the bands and get a good look of the layout for the festival, which could be useful when DeMarco makes his move.

They all climbed aboard the gigantic Mikkle Bird and waved goodbye to the scientist and his assistant, Stravinsky, as they flew off in the direction of Praxim 7. Before they had a chance to come up with an actual plan to defeat DeMarco, the Mikkle Bird was in Praxim 7's atmosphere and headed toward the festival site. Mikkle Birds were so enormous that people could sit on their backs in rows on four, and the bird would still be comfortable. As they flew close to the festival site, the band began to imagine how the rest of the day would pan out.

"So what time are we on?" Riff asked, totally oblivious to their obligations.

"We're on last." DK replied, not being very specific.

"I know that, but when?" Riff was slightly irritated.

"We're on as the clock strikes 15."

"Wow, that's late." Riff stated.

"Well, we're headlining, Riff." Jenken added.

"We're headlining?!" Riff became animated, very quickly. "That's fantastic!"

"It's great, but it does mean this thing he's going to do is straight after." Jenken explained.

"Yeah...but...headlining!" Riff nodded, smiling, thinking that if he had a bucket list, he had just scored another triumph for it.

"Who will be on when we get there?" DK was being more practical, but just as excitable.

"Let's see..." Trent switched on his information streaming device, and logged onto the information for the festival. He silently read what was on his screen for a while, and then turned to the others;

"Actually, there are some good people here." He said.

"Like who?" DK asked.

"Did you know that Hairy Helen is playing?" Trent said, smiling.

"Is she still going?" Jenken was amazed.

"Apparently so. She is doing a longish set, just before The Flying Mikkle Bird Brothers."

"The Mikkle Bird brothers?" That got Deet's attention. "I haven't seen them for years. I learned the alternate crisscross rhythm from their song, 'The Crisscross Rhythm Song.' It was a classic." Deet was paying attention now after hearing their name being called out.

"That's crazy!" Trent was stunned, by something.

"What?" Riff was curious, and irritated by the secrecy.

"Riff, your hero is playing."

"What hero?"

"The one that you said you made you want to grow your beard and play the drums."

"I don't play the drums!" Riff replied, confused.

"I know, to be honest, I don't know why you said that, but you did."

"Shall I try and guess who you mean?"

"You know who I mean, Riff." Trent was looking at him with raised eyebrows as if he was willing Riff to say it.

"I don't think I do. Is he alive or dead?"

"He's playing at the festival, Riff."

"Oh yeah, so he's alive." There was a short pause. "Yes?"

"Yes, Riff, he is alive."

"Okay, so that's taken some of my heroes out of the frame." Riff continued to ponder the possibilities. "Is it someone with one leg?"

"You what?" Trent was hoping for a better elimination than that. "How many people do you know with less than the limbs they should have?"

"I guess..." Riff thought for a moment more, "I guess we're talking four bands have got members with missing limbs."

"So it's not the best way to eliminate the bands in your head."

"Fair enough. Is it Melvin and the Melvins?"

"It is, my friend." Trent knew this would get him excited. "He's on in a few hours."

"Aww man. That's a good thing, that. I haven't heard Melvin and the Melvins since before I gave up Pulling Water."

"You haven't given up Pulling water." Trent stated, trying to trace the logic with his deeply concentrated mind.

"Exactly!" Riff said, shouting it cheerily but loudly, as if he had made a great point in an argument.

Silence gripped them again as they descended on the festival site. The Mikkle Bird flew to the backstage area of the main stage and gently landed beside the artist catering area.

"Nice landing birdie!" Riff shouted, licking his lips at the food counter to the right.

"Hey, look at that!" Trent pointed to the wire mesh fence that circled the festival site, specifically directly opposite them, where he could see a woman standing on the other side of the fence holding up a sign. She was a resident of the nearby town, and had walked down to protest. She was frowning at the festival from the other side of the fence, holding up a sign that simply said, 'LOUD NOISE SUCKS'.

"You can't please all the people all the time." Trent said, giving a shrug to the rest of the band.

"I think the phrase is 'you can't please some of the people some of the time'." Riff interjected.

"Surely it would be something like, 'you can't prove you've pleased all the people if they weren't there all of the time?'" Deet was trying to be helpful but he hadn't heard the original quote in the first place.

"I don't think that's right." Nod got involved. He was the least aware of any quotes, words of wisdom or idioms.

"You're all wrong. It's 'you can please the people sometimes but you can't please the people if it's a man'. It's from a song."

"Oh yeah, who sang it?" Trent knew the song that Nod was talking about, but couldn't place it.

"Lizzy Pedigree, from a few years back." Jenken joined in. He knew the song and actually managed Lizzy Pedigree in the first few years of her career. "You can't please Lizzy any of the time!"

They all laughed, and glanced back at the resident protesting again.

"If I get a chance, I'll get her autograph." Riff said, being typically cryptic.

"Priority is to play your set well, and then deal with whatever this 'Great Remix' is!" Jenken reminded them all.

"Me and Penny will stand on opposite sides of the stage and keep an eye out." Lilly said, immediately nodding to her sister. They both ran off to find their stake out positions in front of the main stage. There were only 3 acts now before The Brown Yelp Gang set, so it wasn't going to be a long wait; the girls were looking forward to seeing the three acts before The Brown Yelp Gang anyway, as was everybody else gathering around the main stage.

First would be the hour set from Hairy Helen, known for her extremely lengthy hair that covered most of the stage, and her unique wailing that pulled everyone into a strange trance that the audience was absolutely powerless to resist. Then the Flying Mikkle Brothers would be on for their slightly shorter set, where they'd be running through their biggest hits, as well as their new song, 'I can't believe we're

365

still churning out shit like this'; a guaranteed classic. Then, owning the stage before The Brown Yelp Gang would be Riff's heroes, Melvin and the Melvins. Those guys were set to light up the stage and get the crowd going before The Brown Yelp Gang hit the stage at 15 O'clock.

Deet and Teddy were discussing something with an anxious tone, within ear shot of Jenken as they disembarked from the plane and watched Lilly and Penny run off to the front of the stage.

"Are you okay, guys?" Jenken asked.

"Well, yeah, we're fine...except that we're supposed to be headlining the other stage too. We were given the slot by the Dramatic Spleen band, a few nights ago." Deet explained.

There was a moment of silence. Trent, Riff, DK and Aria looked at Jenken to see how he was going to fix this.

"Leave it with me." Jenken said, smiling. "I know what to do."

"Eh?" Deet replied, not convinced that he did. "Just go to the stage to prepare for our set?"

"Absolutely."

"- and you have a plan? I don't want to miss the Brown Yelp set, Jenken."

"Of course you don't."

"- but you don't want me here with the others? Or Teddy?"

"Honestly, go to the other stage with Teddy and wait for my cue."

Deet and Teddy looked at each other, then shrugged and waved goodbye to the rest of the band.

"See you on the other side." Riff shouted out to them as they left.

"Have you got a plan?" Trent asked Jenken, quietly, leaning into Jenken's physical space.

"It's fine, Trent. It's going to be awesome!" Jenken's grin didn't always reassure them. This was one of those times. He gestured to the audience side of the stage;

"You guys go on and get settled. Buy a pancake or something. I will sort out the whole 'band playing on two stages at the same time' thing. Ursulas, Nod, you go and scope out the area around the exit in case there's anything happening there."

"Will we be playing together then?" DK asked, innocently.

"Oh yes, my friend. We are going to blow the ozone layer clean off this planet!"

Fortunately, that last declaration from Jenken was a metaphor; if it wasn't, their popularity would have suffered enormously.

Carlo DeMarco was lapping up the atmosphere and mingling with the crowd. He sadistically found great delight in saying to his customers advice like, 'live today like it's your last day', knowing that he was going to be bringing chaos to the festival at the end of the night. His men were stationed at various places around the site, ready for the 'Great Remix DJ' (DJ standing for Death Jockey) to appear, rising out of the ground from under the merchandise stalls. He was enjoying the music, although had some reservations over some of the acts that Dramatic Spleen booked for their stage. Who would book someone like The Space Fairies of Nern, a band so laid back that the audience isn't sure the set has started? He thought for a moment about discussing that decision with Dramatic Spleen at some point after the festival, and then remembered they would probably be dead. Then as he remembered this, he let out a maniacal cackle that resounded around the cheese stall to his left. The cheese customers stopped what they were doing for a moment, distracted by DeMarco. Likewise, the cheese vendors halted in the cheese extracting, removing their legs from the suction machines that produced the cheese.

"It's a good day!" DeMarco shouted to the people milling around the cheese stall. "Have a wonderful cheese...time!" DeMarco continued, awkwardly.

This was enough to reassure them that there wasn't a problem, and the cheese consumption resumed to its natural rhythm. Occasionally, DeMarco checked in with his engineers, just to be comforted that there was nothing in the way of the big plan, and the 'Great Remix'.

Hairy Helen was a delight, as always. Her spellbinding vocal talent was wrapped up in a vortex of sound that her band of Movines all beautifully produced from their snouts. Helen hadn't employed a band of Movines before, but was on record recently as saying she's never going to use anything but Movine musicians from now on. DK had become an instant fan when she said this. She played many of her popular songs, with embellishments and a range of intense bursts of improvisation, before ending the set with the song that made her famous, 'Gah!' True to form, as every gig audience before them, the crowd blissfully and loudly sung along, even with the bizarre impenetrable accent that she adopted for that song.

As she sang those legendary lines across the festival site, the crowd joined in below her:

"Gah! Gah! Gah! Gah! Gah!"

Her final note, that lasted several minutes, was met with a standing ovation, more whoops and cheers from the crowd than had been heard that day. After bowing a number of times, amongst the hysterical cheering, Hairy Helen retreated to the artist enclosure for a cup of herbal Vestrell tea.

The Bask Lizards that DeMarco had hired to act as security walked through the crowds to settle them down, after them being overwhelmed with unadulterated joy; a condition that is hard to recover from without the help of qualified assistance. The calming music recorded by the

Tree People of Eliquinox wafted through the festival site, as the main stage changed the staging to prepare for The Flying Mikkle Brothers. Their set went without incident; the risk with them was whether they had arrived in a state of psychosis or not. These psychotic episodes within the band, that would make their gigs infamously unpredictable, had been reduced by the band decision to add Dr Franklin, a renowned surgeon on New Earth as their bassist. He wasn't a great bassist, but looked after them much better than other bassists. So the audience had the enormous pleasure of one of the most successful bands to come out of the hardcore junkgrass genre from New Earth, without any missing notes, random tangents that lost the song for a while or any confused melodies. As expected, their song, 'I can't believe we're still churning out shit like this' created a tidal wave of emotion from the crowd. The band loved it and couldn't stop saying goodbye; the Bask security had to unplug the instruments and carry the band members off themselves, as they were enjoying the interaction with the crowd so much. The Mikkle Brothers were apologetic when they were offstage, away from the crowd, as their adrenalin dissipated. They felt that it was an embarrassing moment for them, as they were so pleased to finally be performing in a drug-free sober condition.

The usual set up time was required to get the stage ready for Melvin and the Melvins, and as it worked so well in the previous intermission, the music from the Tree People of

Eliquinox was utilised again, with the same, successful effects.

Meanwhile, back on Dramatic Spleen's stage, there were some scheduling issues, as the Space Fairies of Nern had overrun by 45 minutes. The initial 20 minutes were seen as an understandable result of the fluid, amorphous nature of the music. Once the issue approached the 30 minute mark, the members of Dramatic Spleen began to panic. All three members were at the sides of the stage shouting at the band;

"Get off!"

"You've run over!"

"Wake up!!"

"Get off the stage!!!"

"Oi! You're done!"

Burgundy, Mauve and Crimson were shouting at the band as loud as they could to get their attention. It could be that the band was deliberately ignoring them. It could be that they were too lost in their mystical metaphysical exploration, within the music, to notice. Either way, they weren't paying any attention.

"Shall I just get up there and take them off?" Crimson was the drummer, so was inevitably more of a man of action.

Burgundy hesitated, looking around for inspiration.

Behind him, he spotted Carlo DeMarco, the big chief, who had appeared at the back of the stage, aware that there was an issue developing on their stage. He was grinning at them, confident that he could solve it.

"It's fine." He said to Burgundy, proudly. "I've got this." DeMarco produced a gun from inside his jacket, smiled as the members of Dramatic Spleen reacted with shock at seeing the gun, and promptly shot the members of the Space Fairies of Nern with the gun. It was a tranquilliser gun, which he decided to use so there was no panic amongst the crowd yet. He wanted to pick his moment for the carnage that he planned. Burgundy, Mauve and Crimson released a long, loud sigh of relief. DeMarco's Bask stage hands leapt onto the stage and dragged the unconscious musicians off the stage. He then gestured to Burgundy to get on stage and make an announcement; "You're on, Burgundy." DeMarco said, smiling at him. "It's your stage now; let them know that no-one has died." Burgundy ran on stage and immediately grabbed the mic and, with the energy and enthusiasm that had given him the compere job in the first place, addressed the crowd. "How about another round of applause for the Space Fairies of Nern!"

The crowd went wild.

"They travelled for weeks to get here from Nern and played a blinding set. I was barely conscious for most of it!" The crowd cheered and whooped accordingly.

"Give us a few minutes, then we'll have 'The Slime Gits' up on stage for you for the penultimate set of the day! Are you ready for the 'Slime Gits'?"

The crowd erupted again, reacting well to Burgundy's stage presence.

"- and then we'll have our finale act!" His voice was rising in volume and pitch to further incite the audience. "THE BROWN YELP GANG!!!"

Those words were met with a cacophony of excitement that had DeMarco grinning at the side of the stage. Burgundy was mostly just happy with how they had managed to move on with the schedule and get the Space Fairies off the stage. He didn't want to incur the wrath of DeMarco and knew his life depended on it.

Ironically, there was a much bigger threat looming, under the merchandise stalls, waiting to rise up at the end of The Brown Yelp Gang set.

Chapter Sixteen

DeMarco's plan was going well. The festival was thronging with people, all happily eating, laughing, chatting, playing and, most importantly, listening to the music being played on the festival stages. He was becoming giddy with excitement about the destruction he would be causing once The Brown Yelp Gang had finished. He was impressed with how the band had solved their double booking. Jenken had made it his mission to make sure they honoured the bookings for both stages of the festival as soon as he departed the saddle of the Mikkle Bird. He made a bee line for the Bask Lizards roadies working behind scenes on both stages, to suggest his plan of combining the sound coming from both stages. Deet and Teddy would stand on The Little Beat Stage, run by Dramatic Spleen, and the other members of the band would stand on The Great Big Beat Stage, but they would be performing the songs together, in synch, with the cables from both stages hooked up together for one almighty Brown Yelp blast. Once Teddy had heard the plan, she got very excited about having most of the stage to herself, having no platform before for her body popping dance moves that she desperately wanted to reveal to the fans. DeMarco got word of the plan from his engineers, and loved it. Ursulas and Nod were busy mingling in the crowds closer to the exit, in case there would be some kind of trouble at the opposite end to the stages.

Melvin and the Melvins had performed with style, charisma and extremely slick movement within and between the songs. What had made the band famous on their native New Earth was their unique approach to dividing the vocal duties in the songs. There were 16 members of the band; 13 of them were the singers. Each member of the band was responsible for one note in the chromatic scale. When that note appeared in a song, they sang it. This meant that each line was sung by various members of the band; the trick that they always pulled off so well was their ability to sound like each other. You could never tell which individual was singing the notes despite those notes being sung by 13 people. It was fascinating to watch, but gloriously uncanny to hear. No other band had ever sung like that, and finding a niche amongst thousands of species across several star systems is no mean feat. Their last notes were met with rapturous applause, with one member shouting jubilantly, 'I don't think I can take any more!'

Whether that member of the audience could take any more or not, there was still more to come. The headline act spread across two stages, riding the release of their new album, 'Warm and Tasty', The Brown Yelp Gang. Both stages had fully aligned themselves with the schedule, and

Jenken's plan to blend the performers from both stages together seemed to be working. As they all walked on stage to begin their set, the crowd broke out into a tsunami of affection and unbridled joy. On the Little Beat Stage, Deet shouted "How are you all doing?!" to the cheering crowd as he waddled on to his platform at the back.

Hundreds of yards away, connected by the longest cables on the festival site, Trent shouted to his waiting crowd; "Well, good evening Praxim 7!"

The crowd released uninhibited joy on cue.

"How are you doing, Deet?" Trent shouted to the other stage with a knowing smile on his face, loving the audacity of their stage configuration.

"I'm all good at this end, my friend. Let's rock Praxim 7 into oblivion!" Deet's shout warped into a scream as the last words were met with an eruption of sound from the adoring crowd.

Then they began.

First, the opening riff of 'Come out with your hands up' was played. They teased the audience after the first 16 bars, hesitating for a second, as if they were stopping the music. For an uncomfortably long amount of time, they stared at the audience, like frozen statues. Then after a scream from Deet, on the Little Beat Stage, they all came in, together, for the rest of the song. The crowd were loving it, being seduced by the familiarity of these iconic Brown Yelp classics and being intrigued by the new members, Aria and Teddy both stunning the crowds on their respective stages. Hit after hit assaulted the sensibilities of the two crowds in front of the band. The opening song was followed by 'Show me where you put it', 'Kiss your proboscis' and 'Cheese Dream' from the new album. They continued to alternate between old classics and songs from the new album, always whipping up a frenzy from the participating, interactive crowds. Occasionally Aria would look at Riff with the kind of love in her eyes that almost says 'you're forgiven for everything'. He looked back at her with a look that said, 'did you just see my solo I just played?' The blissful feelings on the stage were being alchemically transformed into the best performance The Brown Yelp Gang had ever played. Trent's three heads were laughing in their dizzy enjoyment of the moment they thought they would never forget. DK was blowing melodies through his snout that were turning his band mates heads; he was floating on the intoxicating feeling of breathtaking delight and were playing his parts in the songs like it was their last gig. Teddy was expertly anticipating what DK was playing and bringing harmonies into the ad-libs that were shocking the band and almost distracting them from their faultless performance. The physical distance between the two stages were irrelevant to the unified, tight sound coming from the band. Jenken stood on the side of the main stage, grinning

377

from ear to ear and occasionally laughing to himself when someone on stage played something unexpected.

"This is the life." He mumbled quietly.

The set continued to wow the audience in a life changing, historic way. DeMarco whispered to his security officers as the band reached the last couple of songs, to get the 'Great Remix' ready. As the band approached the penultimate song in the set, Trent's left head began the first note. His middle head added a harmony with the third note interval, and then the right head added the fifth interval. They held the note for a few minutes, then, after what sounded like a physically impossible drum fill from Deet's versatile belly, the infamous classic 'How is your hair' began in full force.

"How is your hair?" The crowd screamed.

"How is your hair?" They continued...

The repeated phrase was a major feature of the song and the main reason the band didn't rate it very highly. It was also the reason why it was so popular. Their biggest hit was that one four word phrase repeated throughout the song. Now, at this festival, it was a powerful moment of unity that would remain in people's minds for the rest of their lives. As if they couldn't top that, The Brown Yelp Gang decided that their last song would be a song from their second album that they thought was the perfect song for the occasion; it was called, 'We were going to say goodbye but we thought we'd sing you this song first'. It, naturally, ends with a rousing chorus of 'Goodbye, Goodbye, Goodbye, my friend, I'll see you when I'm thirsty'.

As the crowd sang the last choruses, waving their hands left and right and smiling at the people around them, DeMarco prepared himself for the moment he had been waiting for since he had conceived the 'Great Remix' 7 months before. He chuckled under his breath as he attempted to contain his sociopathic excitement. Then, as the final moments of the song died down, and the big rock n roll crescendo filled the stage and the crowd were shouting their love at the band, DeMarco walked on stage and grabbed the microphone from Trent.

"Well, how about that, folks of Praxim 7," he began, "and all other places you people have come from!"

The crowd responded with clockwork adulation.

"The Brown Yelp Gang finishing off a great day of..." He paused as he paused for dramatic effect. "FREE MUSIC!"

The crowd stepped up to an even bigger frenzy.

"Now...people of Praxim 7...I want to talk to you about a new world." His voice simmered down to a conversational tone, and the crowd's cheering levelled down to the occasional murmur. The band standing around him watched patiently, smiling, unaware of where his speech was leading.

"...a new world filled with great music, great food, great big events like this..." He was building up to a louder, more passionate delivery again with each new phrase.

"...and ALL UNDER MY COMMAND!" These last words were shouted to the crowd, followed by a maniacal laugh, which was the cue his Bask engineers were waiting for to release the Death Jockey from under the merchandise stand.

Members of the crowd began screaming in horror as the Death Jockey rose up from under the ground, sending the merchandise stand flying into the crowd, with all of its clothing and accessories falling to the side and with people scattering in their fearful disbelief. The Death Jockey, in his colossal 50 foot frame, and huge, metallic limbs that brought with them the threat of instant destruction clambered out of the soil and stood up to survey the crowd around him. It's cold, black eyes surveyed the crowd with murderous intent. The frightened members of the audience didn't waste time and ran as fast as they could away from the danger that had suddenly appeared without warning from under them. DeMarco was cackling with psychotic glee as the festival site became filled with the sounds of hysterical screaming, this time based on fear rather than extreme fandom.

The Death Jockey stamped its foot on the ground around it, managing to hit some poor souls that hadn't moved far enough, and swung his arms across the main stage area, decimating it in front of the fleeing music fans.

"This is the new day. The day of the Great Remix!" DeMarco declared from the ground near the stage, through the microphone that was still miraculously working, despite the devastated stage area.

The members of The Brown Yelp Gang from the main stage had reached the Little Beat Stage where Burgundy, Mauve and Crimson were cowering in fear, under the protection of the metal and wood stage frame. Lilly and Penny stayed where they were, closer to the huge machine that was causing devastation around them, but far enough away to not be in the immediate firing line. Trent crouched and turned to Burgundy with a wink;

"Don't worry my far out friend. We will be fine."

"What the hell is that?!" Burgundy shrieked, from under the stage.

"It's something we've prepared for." Trent answered confidently.

"Basically mate." Riff interrupted. "Your boss is a first prize nutter!"

Then Jenken turned to the band gathered around him, knowing that they were the line in the sand between this huge havoc wreaking robot and the innocent music lovers around them.

"Let's buckle up and focus on the job at hand now, lads." Jenken had never been more serious. "This is it. Ray asked us to check out what he was doing, and we know it was far more serious than he thought. We need to stop this loon before he does any more damage!"

"Agreed!" Trent's heads said in unison.

"I'm with ya." Riff nodded, switching his guitar to weapon settings.

"Let's get closer." Aria said, adjusting her flute for battle mode.

"Agreed." Jenken replied, and waved his arm to initiate a confrontation with the Death Jockey.

As the Death Jockey continued to plough into the crowd and flatten any stall or artistic structure that he walked across, The Brown Yelp Gang all got into position. As they ran closer they could see that Lilly and Penny were concentrating, frowning with closed eyes for mental clarity. Riff and Aria began to shoot missiles into the torso of the Death Jockey, which appeared to leave little damage. It did, however, alert the Bask guards that were scattered around the site. DeMarco's security guards all assembled in a semi-circle formation facing the position the band had taken up, in front of the Death Jockey. The Lizard security fired shots at Riff and Aria first, as they were the first members of the band to send shots to the Death Jockey, and Riff and Aria took cover behind an upturned table. Jenken, DK, Deet and Teddy followed suit, finding a meat and onions stall to hide behind while the guards were shooting at them.

DeMarco was shocked that there was any resistance, and even more shocked that it was coming from the headline band! ('What gratitude' he thought!) He was keen to join the shootout, to rid himself of the hassle that the band were

382

creating for him. When one of his Bask guards was killed by one of Aria's shots from the flute, DeMarco ran to the body and grabbed his pulse rifle. He then stood behind a clothing stall on the opposite side of that area of the site and shot at the Brown Yelp Gang. Jenken and Teddy had been given conventional weapons by Dr Schoenberg, and used them in this melee against the large robot and its master, Carlo DeMarco. Once DeMarco's shots had got close to the band members, Riff and Teddy aimed at him, while Trent and Aria continued to aim at the Bask guards and the Death Jockey. There were few people around now, with the initial terror of the robot's first actions being enough to clear the site. It was a confrontation between the band and the gangster's men, and a 50 foot robot. Sparks flew from every moment of contact on the metal structures around the battle zone. Canvas shields were useless for either side, as the plasma bursts from the pulse rifles burned gaping holes in the 'defences'. The shots coming from the band's modified instruments were hitting the security guards and causing DeMarco to take cover more than he was firing, but the gigantic robot that was DeMarco's chief weapon of destruction wasn't getting affected by the firearms. Trent could feel that their efforts were in vain;

"Jenken," he shouted, "it looks like these weapons we got from that doctor are useless against that thing."

"Yeah, I think you're right." Jenken shouted back. "We're making a difference to the guards though!" Jenken replied, positively.

There was damage everywhere. The firing on both sides continued. The initial advantage that the band felt they had with their confidence and element of surprise was lost as the reality of their lack of experience began to creep into their consciousness. This badly affected their success rate with the shots they were firing, and a stalemate was establishing between both sides. Occasionally one of the Bask security force would get a close shot to the band, but luckily, as the band spent a lot of time hiding behind the pieces of the festival infrastructure, they were hard to hit. The security guards were penetrating the festival staging and stalls that the band was using. It wouldn't be long before they had no shielding at all. Deet and DK were watching this confrontation with an unavoidable feeling of inadequacy. They had left Schoenberg's castle without weaponised instruments, and felt completely useless in this intense, life or death, situation.

"Do you feel duped?" Deet asked DK from behind the upturned stage platform.

"Well, I certainly feel left out!" DK replied, feeling sorry for himself.

"What did that doctor say he had done to us?" Deet tried to recall, while dodging the crossfire.

"Enhanced us!" DK replied.

384

"Yeah, what does that mean?"

"Who knows!"

"Well, what do we do?"

"We play music."

"Yeah..." Deet thought for a moment. "Should we play harder than we normally would and see if it makes a difference?"

"I guess we could..."

Deet laid back on the floor behind the stage platform and began to emit polyrhythmic beats from inside his enormous belly. DK sat next to him, closed his eyes and blew a raspy, thunderous note from his snout.

Unknowingly, Deet and DK had made a powerful, game changing difference. Dr Schoenberg had made some calculations and a few assumptions that gave him the idea of boosting the frequency of DK's notes, so that they were created with relative octaves that were so high that they would only affect the stability of glass and metal. Similarly, Schoenberg did the same with Deet's beats, this time, for him, they were enhanced to cover the lower octaves. The Death Jockey held his head with his bulky and intimidating metal hands, as the noise from the two unarmed Brown Yelp Gang members burrowed into his circuits.

Lilly and Penny had been attempting to topple him, or even crush him if they could, while the others were busy with the guards and with DeMarco. This new development from Deet and DK gave them less resistance from the

385

indiscriminate robot and more of a chance for stopping it once and for all. They both looked at each other with a determined stare, both reading in each other's minds that they should make one last, big concerted attempt to fry the circuitry causing all this mayhem. Aria would see what was happening from her vantage point, where she had moved to behind a big polystyrene letter 'G' and smiled as she saw the girls work together to fight the Death Jockey.

The Bask guards stopped firing as they noticed the ground around them shaking. Wooden panels flew off the displays that were still standing, and canvas marquees flew across the festival site. These new disturbances on the site were being caused by the combined efforts of the twin sisters, Lilly and Penny, using their powerful, and now enhanced minds, to create psychokinetic turbulence. More specifically, the girls were aiming their enhanced cerebral powers at the robot DeMarco had released onto the festival. DeMarco had noticed that the girls seemed to be doing something to the physical world around them, and when he put that with the struggle that the Death Jockey seemed to be having from Deet and DK's new music, he figured he could watch the destruction from a further distance and decided to run in the opposite direction. For a couple of intense minutes, Lilly and Penny continued to burrow inside the robot's circuitry, snapping its connections and sparking some of the internal wiring inside it.

Within seconds of the girls reaching the internal machinery of the colossal robot, its head shattered into hundreds of small, harmless pieces, leading to the collapse and stillness of the metal body that carried it. The band and Bask security around the robot all shielded their faces from the falling pieces. The girls had done it, with the aid of the powerful frequency emissions from Deet and DK, and of course the enhancements from Dr Schoenberg.

The Bask engineers had noticed that DeMarco was nowhere to be seen and, on seeing the Death Jockey falling to its conclusive demise, simply put their arms up in the air in surrender and shouted at the band to cease fire. DeMarco wouldn't have been pleased, but he hadn't noticed as he was on his way out of the festival site.

DeMarco had run in the direction of the only exit on the site. Ursulas and Nod were there, scouting for any trouble. Ursulas saw DeMarco coming up through the pathway toward them and couldn't help but smile.

"Well, well, well." She began. "How lovely is this?"

DeMarco looked up from his strides toward the exit and sighed, in annoyance.

"Ursulas." He almost spat the name out. "What the hell are you doing here?"

"Carlo." Her voice was as arrogant as it always was; DeMarco may have had the upper hand before, but now she felt that she could be the feisty woman people were used to seeing. "I couldn't miss this."

"What? The festival?"

"No, you idiot." She was on a roll. "I mean watching you finally get justice. You have intimidated, threatened, plotted and humiliated everyone you have met and worked with on a regular basis."

"True dat." DeMarco agreed, proudly.

"- and now you have shown your true colours with your ridiculous Great Remix nonsense."

"I wouldn't say it was nonsense."

"Well, look!" Ursulas spread her arms out, to illustrate the chaos that his violence had produced.

"I didn't know the bloody Yelp Gang was going to be armed."

"No, I guess that's an unusual thing to happen."

"Yeah, well I would have been fine if they had just played their songs."

"Well, what are you going to do now?" She was staring confidently at DeMarco, feeling that she had the upper hand.

She was, of course, too self-assured and didn't see DeMarco raising his pulse rifle in her direction and shooting it squarely at her upper body. Nod did see it and speedily pushed her out of the way with his large bulk of a body. Ursulas was sent falling to the right and landing awkwardly on the grass beside them. Nod, in his bid to save Ursulas, received the impact from the rifle blast. His large frame meant that the shot meant for Ursulas' chest was being sent in the direction of Nod's upper left thigh. Nod buckled as he felt the force of the pulse blast on his thigh. Shouting out in pain, he crouched down, steadying himself with his right arm firmly on the grassy floor and snarling bitterly at DeMarco. Ursulas was leaning up from her knees in an instant, with her gun pointed at DeMarco. With a rapid reaction time more fitting to her underworld reputation, she hit DeMarco squarely in the middle of the forehead with her pistol blast. He immediately slumped to the floor, dead. Carlo DeMarco had lived by a ruthless moral code and an unparalleled arrogance that brought with it an equally intense feeling of disappointment in the split second he had to consider his death. Ursulas, with her tough exterior and self-assured swagger, was still shocked by the sudden end to DeMarco's charmed life.

She stared for a moment at the lifeless, now powerless body of the great crime lord and music aficionado Carlo DeMarco. In a flash, her memories of protection bullying, strong arm tactics, cocky audacity, constant gloating and endless self-promotion were now reduced to a horizontal body that led to a pathetic face with its tongue hanging out. It wasn't glamorous, it wasn't sexy and it wasn't the kind of thing you'd see in his publicity. Carlo DeMarco was now banished to the annals of history, and his music endeavours would be forgotten as quickly as any other music promoter would be. His grip on the crime in the system would take some unravelling, and Ursulas was aware of the can of worms she had opened there, but looked forward to being a part of the new, less autocratic, order. As quickly as these thoughts sped through her racing adrenalin filled mind, her thoughts returned to her friend and trusting protector, Nod.

With his bulky shape and size, she couldn't lift Nod up but could see that he would have difficulty walking. The gaping hole in his thigh was making him stagger on his feet and wince with pain as he tried to move toward the others. They both heard an almighty crash and looked up to see the 50 foot robot now motionless along the floor of the main stage area. Ursulas was concerned for Nod, but knew that, with DeMarco out of the picture and the big robot weapon decommissioned, she could leave him for a moment to get help.

"Just sit here on the grass for a moment, Nod. I won't be long."

"It could be worse," Nod smirked, bravely.

"Absolutely." Ursulas smiled back. "I won't be long." She repeated.

Nod agreed and slowly placed himself on the grass, growling through gritted teeth as the pain shot through his body. Ursulas hurried to where the others were, hoping that they could help Nod before he lost too much blood. She could see that a lot had happened at their end, and hoped the band and the girls were not harmed; she surveyed the debris that had been left by the thrashing of the Death Jockey and the melee between the band and DeMarco's Bask security, as she briskly walked through the grassy path. Her priority was Nod, but she had a long history with Trent that was pulling at her too, as she looked ahead of her to see if he was hurt.

Trent, Riff, DK, Deet and Jenken were inspecting the robot body, mostly making sure that there was no life left in it. The Bask engineers had been instructed, by Jenken, to kneel on the floor with their hands behind their heads and await more instructions. Lilly and Penny were leaning on each other, against a canvas sheet that used to be part of one of the marquee stalls, recovering from the exhaustion that their overpowering release of psychic energy would give them.

"That was awesome, girls." Riff said, raising a slight smile from their young faces.

"I wasn't sure we'd do it." Jenken said.

"Rock 'n' Roll, mate." Riff replied, philosophically.

"We need to get these engineers bound and sent off to get tried." Deet suggested.

"Well we have to get them out of here somehow." Aria agreed.

"Where the hell has DeMarco gone?" Trent asked, with all three of his heads looking around for any sign of him.

391

"He scarpered off somewhere, the coward." Jenken scoffed, deeply irritated.

"He didn't get far." A low, familiar, female voice was heard from 20 feet away.

They all looked up and saw Ursulas strutting toward them with a smile on her face, unwilling to break the image she has of an arrogant, no nonsense, spirited woman who will always finish on top.

"Where is he?" Jenken asked, with an animated sense of urgency.

"He's dead. Over there." Ursulas gestured to the exit, where she confronted him.

"That's wonderful!" DK shouted, ecstatically.

"Nod has been hurt, though. We need to get him some help, or get him out of here."

"Oh crap." Jenken cursed. He looked at Trent and Riff. Then he looked at Aria.

They all hesitated for a moment, wanting to think of an immediate solution to Nod being hurt, but failing to think of a way out of there. Then Burgundy appeared from behind DK;

"Hi guys. Thank you for all that you've done today. Who knows what would have happened if that robot had got any further!"

"Don't worry Burgundy, its fine." Deet replied. "We need to get our friend Nod to some kind of doctor or something, he's been shot."

"Yeah, I heard you talking about that just then. I think I can help. I know someone at The Swamp Beast that can help him."

"What's The Swamp Beast?" Riff asked, having only heard selective parts of Deet's account of their first encounters on Praxim 7.

"It's the place where me and Teddy played when we got here; where we got the slot on the other stage."

"Aw, OK." Riff nodded, almost putting two and two together.

"So where is that place then?" Ursulas asked, now directly facing Burgundy and the potential lifeline for Nod.

"If we grab one of the trucks the engineers were moving gear around in, it won't take more than a few minutes to get to The Swamp Beast."

"That's great Burger Deep." Ursulas replied.

"Burgundy."

"Yeah, Burgundy, sorry." She wanted to remain courteous.

"Let's go then."

"I'll go and get one of those trucks."

Burgundy jogged to the left and disappeared behind some debris from the clash with the Death Jockey.

"Wow." DK said, staring back at the huge robot beside them.

"Wow, indeed." Jenken added.

They all sighed the longest sigh any band has ever collectively sighed after a battle with a 50 foot robot.

"We did it." Trent smiled, and let out a triumphant howl from all three of his heads. Deet sniggered and turned to Jenken.

"So I guess your debt is cleared."

"I guess so." Jenken replied, stifling a laugh.

They all looked at each other, tired but relieved that they managed to get through the ordeal without a death among them.

A few minutes later, Burgundy drove up to the band in an orange delivery truck, smiling with the satisfaction of finally helping out, after a traumatic end to the festival.

"Get in, then. There's room for all of you." Burgundy said, slapping the seat beside him at the front.

"What about the girls?" Aria said, typically more worried about them than herself.

"Yeah, there's loads of room in this thing. It's built to haul massive parts of scaffolding and stage platforms around."

"Okay, great." Aria replied. "Come on, girls. Hop on!"

Lilly and Penny helped each other up and staggered to the truck. The rest of the band helped them up as they all settled in the back of the truck together. They drove up to where Nod was waiting, where they found him with his trousers ripped up and bandaged around the wound.

Nod was taken to The Swamp Beast and immediately given more pressure bandages and some severe pain relief to help him sleep.